# Hotshoe

# Hotshoe

## by Jerry Smith

**Whitehorse Press**
**North Conway, New Hampshire**

Cover illustration by Hector Cademartori.

We recognize that some words, model names and designations mentioned herein are the property of the trademark holder. We use them for identification purposes only.

A Whirlaway Book. Published December 1998 by

Whitehorse Press
P.O. Box 60
North Conway, New Hampshire 03860 U.S.A.
Phone: 603-356-6556 or 800-531-1133
FAX: 603-356-6590

Whirlaway and Whitehorse Press are trademarks of Kennedy Associates.

ISBN 1-884313-14-0

5    4    3    2    1

Printed in the United States of America

To all those racers who pitch it in at 140, lap after lap—as gutsy a way to make a living as there is—and to Larry Headrick, whose 1950 Springfield Mile win I lifted and gave to some made-up guy.

# Hotshoe

# 1

We were standing along the back straight at Ascot, jotting down notes in the yellowish light of the arc lamps that lined the track as the announcer interviewed Shiloh Shootout winner Ricky Poe over the PA system, when a sharp explosion like a split-second peal of thunder shattered the night. I flinched instinctively and ducked my head.

"Holy shit," said Stan Martini, a *Cycle Weekly* staffer. He had ducked, too. "That was a hell of a backfire!" he said, grinning sheepishly.

"That was no backfire," I said. "It was way too loud. And it came from the back pit, not the infield."

"It could have been a backfire," Stan insisted. "One time I saw a Harley backfire and spit a carb clean off the bike. Hit a guy in the leg so hard it drew blood . . ."

Stan was well into an account of all the weird stuff he'd seen happen to badly tuned bikes—he could go on like that for hours—when a kid about eighteen or so wearing a red nylon windbreaker emerged from the open pit gate in the outside wall. His face was as pale as a corpse's.

"He's dead," he said. "Back there. Dead." Then he doubled over, dropped to his knees, and threw up.

I looked around. Nobody else had seen him. They were either getting their bikes ready for the main event or facing the front straight, listening to the interview. Stan stood gaping, his notebook and pen poised in mid-air.

"Get the paramedics," I said, and sprinted across the track.

The kid was on his knees, retching.

"Who's dead? Where is he?" I said.

He looked over his shoulder, made a gagging noise, and doubled over again. I left him and went through the pit gate into the darkness.

Ascot Park Raceway was a half-mile dirt oval lined with splintery grandstands and leaning catch fences, low-rent, squalid, and utterly wonderful in that way only old, beat-up race tracks are. It was busy at least three nights each week with sprint cars, motocrossers and flat track bikes. The infield always looked like a construction site at the foundation-leveling stage, with banked curves and jumps and a smaller oval track inside the bigger one. It's a little-known fact that they got the dirt for the track from a nearby cemetery.

When the gates opened in the afternoon, the racers drove in through the gate in the wall behind the back straight, unloaded their bikes and gear in the infield, and then parked their trucks and vans in the back pit, where I now paused for a moment to let my eyes adjust. After sundown it was as dark as the inside of a goat out there. All the lights—and "all" wasn't that many—were pointed at the track, which was almost well-lit enough for a decent mugging.

A flashlight's beam bounced toward me, flitting across the flanks of the boxy shapes parked along the chain link fence that bordered the concreted banks of the Los Angeles River. A jingling sound grew louder, oddly merry in the inky gloom. A bright light dazzled my eyes.

"Who're you?" a voice said between ragged breaths. "What're you doing back here?"

The security guard was in his sixties, about five-foot-six and lean as a stick of beef jerky. His left leg was shorter than his right and had a pronounced outward curve at the thigh. He wore a neat light blue uniform shirt with dark blue flaps over the pockets. Around his skinny waist hung a wide leather belt with a holstered revolver the size of a small cannon. He was breathing hard, and his hat sat askew on a head thinly covered with grey hair.

"I heard a noise like a shot," I said. "Then a guy came out of the pit gate and said someone was dead."

"Did he say where?"

"He just pointed back here."

"All right. Stay with me."

He took off like a starving lab rat in a maze, scuttling between vans, playing the light on each for an instant before moving on to the next. The gimp leg didn't slow him down much. I had to hustle to keep up.

"Lookee here!" he called suddenly from up ahead.

Centered in the flashlight's beam was a bright stainless steel revolver on the ground under the driver's side door of a long-wheelbase Dodge. He sank stiffly to one knee and bent over it, sniffing like a bloodhound.

"Been fired in the last few minutes," he said. "Nitro powder smell's still strong. Now, if we—"

A man's arm hung out of the window of the Dodge. The beam followed it up into the cab.

"Jackpot," he whispered with a kind of fierce glee.

There was a man seated at the wheel, or rather slumped over it. His left arm hung out the window. There was a dark, wet hole in his left temple. The silver-grey hair around it still smouldered from the powder blast.

I looked inside and immediately wished I hadn't. Blood glistened obscenely on the passenger seat, the dashboard, and the inside of the windshield. A round, starred hole in the opposite window marked the bullet's path after it blew out the right side of the man's head and sprayed the interior with his brains.

The sight and smell twisted my stomach like a wet dishrag. I sank down onto my heels and put my head between my knees.

Some time later the cops showed up, preceded by flashing blue lights and the muted crackle of static on the radio. Two uniformed officers climbed out of the car with the slow, bored uncoiling of lazy snakes. They hitched their belts, slid nightsticks into them, and after a cursory look at the dead man began stringing yellow plastic tape between vans to seal off the area.

In the meantime a crowd of curious racers and mechanics from the infield had gathered. The security guard swaggered over and insinuated himself into the action, barking gruffly at them to stay back. It took both cops and the guard to open a path for the infield ambulance.

One cop took out a notebook and motioned the guard over.

The guard was playing to the crowd, answering the cop's straightforward questions with cliches lifted out of TV police dramas.

I was sucking in lungfuls of cold night air when the cop came over to me.

"You all right?" he said.

I nodded.

"I have to ask you a few questions."

"Sure. Go ahead."

"Your name?"

"Jason Street."

"Address?"

I gave him my Lakewood home address, and the Seal Beach address of *Motorcycle Monthly.*

"*Motorcycle Monthly,*" he said. "What's that?"

"A motorcycle magazine."

"What do you do there?"

"I'm features editor."

"What does a features editor do?"

"A little of everything. I write stories, do road tests, cover races . . ."

"Were you here covering the race?"

"Uh huh."

"Tell me what happened."

"I was standing just across the track from the back pit gate. I heard a noise like a backfire. A guy came through the gate and said someone was dead."

"We talked to him already. He was scared out of his socks. When I asked him what he was doing back here he said he was stealing radios, just like that. Didn't get any."

"Then I met the security guard and we found him." I stopped to think. "That's about it."

"You know the man?"

"Never spoken to him before tonight."

"Sorry, not the guard. Haffner's his name, Gus Haffner. I mean the guy in the van."

"No. I mean . . . I didn't see his face," I said. "Who is it, anyway?"

"We're waiting on a forensics team."

The cop and his partner leaned on their car smoking while Haffner strutted importantly. A while later a plain sedan pulled up and two men in suits got out, nodding to the cops. One hauled a suitcase from the trunk and both donned latex gloves. The ambulance crew stood out of the way while the suits took pictures and put things in plastic bags.

When they were through, the body was removed, covered with a sheet, and wheeled into the ambulance. With the drama over, the gawkers thinned out and filtered back to the infield.

"Are you through with me?" I asked the cop.

"Sure, Mr., uh . . . sure. Thanks."

I started away, then stopped.

"Yes?" said the cop. "You remember something else?"

"No, I . . . it's nothing. Never mind."

"Mr.—" he flipped through his notes— "Street, if there's something you want to tell us . . . "

"I was curious, that's all."

His eyes narrowed. "About what?"

"About why someone would do that." I nodded toward the van.

"Suicide?" He pushed his hat back on his head and looked at a faraway point over my shoulder. "Most of the time it's something like a guy's business goes belly-up, or he finds out his wife is screwing around on him. Or it could be the guy gets up one day, reads something in the morning papers that doesn't agree with him, and he snaps and decides to ring for the big check." He shrugged. "Tell you the truth, it beats the hell outta me."

Stan Martini was waiting behind the yellow tape.

"Who is it, Jason?" he said. "Was it a suicide? Where—"

"I don't know who it is, Stan, and I really don't want to talk about it, okay?"

"Come on, give me a break." He laid his hand on my shoulder. *"Motorcycle Monthly* can't use this story. With your lead time it'll take you three months to get it on the stands. We're a weekly. If I call this into the office in the morning—"

I shook off his hand and shoved past. "Screw your deadline, Stan."

Just then I heard my name called. The cop was ducking under the tape, holding something in his hand.

"Mr. Street," he said, "you say you don't know the dead man, is that right?" he said.

Stan went on point like a retriever and whipped out his notebook.

"No, I said I didn't see his face so, I don't know who it is."

"It seems maybe he knows you. Did you write this?"

He held out a plastic bag with a blood-spattered object inside and shined his flashlight on it. Stan started scribbling, his pen scraping audibly on the paper.

It was a copy of the latest issue of *Motorcycle Monthly,* folded open to the lead page of an article I had written, a multi-brand evaluation of sport bike tires. The test, conducted at Willow Springs Raceway, had been a three-day hell-march in hundred-degree heat, busting our knuckles changing tires, downing a gallon of water at a gulp, and sweating it off in ten minutes on the track.

Scrawled across my by-line in the bold black strokes of a felt-tip marker was the word LIAR.

"It was sitting on the seat next to him, folded open just like this," the cop said. He pried open the bag and ran his thumb along the seal. Holding the magazine gingerly between his thumb and forefinger he flicked his wrist until it refolded itself with the cover showing.

"You know this man?" he said, indicating the subscription label. "A Mr. Sherman Case? Of Case Tire and Rubber Company, in Torrance?"

Case Tires, of which Sherman Case was president—correction, late president—had given us several sets of his company's Sport Magnum tires for the tire evaluation. When everyone's notes were turned in and the results tallied, every tester's least favorite tire was—ta daa—the Case Sport Magnum. The results were as unambiguous as they could be. When I wrote up the test, I said so, concluding that the Sport Magnums had a lock on the bottom of the heap, with no other challengers for the honor anywhere in sight.

The words the cop had spoken only minutes before echoed in my mind.

*Or it could be the guy gets up one day, reads something in the morning papers that doesn't agree with him, and he snaps and decides to ring for the big check.*

The morning papers. Or the latest issue of *Motorcycle Monthly.*

Sherm Case had rung for the big check, all right. Only I was the one who was about to be stuck with the tab.

# 2

"Jason, sit down," Barry said. "We've already been over this—"

I planted my fists on the conference room table and leaned toward the little man in the suit sitting next to Barry.

"I want to hear it again, Barry," I said, "but this time I want to hear it from *him.*"

Barry Meriden, my editor at *Motorcycle Monthly,* ran his fingers through his thinning hair—which was getting visibly thinner as this particular meeting progressed—and pushed his glasses up onto his forehead while expelling the patient, long-suffering sigh of a substitute teacher with a rowdy class on his hands.

The little man in the suit, a Mr. Peters, glanced nervously at Barry for reassurance that I wasn't about to tear off his head and throw it in his face. He was a partner in *Motorcycle Monthly's* law firm. He and Barry shared a retreating hairline and a bemused, somewhat professorial expression. Where Barry was broad-shouldered with forearms like a blacksmith's below his rolled-up shirt sleeves, Peters was short and round and soft, and moved and spoke with a fussy, lawyer-like precision.

"Really, Mr. Meriden," he said, shooting his cuff and eyeing his watch, "I must be going soon. The traffic, you know . . . "

"Give the widows and orphans a break," I said. "The foreclosures and evictions will wait. Talk to me."

"Jason," Barry snapped, putting a warning into it. "Mr. Peters, I think Jason is right. You owe him an explanation. After all, it's his job we're talking about."

"My *former* job, you mean," I said.

"You misunderstand, Mr. Street—"

"Make me understand. Please."

"Jason—"

"I'm trying," Peters said petulantly, "if only you'll let me."

I sat down.

He cleared his throat. "The suit brought against *Motorcycle Monthly* by Case Tire and Rubber Company alleges a breach of an implicit agreement of fair comment—"

"A what? Barry, make him speak English."

"An implicit agreement of fair comment," Barry said, "is created when we do stories like the tire comparison, or whenever we contact a number of manufacturers of a certain type of product and invite them to participate in an impartial comparison. By so doing we are implying that no one manufacturer will have an advantage over another."

"That's standard operating procedure around here." I turned to Peters. "What exactly is Case Tires' problem with the way I conducted that test?"

"Case Tires alleges that . . ." He rummaged through his pigskin briefcase, pulled out a sheaf of paper, ran his finger down the first page, then flipped to the second page.

"Well, to summarize," he said at last, "Case Tires alleges that you, Jason Street, acting for *Motorcycle Monthly,* solicited an inducement from the representative of Blazer Tires, Incorporated, in return for which you slanted the results of the tire test to reflect favorably on Blazer's products, to the detriment of Case Tires' products."

"Says who? And what the hell kind of inducement am I supposed to have solicited?"

"Ah . . ." he flipped through a few more pages. "Here it is. According to a deposition given by a Mr. Cameron Batchelor, who is employed as public relations manager by Case Tires, you, Jason Street, requested—in Mr. Batchelor's hearing—that the representative of Blazer Tires, a Mr. Chad Kennedy, give to you various items of merchandise, in return for which you agreed to alter the test procedures that had been previously agreed upon by all the participants to favor Blazer Tires' products and to reflect favorably upon them to the detriment of Case Tires' products and those of the other manufacturers." He looked up from the page and blinked owlishly. "Is that substantially correct?"

"It's substantially bullshit!" I said. "Chad was sitting in his van listening to his Walkman while the other tire company reps were busting their asses helping us change tires. We were out of Gatorade, it was hot enough to fry eggs on top of the ice chest, and it was two hours past lunchtime. I jokingly—repeat, *jokingly,* as in not seriously—told him if he got up off his sorry ass and drove into town and filled the coolers with drinks and sandwiches, I'd write up Blazer Tires as the greatest thing since the invention of the wheel itself."

"They can't be serious," Barry said. "Jason was obviously joking with the man. There's no way any reasonable person would interpret his statement otherwise."

"If Mr. Street's comments to Mr. Batchelor were the only allegation, I would tend to agree," Peters said. "But Case Tires is also alleging that *Motorcycle Monthly* informed Blazer of the test procedures in advance so that Blazer could build special, er, 'ringers' that perform better than their over-the-counter tire."

"What proof do they have for that?" Barry asked.

"It's only circumstantial, but Blazer, which has refused to comment, by the way, and is referring the matter to its own legal department—as I was saying, Blazer, as determined by a count of the number of pages of advertising over a twelve-month period ending last month, is *Motorcycle Monthly's* largest tire advertiser. Case Tires, on the other hand, does not advertise extensively in *Motorcycle Monthly.* But they do so in another motorcycle magazine called *Cycle Journal,* in sufficient quantity to qualify as that magazine's second largest tire advertiser."

"What's that got to do with anything?" I said. "Who cares how much they advertise with *Cycle Journal?*"

"Case Tires' products have received mostly favorable reviews in *Cycle Journal* in the recent past, while they have not fared as well in *Motorcycle Monthly.* Case alleges that their products' poor performance in your tire test is a direct result of their refusal to advertise more heavily in *Motorcycle Monthly,* and your subsequent actions to make Blazer aware of the test procedures before the fact."

"Or maybe their tires are junk just like I said they are," I said, "and they get good write-ups in *Cycle Journal because* they advertise so much! Has anyone thought of that?"

"Oh, really, Mr. Street," Peters said, looking mildly scandalized at the suggestion, "that would be most difficult to substantiate . . ."

"It's no more far-fetched than what they're claiming *we* did. Besides, *Cycle Journal* has done that sort of thing in the past. You remember, Barry, what happened with all those bogus product evaluations they printed—"

"Let's not get into that now, Jason," Barry said. "Mr. Peters, perhaps you could explain why Jason is being put on leave."

"Leave, hell," I said. "It sounds like 'fired' to me."

"Not at all, Mr. Street," Peters said. "You'll remain on the payroll for the duration of your leave, on full salary. You will not, of course, participate in the day-to-day business of the magazine, and you will clear in advance with Mr. Meriden any visits you find necessary to make to these offices—"

"We have to do it this way, Jason," Barry said. "Just be thankful the suit is aimed at the magazine, and not you personally—"

"Although I would not be surprised," Peters butted in, "if Mr. Street were named as defendant in an additional action if—"

"Mr. Peters," Barry said mildly, "thank you for your time. Hadn't you better be going now? The traffic, you know . . ."

"Doesn't anyone see what's really going on here?" I said after Peters was gone. "Sherm Case killed himself for who knows what reason, and the callous bastards are trying to cash in on it by blaming me."

"It's a good gamble," Barry said. "There isn't a jury on earth that won't be sympathetic when Case's attorneys claim he shot himself because we doctored the results of the test to make him look bad."

"But they're making it sound like I pulled the trigger myself! It's not just them, either. Did you see that piece in *Cycle Weekly,* the one that weasel Stan Martini wrote, about how they found 'the blood-soaked copy of *Motorcycle Monthly* next to the dead man, opened to the tire test that unfairly slammed the Sport Magnum tire?' He practically accuses me of driving Case to suicide all by myself! The bastard even—"

"Jason, calm down," Barry said. "I have no doubt that you

conducted yourself in an ethical and professional manner. But this is turning ugly fast. The magazine doesn't have the resources to fight a protracted legal battle. We're losing ad pages as we speak. The publisher has momentarily snapped out of his customary stupor and is practically foaming at the mouth. He wants to fire you."

"What's stopping him?"

"I said if you go, I go with you."

"Now hold on, Barry, I won't let you stick your neck out for me if—"

"It was my decision. I won't have him usurping my editorial prerogatives or dismissing valued members of my staff on the basis of fanciful allegations of misconduct that wouldn't pass the smell test on 'People's Court.' Besides, either I'm editor or he is. For God's sake, the man doesn't even read the magazine he publishes."

"Thanks. But why the leave? Why can't I keep working while we fight this?"

"Letting you keep working amounts to *Motorcycle Monthly* saying that Sherman Case's death is of no importance. On the other hand, firing you is as good as admitting you did what Case Tires is alleging. We have to make some gesture of good faith, so we're issuing a press release, something along the lines of 'We have every confidence that *Motorcycle Monthly* and the editor in question will be cleared of any charges of wrongdoing. In the meantime we are conducting an investigation of our own into the matter and until such time as the investigation is completed Jason Street will be placed on leave,' and so on."

"So I just sit home by the phone waiting, is that it?"

"Take a vacation. No one said anything about taking you off the insurance. Pick a test bike from the garage. Get away for a while until things calm down a little. Take Sara with you."

After I cooled off I decided he was right. Sara and I were going through a rough patch right then, the worst since she moved in with me a year ago. A road trip might do us both good, give us a chance to get away from familiar surroundings, get out of the rut, and find out what was bugging us.

There was a Yamaha Venture touring bike on long-term loan

to the magazine in the garage. I rode it home and spent the afternoon cleaning it up and checking it over. We took off early the following morning under bright skies, shooting for the north shore of Lake Tahoe by sundown the next day.

An hour after lunch we were on a secondary road between 101 and Interstate 5 when the rear tire went flat. I hoisted the bike up onto the centerstand, rotated the wheel until I found the problem, and pulled a nail the size of a harpoon out of the tire with the toolkit pliers. There was an emergency tire repair kit in the saddlebag. I used it to plug the tire and inflated it with $CO_2$ cartridges. We were on our way half an hour later.

Ten miles later the bike was on the centerstand again, the rear tire once more as flat as week-old beer. Either I had missed the second nail when I plugged the hole made by the first, or we had picked it up since the change. Either way, we were out of $CO_2$.

I left Sara with the bike and rolled the wheel to a farm house. A pimply kid in overalls threw the wheel in the bed of his pick-up and drove me to a gas station on I-5 where I had the new hole plugged and the tire inflated.

When he dropped me off at the bike, Sara had comic-book daggers coming out of her eyes and that look on her face that signals storm clouds gathering on the relationship horizon. I wasn't in a very festive mood myself. I horsed the wheel into place and we rode well into the night to make up for lost time, stopping at last at a motel with a framed picture of Norman Bates over the registration desk.

The next day I fell victim to the male human's genetic inability to ask for directions despite being hopelessly lost, taking us miles up a two-lane back road that petered out into rutted dirt before I admitted the obvious and turned around. Sara had given me the silent treatment all day over the previous day's tire fiasco. It came to a boil that night over a late dinner in a restaurant on the north shore.

"Good salmon," I ventured at one point just so I could say we hadn't eaten the entire meal in complete silence. "Don't you think so?"

"It's all right," she mumbled.

"Just all right?" I said. "It's great. It's king salmon. It's emperor salmon, it's ruler of the known universe salmon—"

"Fine. It's the best goddam piece of salmon the world has ever known." She picked hers up and threw it toward my plate. It landed in my lap. "Are you happy now?"

I put it on my plate and wiped my fingers on my napkin with exaggerated care and plastered a wide, sappy smile on my face.

"Yeah, I'm happy as hell," I said. "Why wouldn't I be? I mean, this has been an absolutely fantastic trip so far, hasn't it? Although I have to tell you I'm a bit disappointed you didn't see the humor in me throwing those two nails out in front of the bike while you weren't looking just so I could run off and have a jolly outing with some hick whose idea of a good time is getting drunk with a bunch of his buddies and throwing up on the high school principal's lawn!"

She glared at me and gripped her fork like she was picking out a place on my forehead to stick it. My foot was in my mouth all the way up to the ankle anyway, so I opened wide and went for the knee.

"What the hell's wrong with you anyway?" I said. "What's wrong with us? Why are we fighting all the time? We never used to be this way."

"I was always this way," she said. "You're the one that changed."

"How? What am I doing that I didn't do before?"

"You always have to be in control. You always have to do things your way."

"Asking you to roll the garden hose up on the reel when you're through with it isn't control. It's just the way things are done. And speaking of control, what about you? You flip out if I don't fold the towels just the right way. What's the big deal about towels, anyway? Is there some secret fold I don't know about?"

She threw the fork at me with a neat flick of her wrist—lucky for me she was too angry to aim straight—knocked her chair over standing up and stalked out of the restaurant. Every pair of eyes in the place followed her, then swung to where I sat in utter bewilderment.

I paid the tab and walked to the room. She wasn't in it when I got there. I sat down on the bed and waited. Ten minutes later I heard a rap on the door. She brushed past me and went into the bathroom. The lock on the door snapped home like a rifle bolt.

I sat down on the bed again to wait her out. It was a familiar pattern of inaction, one I fell back on often when I was a kid and Dad came home drunk or my older brother decided it was time to beat me up. Sitting and brooding hadn't gotten me very far with my family—Dad was still a drunk and my brother had died before I could make peace with him—and it wasn't shaping up as the shining salvation of my relationship with Sara, either. It was time to try something else.

"Sara," I said through the bathroom door. "Please come out. Let's talk."

"Go away."

"You can't stay in there all night. Come out. Talk to me."

"I have nothing to say."

"Well, I have plenty to say. I love you. Can you hear me? You're the best thing that ever happened to me. I don't want to lose you. But I'm afraid I will if we don't figure out what's wrong."

No reply. I jiggled the knob.

"You're being childish. Open the damn door."

"Don't touch that knob."

I jiggled it harder. It wasn't a quality piece of hardware to start with. It gave a little. The door rattled in the frame.

"Don't!" she screamed in a thin, high voice. It sent shivers up my spine. "Don't you dare! I'll tell!"

The door flew open and she lunged at me, her fingers curved like claws and her lips drawn back from her teeth, a shrill, keening sound coming out of her mouth.

I caught her wrists and used her momentum to throw her onto one of the double beds. She exploded under me, kicking and clawing at my eyes. I had never seen her overcome by such fury. I let go and leaped back, expecting another charge and not having the least idea what I would do when it came. Instead she hugged herself and rolled up into a ball, with her knees pulled up in front of her chest, and sobbed.

She cried herself out after a few minutes, rocking slowly and humming tunelessly to herself. I stood across the room with my back to the wall, afraid to touch her, afraid to leave her alone.

She seemed to come around, as if awakening from a bad dream. She knuckled her eyes, groped for a tissue on the nightstand and blew her nose. Her eyes were red, her cheeks tear-stained. She sat up and blinked at the room as if she had no idea at all how she got there.

It was over. Her body relaxed, her familiar posture—lithe, graceful, almost cat-like—returned. She swept her long auburn hair out of her face and ran her fingers through it.

"What happened?" she said.

"Don't you remember?"

She frowned, shook her head.

"I tried to open the door. You came at me like a tiger."

She nodded, matter-of-factly. Like . . . *Oh, a tiger. I see.*

"What did you mean, 'I'll tell'?"

"What?"

"You said you'd tell. Tell who?"

"I said that?"

"Sara, what's going on?"

Her eyes went liquid, unfocused. Her voice was small and weary.

"It was like the dream," she said. "I have this dream where I'm a little girl and I'm in a small dark place and something is outside and it wants to get inside and hurt me. And I yell at it to go away or I'll tell . . . tell my mommy, I guess."

"How long have you been having this dream?"

She shook her head, her brow wrinkled in thought. "Since a few months after we moved in together, I think. Not before, I'm sure."

"Why haven't you said anything?"

"I was afraid."

"Of what?"

"Not what, who. You."

"Me?"

"I was afraid you wouldn't want me any more."

"Not want you any more?" The notion was so absurd I almost laughed out loud. "Are you serious?"

"When I was on my own, I was in charge of my own life," she said, as if she were only now realizing the truth of what she was saying. "When I moved in with you, something happened. I lost control. I had just been laid off from Bartlett, remember? And I couldn't line anything else up right away. In the meantime you paid the bills, you bought the food, you went to work every day while I sat around watching TV in my sweats. And since I wasn't contributing anything to the household expenses, I felt like I had to be there when you got home, and have your dinner ready, and go out when you wanted to, and . . . have sex when you wanted to, even if I felt like being alone. I had no job, no privacy, no control. If you got mad at me and threw me out, I wouldn't even have a home. So I walked around all day on eggshells, terrified I might do something to make you want me to leave."

"All that about me paying the bills and all, that's okay with me. You're between jobs, that's all. I don't mind. I make enough to take care of both of us."

"And that's part of the problem. See, from the day they're born, women are taught to be good little girls, and then good little wives. Let the man make the money, do what he wants, keep him happy. No one ever told us we can have jobs we like, make money of our own, make our own choices."

"I never said you couldn't. You were when we met, and doing a damn fine job of it, too."

"Was I? Those days seem like so long ago, if they ever really happened at all. Lately I'm tense and scared and I feel like something bad is about to happen. This dream is at the center of it. Or the dream is the center, I don't know which. It's always the same, it never changes. And it scares me to death every time. No one and no place is safe for me. Not even you."

I could scarcely comprehend what she had said except on the most superficial level. That she was afraid of me was shocking, that she didn't feel safe in our house a complete surprise. The only thing clear to me was that she was in the grip of something neither one of us understood. Unless she came to terms with it, it would tear her—and us—apart.

We rode home and spent a futile week trying to identify when and why she felt afraid or threatened, what it was I did that made her feel as though she had no control. We were trying to scratch the surface of a diamond with a dry twig. I offered to pay for counseling. She refused angrily, saying she could pay for it herself. We both knew she couldn't, and therefore wouldn't go. Another dead end.

I was starting to feel as insubstantial and unconnected as she was. Because of the lawsuit I was disgraced in the eyes of my peers, shunned by people I had worked with for years, and my own self-worth—never a high-yield stock to begin with—was scraping rock bottom.

We stopped having sex altogether. Even though I knew more or less that it had to do with control, and little to do with me as a person or how much she loved me, it hurt. We drifted apart, separated by a thousand miles in a twelve-hundred-square-foot house, strangers to each other more and more every day that went by.

One night when Sara was at her sister's apartment, and I sat in front of the tube watching two-dimensional people living two-dimensional lives that still seemed better than mine, the phone rang.

"Hello," I said, my eyes still glued to the screen, fascinated at how easily the two-dimensional people solved all their problems and exited stage left arm in arm, smiling.

"I'm looking for Jason Street," a woman's voice said.

"You found him."

"I need to talk to you."

"You are talking to me."

"In person. Can you meet me in half an hour?"

"Meet you—Who is this?"

"How about the Long Beach Sheraton on Ocean Boulevard? I'll be in the lounge."

"Hold on—do I know you?"

"My name is Sherry Case. Sherman Case is—was—my father."

# 3

I felt like the poster child for the fashion-impaired as I walked into the Sheraton later that night in my jeans and leather bomber jacket. Some black tie fundraiser was just winding up in one of the banquet rooms. As I walked down the corridor leading to the lounge, a set of double doors swung open and out spilled a few zillion dollars' worth of SoCal notables, washing over me like a perfumed tsunami. It was like swimming upstream in a river of pearls and silk. I flattened myself against the wall until the crowd thinned out.

A lot of people headed for the lounge. By the time I got there it was filling up fast. I stood by the door, craning my neck for Sherry Case, who had described herself as blonde, wearing a dark skirt and jacket over a light colored blouse, when a hand touched my elbow.

"Jason Street?"

She was blonde, all right, devastatingly so, and in great quantities. Her hair spilled over her shoulders with that tousled, just-got-out-of-bed look that takes some guy named José or Earl hours to achieve. The jacket and skirt were dark blue with subtle pinstripes, the blouse silk or something equally gossamer.

Under other circumstances I would have been totally knocked out. But considering the hell her late father's company was putting me through, I wasn't inclined to be gentlemanly. I disliked her instantly. The feeling was obviously mutual.

She led me to her table and summoned a waiter with an imperious snap of her fingers. The waiter glided over on ball bearings, nodded approvingly at her order, confined his reaction to my or-

der of a Perrier to a single hoisted eyebrow, and glided away as silently as he had appeared.

Sherry Case drew a gold cigarette case out of her purse and lit
up.

"Do you mind?" she said in a tone that clearly said she didn't
give a good goddam if I did or not.

She tapped her perfect fingernails on the table until the drinks
came, staring at a spot on the wall and blowing smoke out of the
corner of her mouth. She had on too much makeup for my taste,
and probably looked far better without any at all. She might have
been a perfectly pleasant person under the hair and the tailored
suit and the don't-mess-with-me attitude. I never got the chance to
find out.

When the drinks came she took a discreet sip of hers, followed by another not-so discreet gulp.

"This is very awkward for me," she said. The glowing tip of
her cigarette trembled like a wary firefly. I tried to guess her age.
She was acting a lot older than she was. Not doing a bad job of it,
but it was an act all the same.

"I know how you feel," I said. "What can I do for you?"

"Do you want your job back?"

"I still have my job."

"You're on leave. From there it's just a few steps to the unem-
ployment line. How long do you think it'll be before your publisher decides you're dead weight and lets you go?"

I started to say something. She held up her hand, palm forward, to silence me.

"It might not be too long before nobody at *Motorcycle Monthly*
has a job. My father's company is suing your magazine for more
money than the miserable rag can possibly be worth."

"Was there some point to this meeting, Ms. Case?" I said. "Or
did you just need someone to watch you drink? You could have
insulted me over the phone and saved us both the gas."

The cigarette on its way to her lips stopped in mid-air. Her
eyes narrowed.

"I don't care if you don't like me, Mr. Street," she said.

"That's handy. Anyway, if your usual method of striking up a
friendship is to drop a ton of lawyers on me and my magazine—"

"A word from me might change that."

That caught me flat-footed.

"I'm listening," I said.

"Everyone thinks my father committed suicide. Isn't that right?"

I nodded.

"You do, too, don't you?"

"I'm no expert. But that's what it looked like, yes."

"My father did *not* kill himself." She stubbed her cigarette out in the ashtray in the middle of the table, bearing down so fiercely that the ashtray shot out from under her hand and rocketed off the table onto the carpet. The ball bearing waiter appeared, whisked it away, fetched a new one, and vanished noiselessly. She had another cigarette going before he returned. She waited until he was gone, then took another gulp of her drink.

The booze seemed to be getting the better of her. For all I knew the drink in front of her wasn't her first that night. I have this thing about letting drunks waste large chunks of the only life I'll ever lead. I pissed away years of my childhood cleaning up after Dad, covering up for him, enduring the daily shame and nightly terror of living with an alcoholic. When I moved out I swore nothing in the world would make me put up with it again.

I tossed a couple of dollars on the table for my drink, slid around the soft leather booth, and stood up.

"Where are you going?" she demanded. "I'm not through talking to you."

"The hell you're not. If you have something to say, get to it. Otherwise I have better things to do than sit here and watch you get shitfaced and blow smoke in my eyes."

A couple in the next booth stopped their conversation to stare at me.

"Can I help you?" I barked at them. "Bowl of pretzels? Freshen up those drinks for you?"

"Please, sit down," Sherry said, crushing her cigarette out. "I'm sorry. I've been under more than a little strain lately. I won't waste too much more of your time."

"I'm sorry, too," I said, sinking heavily into the booth.

"Things have been . . . strange at home. I was itching to tee off on somebody on general principles. You were convenient."

"I know you think I deserve to be teed off on, and why. But hear me out first. The lawsuit was the acting CEO's idea. Case Tires is in trouble. We're deep in debt, and in the middle of a recession and a slump in motorcycle sales on top of it. My father's death couldn't have come at a worse time. He was very much a hands-on businessman. He thought paperwork was for sissies. He left an awful mess behind."

"What has this got to do with me and *Motorcycle Monthly?*"

"Tyler Wallace—he's the acting CEO—has this idea that he can settle with your magazine out of court, and, with the settlement, help prevent a takeover by another tire company that's been trying to buy Case Tires for years. Not everyone in the company agrees, me included. Not only will it take too long—these things drag on in the courts for years—" She started to light another cigarette. As the flame neared the tip she caught my eye. She snapped the lighter shut and replaced the cigarette in the pack. "At any rate, it wasn't your fault my father died, nor the fault of your magazine."

"Tell that to this guy Wallace."

"I have. He isn't listening. My father left me his shares in the company—fifty-one per cent—but until the estate is settled, I'm a non-entity."

"How long before you're not?"

"Wallace is making it as difficult as he can, but with the shape things are in, he doesn't have to try too hard . . . I don't know. But I'll tell you this, and you have my word on it." She leaned across the table. Her eyes, the deep blue of far-off oceans, met mine.

"My father did not kill himself," she repeated, her voice steely.

"You already said that," I observed. "What makes you so sure?"

She stuck out a defiant chin. "He was not the kind of man to surrender to a problem. He would attack it, pummel it, wrestle it to the ground. He was beaten sometimes, but he would never give up. Which brings us to you."

"Me?"

"I told you my father left me his stock in Case Tires. Something else he left was an insurance policy on his life, in the amount of one million dollars, payable to Case Tires in the event of his death."

"Well, hell, there's the money you need to stop the takeover," I said. "What's the problem?"

"The problem is the policy doesn't pay off in the event of suicide. If my father's death is ruled as murder, however . . ."

I was waiting for her to finish when the little light bulb came on over my head.

"You see, don't you?" she said. "The police are calling it a suicide. I know it wasn't. I can't prove it. But you might be able to."

"Me?" Now I knew she was drunk. "You're joking."

"I'm serious. You're in the motorcycle business. You know people, you know how things work. You're a journalist. You can ask questions without arousing suspicion."

"Ask who—"

"The company that's trying to take over Case Tires is owned by a man named Max Bauer. His father, Heinrich, and my father used to be partners until my father forced him out. Heinrich died soon after that, and Max—who should have inherited the company—never forgave my father."

"You think Max Bauer killed him?"

"I wouldn't be at all surprised. Anyway, it's a place to start."

"You need the police. Or a detective agency. There must be a dozen in the phone book."

"I already tried them. They won't touch the case."

"Why?"

She fidgeted with her lighter.

"Go ahead," I said. She lit up gratefully.

"They, ah, wouldn't take the case for financial reasons," she said through the smoke. "Actually, right now I'm rather short of funds. My . . . income was based on a, uh, money from my father—"

"An allowance?"

"All right, yes. But I can make cash withdrawals from my credit cards to cover your expenses. Just phone me from wherever you are and I'll wire the money."

"Whoa, back up. You're a couple of jumps ahead of me. Just exactly where am I going? And why?"

"You've heard of Rusty McCann, haven't you?"

"McCann the flat track racer? Sure, second year Expert, talented but erratic, might win the Grand National Championship someday if he ever settles down and gets serious about racing. What about him?"

"Case Tires is his primary sponsor. Oh, he has others, but we pay most of the bills. I've arranged for him to take you on as a pit helper. I told him it's as a favor to me, because I don't blame you for what happened and want to give you the chance to clear yourself. He doesn't know anything about our financial situation, and I'd prefer he didn't find out."

"Hold on. The flat track circuit heads for the midwest tracks any day now, and it won't be back to the west coast until the San Jose Mile in September. What am I supposed to do, follow these guys?"

"Exactly."

"You're crazy! I can't just take off and hare around the country looking for your phantom killer."

"What else are you doing right now that's so important?" she said.

"She has a point," Sara said later that night over hot chocolate in the kitchen.

"Oh, not you, too," I groaned. "Sara, this is the most lamebrained scheme anyone's ever trotted out in public. First off, odds are a thousand to one against that Sherm Case was murdered. If she wants to believe otherwise, that's fine with me. Personally, I think she's more interested in the million bucks. Second, how the hell does she know the killer—that's assuming there is one, which I'm not, you understand—how does she know the killer has anything to do with flat track racing? If he'd killed himself in the parking lot of Dodger Stadium, would she ask me to sign up for spring training, for crying out loud? And third—"

"It would do us both a lot of good if you got away for a while," Sara said, looking down at her mug.

I pulled up short. "What the hell do you mean, do us both a lot of good?"

"I need some time alone," she said, "to work out what's wrong with my life, with our life together. And you're going crazy, knocking around here with nothing to do all day but yell at the TV and play with the dog. If she's willing to pay your expenses, what's the harm?"

"It'll never work. People will recognize me."

"Don't flatter yourself. How many times has your face appeared in the magazine?"

"They'll know my name."

"Pick an alias. John Smith. Bill Williams."

"Are you serious?"

"Go. Have an adventure. I'll take care of everything here."

"I can't. I'm scared," I said, sensing a faint, eerie echo of Sara's fear.

"Of what?"

"That you'll be gone when I come back."

She slumped down in her chair and sighed.

"I don't know what's happening to me," she said. "Every day I'm more confused and frightened. All I know for sure is I need some time by myself to think about it."

"What if you think about it and decide you have to leave?"

She covered her face with her hands. I stood behind her stroking her hair.

"Jason, I can't promise that I'll be here when you get back. But I'm going to try my best to be. I have to do what's best for me. Can you accept that and not hate me?"

"I don't hate you," I said, pulling her to her feet and wrapping my arms around her. "I could never hate you."

It's funny how love persists even if its object inflicts unbearable pain. I would always love her, whether we were together or apart. I wanted what was best for her, too, which is why I was willing to let her go if that's what she wanted.

# 4

It was a warm summer morning on Tahoe's north shore. The water lapped gently at the sandy beach as Sara and I strolled barefoot, arms around each other's waist, without a care in the world. Suddenly the earth heaved with a mighty lurch and I woke abruptly to a racket like somebody pouring a ton of buckshot on a tin roof. I sat up, bonked my head on the plank of plywood inches from my face, and flopped back onto the bunk.

A grinning, upside-down head appeared over the edge of the top bunk.

"Hey, Hemingway's awake!" it said, addressing me by the annoying nickname that had been settled on me five minutes after we were introduced.

"It's about damn time," said the man in the driver's seat, looking over his shoulder. "We thought you was gonna sleep all the way to Springfield."

Rusty McCann swung down out of the bunk and dropped into the passenger seat beside Ozzie ("Don't call me Harley") Davidson. He reached under the seat and pulled out a nylon pouch full of CDs, and shoved one into the player in the dash. Instantly a deafening guitar solo exploded out of the door speakers at a volume just below the pain threshold.

Ozzie, without taking his eyes from the road, jabbed the OFF button.

"Knock it off, Rusty," he said, in a way that suggested he said it pretty often.

"Mornin'," Rusty said to me, grinning impishly. "Sleep well?"

"Yeah, fine," I muttered. "I must have dropped off for a full twenty minutes there eight or nine hours ago. Where are we?"

"Outskirts of nowhere," Rusty said bouncily. "Be smack in the middle of it any minute now." He had the boundless energy of a puppy and the face of a mischievous kid behind the scraggly blond moustache.

I slid out of my bunk and perched my butt on the edge, wiping the sleep out of my eyes. My clothes felt sticky, my scalp itched, and my mouth tasted like a small reptile had hatched its young there.

Ahead, through the bug-spattered windshield, lay the flattest, dustiest, and least hospitable landscape I had seen since the last time I looked through the windshield, which was right around where Arizona turned into New Mexico. The sameness of the landscape gave me a disquieting feeling of not having moved at all since sundown yesterday.

Behind me, on the other side of a thin plywood bulkhead, the bikes, tools, and gas cans clanked and rattled with every rut and frost heave in the pavement. When Sara had dropped me off at Rusty's house in Thousand Oaks the day before, I had been pleasantly surprised to see the team van, with its plush cab and twin bunks in front of a cavernous cargo box. There was even an onboard water tank and a built-in cooler. I mentally compared it to the aged, cramped, and constantly ailing Dodge short-wheelbase van I used to travel in—kind of a gym locker on wheels—and decided hitting the road again might not be so bad after all.

Ten hours later, as the sun faded in the rear view mirrors and my eyelids started to droop, I wasn't so sure. The van bucked and pitched on its rock-hard suspension sounding like "two skeletons screwing in a snare drum," as Ozzie so colorfully put it. Rusty seemed perfectly capable of sleeping through a nuclear bomb test, and Ozzie didn't look like he ever slept. For me there was no chance of sleep as human beings define the term. The best I could manage was to doze fitfully until the next expansion joint in the interstate jolted the contents of the van off the floor and dropped it down with a thunderous crash.

"We're coming up on Oklahoma City in about an hour," Ozzie said. "Ready for some breakfast?"

We pulled into a truck stop outside the city limits and parked the box van at the end of a row of eighteen wheelers. Rusty bounded into the restaurant like a kid at Disneyland, stopping at the cash register to paw through a rack of belt buckles and key fobs with the names of diesel trucks on them. He was about five-foot-six, just the right height for a motorcycle racer, trim and lean with forearms like Popeye's—handy for wrestling a Harley-Davidson XR750 flat track bike around dirt ovals. Although his bio in the racing series press kit said he would be twenty years old on Halloween, from a distance he barely looked old enough to take out a library card in his own name. He flipped through the revolving racks of trucker trinkets, hardly seeing one before moving on to the next, taking in the entire room in a series of random forays down the aisles like a whirlwind in a T-shirt and jeans.

Ozzie shook his head in wry amusement as he and I trudged to an empty table.

"He reminds me of my Irish setter," I said. "Is he always like this?"

"Nah," Ozzie said. "Only when he's awake."

Rusty slid into the booth just as a passing waitress with a coffee pot in one hand gave us a twangy good morning and sailed three menus at us without breaking stride.

"Howdy, ma'am," he said, mimicking her accent perfectly. A couple of truckers in the next booth looked our way, not entirely amused by the smart-ass city boy makin' sport of their speech.

"I'll have the number one breakfast," Rusty said when the waitress returned for our orders. "By the way, what is it?"

She cocked an eye at him. "Biscuits an' gravy, grits or homefries," she recited.

"Homefries. No, wait—grits. Orange juice, too."

Ozzie and I ordered, and the waitress scurried off.

"Why did you order the number one breakfast if you didn't know what it was?" I asked.

"If you're gonna be Number One, you gotta think like number one," Rusty beamed.

"The Number One number plate," Ozzie said in response to my puzzled look. "Like the Grand National Champ wins at the end of the season? He figures if he eats the number one breakfast, sooner or later he'll win the Number One plate. He's had every damn number one breakfast from San Jose to Hagerstown. Some of 'em been real tasty, too, ain't they, Rusty?"

Rusty stuck his finger in his mouth and made a gagging sound.

"Like I said," Ozzie said.

The coffee was as hot and black as fresh asphalt and strong enough to soak the stripes off a tiger. After two cups I felt more or less alive. The food wasn't half bad. Rusty gulped his down in about three bites, then slid out of the booth and disappeared into the gift shop again. It was wearing me out just watching him.

Just as I was beginning to think Rusty had some weird fixation about gift shops, I saw what it was he really wanted to take home as a souvenir. As I settled the tab from our trucker's wallet, Ozzie disentangled Rusty from the redheaded teenager working the gift shop cash register. He had charmed her right out of her socks and was working his way up when Ozzie glided up behind him.

"'Scuse me, ma'am," he said politely, "but we gotta go. See, if my little brother don't keep up on his medication, the doctor says he'll start in doin' them things to puppies an' kittens again, and the judge'll want him to go back to the—" He leaned toward her and whispered, "We just call it 'the quiet place.'"

I took the driver's seat and Ozzie settled into the shotgun. Rusty was still fantasizing about the freckled little redhead as we drove through Oklahoma City and got on I-44 heading toward Tulsa. After a while he exhausted the lewd possibilities, hopped into the top bunk, put his headphones on, and buried his nose in a copy of *Cycle Weekly*.

Ozzie propped his long legs on the dashboard and slid down in the seat. He was about six feet and change, his face leathery and wind-burned, with arms that rippled with stringy muscles like the village smithy's and scarred, large-knuckled hands. A perpetual five-day stubble covered his creased, narrow face, and a hank of his slicked-back black hair kept falling into his eyes.

We drove along in silence for about an hour, Rusty napping in the bunk, Ozzie draped over the seat like an old sweater, me content just to drive and be alone with my thoughts.

A few miles outside of Tulsa, Ozzie stirred and sat up. He

planted a foot on the engine cover, balanced his elbow on his knee, and propped his chin in his hand. He stared out the window at the bleak landscape for a while, then turned to me.

"Lemme see if I got this right," he said in the country-boy drawl he affected when it suited him to appear slow-witted and gullible. "Everybody thinks you wrote some article in your magazine that made Sherm Case blow his brains out, right?"

I nodded.

"Only Sherry Case don't blame you. In fact she thinks her old man was murdered, and she wants you to find out who did it? Well, I may just be a hick from Bakersfield, but ain't this all a mite far-fetched? I mean Sherm Case had his share of folks he wouldn't want to walk up a dark street with, but hell, who'd want to kill him?"

"Sherry mentioned a man named Max Bauer. Do you know him?"

"Owns Universal Tire and Rubber Company. He's a small-timer in the motorcycle tire business, but a big player in racing. He has his street bike tires made in Japan with his own sidewall markings, but he makes all the racing stuff over here. It's not bad, either. If we weren't contracted to Case Tires, I'd put Rusty on Bauer's rubber at some of the tracks."

"Did Bauer and Case know each other?"

"Sure, back when Sherm won the Grand National Championship. Right after that he hung up his leathers and went to work for Old Man Bauer, that'd be Max's father—Henry or Heinrich or some damn thing."

"I didn't even know Case was a racer, much less Grand National Champ. When was that?"

"Uh-huh, that'd be 1950. Sherm Case won it that year and retired right after. Old Man Bauer took him on as a sales rep, then made him vice-president over his own son—"

"Max?"

"—yep, and when the old man had a stroke Sherm took over and changed the name to Case Tires."

"What did Max have to say about it?"

"Nothing. He was long gone by then. Case gave him the boot."

"Wouldn't that make Max one of the people Case wouldn't want to walk down a dark street with?"

Ozzie nodded sagely. "It might at that."

"Where could I find Max Bauer these days?"

"Just look for Ricky Poe once we get to the track. Max sponsors him. He's been coming to a lot of the races himself lately to keep an eye on things. Word is he's not too happy about Ricky blowing up in every main event so far this year."

"Poe has been winning all the Shiloh Shootouts, though, hasn't he?" The Shiloh Shootout was a six-lap race featuring the top six fastest qualifiers for the main event. "How come he can't keep it together for a twenty-five-lap race?"

"That's what Max and everyone else has been asking themselves. Ed Grimes, his tuner—Fast Eddie they call him, that's a laugh, more like Last Eddie—he better watch his ass, or he'll be watching the next mile race from the outside of the fence instead of the pits, and Ricky'll be back waitin' tables in his old man's restaurant in Redding."

I glanced over my shoulder at Rusty. He had his headset on, but the *Cycle Weekly* was flat on his chest and his eyes were closed.

"What about Rusty?" I said. "How are his chances?"

Ozzie checked to make sure Rusty was asleep. "The pressure's really on us this year," he said. "You guys in the press are partly responsible. Rusty's a second-year Expert, and after that great rookie year everyone's expecting big things out of him, Case Tires included. Nobody's come right out and said so, but I got a feeling our sponsorship depends on him doing real good this year. Top five, something like that."

"Can he pull it off?"

Ozzie frowned. "I give you even money on it," he said at last, "He's got the talent—got it in spades—he just doesn't have the judgment yet." He met my eyes. "Look, since you're along for the ride, I'd appreciate it if you could kinda keep an eye on him whenever you can. Sometimes I gotta be the kid's mother as well as his tuner."

I laughed. "How many redheaded checkout girls has he gotten away with so far?"

"None I've noticed, leastwise not for any length of time. Can't begrudge the boy a little partying after a good ride. But I won't waste my time with anyone who's into chasing skirt first and into racing second. I'm getting too old for this running around stuff, and I'd like to say I took one kid to the top before I hang it up and buy me a farm somewhere and raise chickens and bug the shit outta the neighbors riding my dirt bike out on the back forty."

We pulled into Springfield a few hours later. The happening place to stay during the race was the Holiday Inn East, right off I-55 on South Dirksen Parkway. Some teams got into town a day early to rest up or to race in the preliminary events on Saturday. Vans and trucks painted with team logos and sponsors' names were parked next to dusty station wagons with tourist trap bumper stickers like "Trees of Mystery!" and "Where the Hell is Wall Drug?" Rusty hopped out and sauntered over to a group of people sitting on the lift gate of a box van. High fives were exchanged, and beer offered and accepted.

Ozzie and I took our luggage into the lobby and checked in. Ozzie doubled up with Rusty, and I got a room for myself. I unpacked my duffel bag and was looking forward to some time alone when the phone rang.

"Chow time, Hemingway," Ozzie said. "Meet us in the lobby in ten."

"Listen, you guys go on," I said. "I want to catch up on a few things. I saw a burger place down the street. I'll just grab a quick bite there, okay?"

"Suit yourself. We leave for the track at seven in the morning. Meet us at the van."

What I wanted to catch up on was how Sara was doing. I had had lots of time to think about our situation during the drive. The more I thought about it, the more I feared Sara was slipping away from me. What I couldn't pin down was why. The reasons she had given weren't altogether convincing. The ones I came up with didn't make me feel any better.

The phone rang until the answering machine kicked in. Halfway through the recording Sara picked up and said, "Hello?"

"Hi, sweets, it's me," I said. She sounded sleepy. I glanced at my watch. It was early evening back home. "How are you doing?"

"Okay," she said around a yawn.

"Stayed up too late last night partying, huh?" I joked. "What time did you send the Chippendale's guys home?"

There was a pause, then she said, "Where are you?"

"Springfield, Illinois. Birthplace of Lincoln. The city is crawling with Lincoln this and Lincoln that. Lincoln Burgers, Honest Abe's Used Cars, Log Cabin Liquors, that sort of thing. I even saw a John Wilkes telephone booth."

Another pause. "Uh huh."

"Are you okay? You sound beat."

"I was taking a nap."

"In the middle of the day?"

"Is that illegal?"

"No, it's just that you never sleep in the daytime unless—" I bit off the rest of the sentence.

"Look," she said irritably, "I'm sorry if you have a problem with me taking a nap. But if that's all you called about, I'd like to get back to it."

"That's not all. I called to say hello. And to tell you I love you. And I miss you."

"I miss you too," she said without any noticeable conviction. "I have to hang up now."

We rang off and I sat on the squeaky motel bed staring at the phone. There was a painting over the dresser. It was a wintry scene, with a bare-limbed tree and a frozen river in the background. A snapshot of my life.

The only time I could remember Sara wasting good daylight with a nap was when we made love in the morning and slept in. The slightest change in her normal routine threw her daily clock off by a few hours, and she would get sleepy that afternoon. By the next night she'd be on schedule again, and the morning after that she'd be out the front door at first light running laps around the block.

The empty feeling in my stomach was only partly due to hunger as I walked down the street to the burger stand. I took the food back to my room, ate about half of it, and tossed the rest in the waste basket. I thought about calling Sara again, but couldn't imagine what I would say. Instead I fell asleep watching cable movies.

I overslept the alarm the next morning and didn't have time for a shower. Ozzie was sitting behind the wheel with the engine running when I threw open the door and jumped in, bleary-eyed and unshaven. Rusty was lying in the bunk reading the Sunday comics.

We drove in silence to the fairgrounds on the north side of town. Sign-up was outside the track. I had to buy a thirty-dollar mechanic's license, become a member of the sanctioning body and pay a full year's dues, and cough up another twenty-five bucks to get into the pits. All told I was out seventy-five dollars before I had even had my first cup of coffee. The thought that Sherry Case would cover it later was some consolation. This brainless scheme was her idea, and the more it wound up costing her the better.

We drove through the tunnel between turns three and four and parked in the pits, set in a semi-circle of dirt near the start-finish line, bordered by short, green grass that covered the rest of the infield. Rusty and I laid down a tarp and set up the canopy over it while Ozzie unloaded the bike and arranged his tools and spare parts.

Rusty got into his leathers and sat on the tailgate putting tear-offs on his helmet. The clear plastic lenses fit over the face shield and were torn off during a race as dirt thrown up by the bikes ahead built up on them. A racer would go through two or three of these in twenty-five laps at some tracks. The trick was to time it so the supply would last until the end of the race. If you ran out too soon, you'd be riding the last few laps with dirt and oil smeared all over your face shield. Try to wipe it off with your glove, and you'd only smear it worse.

Rusty affixed a doubled-over tab of masking tape to each tear-off, arranging some to tilt up and others down, all the tabs on the left so they could be reached during the race with the hand that wasn't holding the throttle wide open. The tabs were fanned out to prevent grabbing more than one at a time.

After he finished with the tear-offs he took a bottle of plastic polish and began cleaning his helmet, flicking minute bits of dirt off with his fingernail. He did all this with a nearly ritual intensity, his face slack, his eyes fixed only on the task at hand.

"He's putting on his race face," Ozzie said quietly over my shoulder. "Getting in the mood. You watch. He'll be a different kid until the checkered flag falls this afternoon."

Ozzie was flipping through a loose-leaf binder filled with pages of hand-written notes. I asked him what it was.

"Crib sheets," he said. He held the book open for me to see. One page was headed "Springfield" and was covered with cryptic notations. "See here, this is how far up in the clamps the fork tubes were set, and here's the shock length, what gearing we ran, the wheelbase, that sort of thing. We got a third last year with this set-up, and it ought to be real close to perfect for today."

I pointed to a scribble at the top of the page. "What's this one?"

"Huh?" He squinted at his own handwriting. "Oh, yeah, the weather." He looked up at the sky and sniffed the air like a hunting dog. "'Bout the same. Been a wet year so far, though, wetter than last. The track oughta be pretty tacky."

"You kept track of last year's *weather?*"

"I ain't got time to go re-inventing the wheel here. You'll see why once the show starts."

The first practice was announced over the PA. Rusty strapped on his steel shoe, a flat piece of metal cut in the shape of the sole of his left boot, with a rounded toe cap and a heel counter to keep it in place. Flat track racers drop their left feet off the footpeg in the corners and skim them along the track, ready to support the bike if a slide gets out of control. The steel shoe acts like a speedboat skipping over the water, keeping the boot from catching in holes in the track. Some racers have three shoes, one each for miles, half-miles, and short tracks. The faster the track, the flatter the shoe is on the bottom. Mile-track shoes are as flat as a granite tombstone.

Rusty stomped his left foot several times to seat the shoe and buckled his helmet. Ozzie rolled the Harley off the stand and Rusty climbed aboard. He sat on the bike, bouncing it on the suspension, turning the bars from left lock to right lock, pulling the clutch lever, toeing the brake pedal, making sure everything worked. Dirt track bikes don't have front brakes, and the racers don't use the tiny rear brake for much except setting the bike into a broadslide to scrub speed off going into the corners. There's absolutely nothing on a dirt tracker that doesn't have to be there—no fenders, no instruments, no kick starter. They represent the racing motorcycle in its most elemental form, and have the same stark, menacing beauty as a barracuda.

Rusty put the gearbox into second and pulled in the clutch. When he nodded, Ozzie began pushing him across the pit toward the starting line. Rusty stood up on the footpegs, then simultaneously dropped heavily onto the seat and let out the clutch. The engine coughed once, then caught with a booming explosion like rolling thunder. Rusty rolled to a stop and revved the engine, increasing the revs slowly and backing off, until the oil warmed up. Ozzie knelt by the bike, squinting at the engine and poking at it with a screwdriver.

The officials opened the track gate and let half a dozen riders out to try out the surface. They made a few laps, pulled off near where the officials stood waiting for their verdict, and pronounced the track fit to race on.

For the next hour and a half the racers went out in twos and threes, dialing in their chassis, engines, and tires. Rusty went out twice before coming in and asking for a little more gear, meaning he wanted Ozzie to change the rear wheel sprocket in order to get a higher top speed on the straights. Ozzie obliged and sent Rusty out again. He returned satisfied and declared he'd had enough practice. Ozzie looked like he thought there was no such thing as too much practice, but he nodded anyway.

"Don't want to waste it where it don't count," he philosophized. "Save it for time trials, qualify up front, then kick ass in the main."

With time trials only a few minutes away, Rusty was still deep within himself. Ozzie was busy wiping down the bike with a red rag and rechecking all the things he had checked barely half an hour ago. There was a snack bar under the theater stage in the middle of the pits. I got a cup of coffee there and went over to the front straight to watch the start of time trials.

The racers went out two at a time, half a lap apart. Each one got a warm-up lap, then one lap against the clock, then came in. Every time one came off, another was sent out, and the process continued until everyone had posted a time or waved off their first attempt. The times determined the make-up of the heat races, which in turn determined a racer's position on the starting grid— provided he made the program at all. Only seventeen riders could qualify for the main event. At least fifty were trying.

It was about as riveting as lawn bowling, so I leaned against the fence and sipped my coffee, watching the racers and mechanics and crew.

The day was warming up fast. People were shucking out of sweatshirts and jeans, peeling down to halter tops and shorts. There's a certain anonymity to standing at the edge of a crowd of people. I took advantage of it to stare openly at some of them. I got carried away once and found a particularly attractive woman staring right back at me with a half-quizzical, half-inviting look. *Do we know each other? Should we maybe get to know each other?* I gave her a nod and a smile, which she returned before walking on.

Immediately I felt guilty, as if Sara were watching me. Trouble at home wasn't a license to look for more on the road. I dumped my tepid coffee and walked back to the van.

Rusty qualified fifth fastest, earning him a front row start in his heat and a spot in the six-man Shiloh Shootout. He was a bit more animated than he had been earlier, but still subdued. He accepted my congratulations with a shy grin and retreated into the van and closed the rear doors.

"Is he all right?" I asked Ozzie. "He looks sick."

"Just nerves," Ozzie said as he pulled the air cleaners off and knocked the caked-on dirt out of them against the side of his shoe. "He's thinking about what he has to do out there, breaking the track into segments, figuring out the fast way through each one, then stringing them all together in his mind."

"This is the same kid we separated from a checkout girl with the Jaws of Life yesterday, right? And you want him to concentrate on his racing more?"

Ozzie put the air cleaners on the seat and crossed his arms. "What he's doing right now, he has to do just to get out there and ride. But what he has to do to *win* is do that all the time, not just on race day. This thing he has about thinking like Number One? Well, he's on the right track. But it's more than eating whatever weird breakfast is first on the damn menu. It's thinking like a racer twenty-four hours a day. He ain't there yet. When he gets there, he'll be a winner. Right now he's fast, but he's raw, running on nerves and luck."

"Who was it said he'd rather be lucky than good?"

"I dunno," Ozzie said, "but he ain't the Grand National Champ, now, is he?"

The show began at 1:30 in the afternoon, right on schedule, a rare enough occurrence that it caught everyone off guard. It kicked off with a parade lap around the track by vintage dirt track machines, then the Motor Maids, a Harley-mounted women's drill team dressed in aviator's caps, military-style blouses and jodhpurs, and gleaming knee-high boots. They rode up and down the main straight in formation, an American flag mounted on the forks of the lead bike flapping in the breeze, while the announcer mispronounced the names of the various notables in attendance. Finally the national anthem boomed over the track, everyone got to their feet with hats over hearts, and the heat races were called.

It seemed smart to leave Ozzie and Rusty to do what they did best, so I moseyed out to my spot on the front straight. The way Ozzie explained it, they took the 48 fastest qualifiers and put them in four 10-lap heat races, starting positions determined by qualifying times—the guys who qualified 49th or slower could go home now, or stick around and watch if they wanted to. Since this was a mile-track race, first through third in the heats transferred directly to the main event, while fourth through ninth went to one of two ten-lap semis. First and second in each semi transferred to the main, and third through seventh got to ride the Last Chance Qualifier. The LCQ was sometimes the best race of the day—only the winner transferred to the main. Everyone else was bleacher-bait.

Rusty was in the first heat and got a perfect holeshot, reading the starter like an open book and anticipating the green light a split-second before it lit up. He was first into turn one, but slipped off the groove—a narrow racing line scrubbed clean of loose dirt by the tires, the fastest but not necessarily the only way around the track—and fell to fifth before he could gather it up and elbow his way back into line.

The next lap he tried the cushion, the part of the track outside the groove. At some tracks riding the cushion was like riding on greased ball bearings. At Springfield, the cushion worked passably well, but not as well as the groove. You looked spectacular up there, crossed up and throwing a roostertail of dirt, but the guys down on the groove were leaving you for dead. Rusty swooped high in the corner and tried to blast around the bunched-up pack on the outside, but he couldn't pull it off. He lost another spot, and the next lap was back on the groove in sixth place, three spots from a direct transfer.

By the fifth lap he was up to fourth, and a lap later he drafted the third-place rider across the line, yanked on the bars at the last second, popped out of the slipstream, and pitched his Harley sideways into turn one in third place.

The other guy didn't stay passed for long. He dogged Rusty for two laps and then pulled the same slipstreaming move, cutting it close enough for the two riders to swap sweat. Rusty, who had been concentrating on reeling in the two lead bikes, bobbled and fell back half a dozen bike lengths. He couldn't make up the gap by the checkered flag and finished fourth. He would have to win or place in his semi to make the main.

When I got to the van Ozzie was fuming while Rusty stood, hands on hips, staring at the ground with a frown on his face.

". . . you were in third, you had a direct transfer in your hip pocket!" Ozzie was saying in a low voice taut with emotion. "You should have been paying attention to the guy behind you, not those two guys way the hell up ahead of you."

"I know, Ozzie," Rusty said, kicking the dirt with his toe. "I'm sorry."

"Sorry don't put us in the main."

Rusty unbuckled his steel shoe and, holding it by the strap, tossed it in the van. Then he walked off, shaking his head and talking to himself.

I idly picked up the shoe, just wanting a closer look at it, and dropped it immediately. It was blazing hot.

"Problem?" Ozzie said, grinning.

"Nope," I replied, sucking my fingers. "It just doesn't take long to look at a steel shoe."

There were three other heats to run before the semis. I found a spot at the far end of the pits as close to the corner as the turn marshalls would let me go and watched as the racers thundered down the main straight, laid down flat on the gas tank, left hands wrapped around the fork tube to cut wind resistance. Then in one practiced, perilous-looking motion, each one sat up, grabbed the handlebar, downshifted, tapped the rear brake to scrub off speed and set the bike into a slide, and almost carelessly dropped his left foot off the peg onto the track. The exhaust note dopplered from a high-revving bellow to a muted, off-throttle growl, then climbed gradually to a full-throated roar that echoed off the far retaining wall as the bike negotiated the corner and reached the long back straight, at the end of which the whole hair-raising ballet took place once more.

I once heard it summed up this way by a veteran dirt track racer: "It's easy. All you gotta remember is 'Go straight, turn left, go straight, turn left.'"

I had done my share of racing, but only on the pavement, and only on road racing bikes where a dirt track-type slide was almost always a prelude to a leisurely chat with the paramedics during the ambulance ride to the ER. As I watched I tried to imagine what it must be like to ride a bike with no front brake at 130 miles per hour down a narrow dirt alley toward a curving fence and have to pinpoint a spot on the track about the size of a TV tray in which to execute that intricate leap back from the brink of disaster at precisely the same instant lap after lap . . . and decided there's never been enough money printed to get me to try it.

"Who are you rooting for?" a voice to my left said.

I turned to see the woman I had been caught staring at earlier. Up close she was even more stareworthy. She was about five-foot-six or -seven, half a head shorter than my six feet, had straight black hair falling down over her shoulders, fashionably promi-nent cheekbones, and a wide, beauty-queen smile. Her legs were long and tanned and contrasted her white shorts and polo shirt deliciously. A sun visor with some sponsor's logo on it shaded her eyes. The network of fine lines at the edges of her eyes gave her away as older than she looked. Even so, however many years she had on my thirty-one had been kind to her.

"I'm here with Rusty McCann," I said. "You?"

She shrugged. "No one in particular. Have we met?"

"We have now." I held out my hand while my mind raced. Should I tell her my real name? What if word got out I was here? Or was Sara right about no one knowing me? "I'm Bob." *Bob, I* thought. *Holy shit.*

"Angela," she said. Her grip was firm and she held my hand as she added, "What are you doing after the race, Bob?"

"Uh, I'm not sure. It depends on what Rusty's doing, I guess."

"Maybe we could do it together. You and me, I mean, not Rusty."

The first thought that came to mind was whether she had forgotten her glasses. I must have looked like the mayor of Skid Row—I sure felt like him—but I was willing to entertain a second opinion. Maybe my three-day stubble looked roguish for all that it itched like hell. At any rate it wasn't every day a tanned and leggy woman like Angela left the door wide open for me, and frankly I had had all the male bonding I could stand for a while. I considered a witty reply—then stopped cold.

"I'm flattered, Angela," I said, "truly flattered. But I'm, well, sort of involved with someone right now."

"So am I," Angela said. "So what? Is she here?"

I shook my head. "Home. California."

"California's a long, long way away."

"She'll know. And even if she doesn't, I will."

Angela tsk-tsked. "A conscience. Who'd have thought it in this day and age."

"It's my cross to bear. But—"

"I know, you're flattered. Well, Bob, I'll tell you what. If you think you might want to be more than flattered, I'm at the Holiday Inn East. Room 121. Give me a call."

She patted my hand and added, "Oh, and your conscience? Believe me, you can get over it if you try."

She walked slowly away, leaving me with a tornado like the one that blew Dorothy to Oz whirling the thoughts around in my head.

Ozzie materialized at my right. Startled, I flinched.

"Jesus, don't do that."

"You look like you seen a ghost," he said. "But then ol' Angela will do that to you. She's never done it to me, mind, not that I haven't wished once or twice she would."

"You know her?"

"Sure I do. Don't you?"

"Never saw her before today."

"Well, I'll be damned. And here I thought you was jumping right into your new career as a undercover detective."

"You lost me."

"No shit. That's Angela Bauer," he explained. "Max Bauer's wife."

# 5

Ozzie's dressing-down lit a fire under Rusty. He won his semi, going through the pack to the front like a chainsaw through a chocolate bunny, and earned a place on the starting grid for the main event. But he still had one more race before that, one that neither he nor Ozzie minded running.

The Shiloh cigarette company's trademark cowboy hat balloon floated over the pits, a huge bloated thing like a Stetson-shaped bagel. The face of the flinty-eyed, lantern-jawed photo model—who passed for a cowboy if you didn't know what real cowboys looked like—stared moodily out of banners hung along the front straight, a smoldering Shiloh dangling from the corner of his mouth. The company representatives lounged by the infield stage, guarding the huge cardboard replica of the $10,000 check they would present to the winner of the six-lap Shootout, which paid all six riders a total of $15,000.

Rusty's fifth-fastest qualifying time put him in the Shootout along with the current National Champion, Al Hendricks, and Ricky Poe, riding for Max Bauer under the Universal Tire banner. Poe had qualified second-fastest behind fast qualifier Hendricks. Despite Poe's string of main event non-finishes since the middle of last season, he pretty much owned the Shiloh Shootouts, and the crowd was rooting for him.

With a cool ten grand up for grabs I was pressed into service. Ozzie rolled the bike to the line while Rusty walked alongside, helmet in hand, his steel shoe clanking. I tagged along behind lugging a tray of tools in case any last-minute adjustments had to be made on the grid.

None were necessary—there wasn't much room for last-minutes in Ozzie's way of doing things. I hung back while Ozzie and Rusty huddled over race strategy and the loudspeaker announced the riders and the qualifying times that had gotten them into the Shootout.

Angela Bauer was leaning on the infield fence with a bored expression on her face. I smiled and nodded before I could stop myself. The smile I got in return was more than friendly. *Good luck,* she mouthed silently.

Rusty, Ricky Poe, and Al Hendricks pulled textbook holeshots, leaving Billy Crane, Ted Munson, and Kevin Murdock fighting for fourth through sixth. The front three riders were all over each other until the back straight, when the order sorted out Hendricks, Rusty, and Poe.

Hendricks held Rusty off for two laps, while Poe waited for the right time to make his move on Rusty. It came in turn three when Hendricks went into the corner a little too hot and slipped off the groove. Rusty, riding behind and to the outside of Hendricks, had to roll off the gas to avoid collecting him. Poe slipped under them and took off like a scalded cat.

Poe had motor on both of them. Since the Honda factory's pullout from dirt track racing, almost everyone rode a Harley-Davidson XR750, a limited-production, purpose-built machine that was probably the single most successful race bike ever made. Harley dirt track engines pretty much reached the peak of their development years ago, and there were few tuning tricks that everyone didn't already know. So, exhaust pipe and muffler design notwithstanding, most engines sounded pretty much the same, although some revved a little higher—or wound up tighter, as the racers say—than others.

But Poe's engine had an added frantic, almost shrill quality underlying the trademark booming exhaust note. More than a few people trackside winced as he flew by, as if his engine would burst into a fireball of expensive shrapnel any second.

Hendricks and Rusty joined up in a two-bike draft to try to catch up to him. Through a quirk of aerodynamics, two bikes running nose-to-tail were faster on the straights than a single bike. If a couple of riders cooperated for a few laps, they could catch the leaders where either one alone would have been stranded. But even all by himself in dirty air, Poe left them for dead. On the last lap Rusty used the draft to slingshot past Hendricks coming off turn four, edged him at the line by half a wheel, and settled for second and a $3000 paycheck—not bad for six miles of go straight, turn left.

A couple of riders had complained about a developing hole in turn three, so the main was put on hold while the track crew drove out to see what they could do about it. During the delay I wandered through the pits, watching the riders getting ready for the main event. Some lounged in lawn chairs, shooting the breeze. Others knelt in the dirt helping their mechanics make those last-minute changes Ozzie hated. Those without mechanics made the changes themselves, barking orders to the girlfriends and hangers-on scrambling for tools.

Ricky Poe was accepting congratulations for bagging the Shootout and deflecting questions about the odds of the bike holding together in the main. Eddie Grimes, a small, hunched man with thick black eyebrows, unruly hair, and a bushy beard, was kneeling by the bike, yanking the carbs off the throttle cables. He took them into the van and closed the doors after him.

"Whaddya think, Ricky," someone asked him, "is it gonna last twenty-five laps?"

"Or is Fast Eddie in there tuning you out of another main event win?" another added with a smirk.

It was the sort of leading question a media person would ask. As far as I knew Poe had yet to finish a main event, much less win one. I scanned the faces of the onlookers for the last speaker, wary of running into another press guy who would blow my cover. But if I had ever seen him, I didn't remember where or when. He was half a head shorter than me, had a neatly trimmed salt-and-pepper beard, and wore thick glasses. He had what my editor—who had one himself—calls a retrograde hairline. There was a rolled-up Springfield program sticking out of his hip pocket and he was wearing a white polo shirt with, of all things, a faded red *Cycle Guide* logo over the pocket. *Cycle Guide* had gone out of business in the late eighties.

Ricky was getting edgy under the barrage of questions. But his grin only wavered for an instant.

"Hey, if it runs like it did in the Shootout," he said, "we'll kick butt!" He hopped on his minibike and fired it up.

"Big if," someone muttered. A few laughs.

Suddenly Ricky looked uncomfortable. He stomped the gear lever into first and rode off.

"What's Poe's problem, anyway?" I asked the bearded guy. "Why does he always break in the main?"

"Ricky's problem is Eddie," he said. "The guy doesn't know when he's well off. Did you see the way the bike ran just now? Did it look fast to you?"

I nodded.

"Me, too. Shows what we know. Eddie's problem is he can't leave well enough alone. "

The van door swung open and Grimes hopped out. He reconnected the carbs, checked the slide synchronization, and with a sidelong glance at us, threw a cover over the bike and walked away.

"Enjoying the show?" Ozzie said when I returned.

"I'm getting into it," I admitted. "I was just over at Ricky Poe's pit. A lot of people were ragging on him about never finishing a main."

"It ain't Ricky's fault."

"That was the general consensus. Why doesn't he dump Eddie Grimes?"

"Can't. It's Eddie's bike. Eddie lined up the sponsorship deal with Universal Tires, too. And there ain't a whole helluva lot of bikes or sponsorships going around lately. Ricky's kind of stuck."

"How come Max Bauer doesn't bounce Eddie? Why does he keep on sinking money into a team that can't finish a race?"

"Ask him. If he tells you, tell me."

That reminded me that I would have to talk to Max Bauer—or to someone about him—sooner or later. Although it was tempting to think that Sherry Case had merely provided me with a temporary solution to my domestic problems, I had in fact agreed to look into Sherm's death, and I owed her at least that much for her money. That Bauer might have resented Sherm Case for supplanting him in his father's company wasn't much, but it was all I had to go on.

The track crew came in and the PA called the main event to the starting line. The bikes rolled onto the grid and lined up backward, facing turn four. The announcer ran down the starting lineup, the crowd cheering at intervals. Rusty was completely oblivious, as far inside himself as he could go without coming out the other side. When the announcer called his name, Ozzie swatted him on the shoulder with the back of his hand. Rusty blinked as if waking from a dream, gave the grandstands a wave, and flipped his helmet onto his head.

The introductions complete, the riders and mechanics bump-started the bikes while the officials shooed us non-combatants off the grid. Rusty rode slowly toward turn four while the engine warmed up, then turned around and did a practice start, revving the engine and dropping the clutch. Ozzie caught his eye as he rolled up to the grid and hunched his shoulders in inquiry. Rusty shot him an upraised thumb. Ozzie joined me on the sideline.

"It's up to the boy now," he said.

Only a few racers had yet to take their places on the grid. By chance I had my eye on Rusty's bike when a drop of something hit the hot header pipe and vaporized in a puff of thin smoke.

"Ozzie, get 'em to hold the start!" I said, snatching up the tools.

"What?" he said. "Why? Whaddya see? What's wrong, goddammit?"

I sprinted out to the grid and skidded to a stop on my knees beside the bike. Out of the corner of my eye I saw Ozzie grabbing the referee by the sleeve, pointing toward me.

I flipped the petcock to "off," pulled a pair of wire cutters out of the tool tray, and snipped the rubber fuel hose off right at the filter. Because Ozzie had plumbed each tank petcock to feed both carbs, the engine kept running. I held the cut end away from the header as the fuel in the filter spilled onto the track.

Rusty shouted something that got lost inside his helmet. Ignoring him, I pried the split section of hose off the filter and pushed the freshly cut end over the filter spigot. Then I wrapped a zip-tie around the hose, clamping it to the filter. I flipped the petcock to "on" as I leaped up and clapped Rusty on the shoulder, giving him a thumbs-up.

Ozzie, who was still shouting in the referee's ear, saw me jogging back to the sideline. He nodded to the ref, who nodded to the starter, who picked up the starting light switch and surveyed the grid. When all the bikes were lined up to his taste, he hit the switch, the green light lit up, and seventeen clutches dropped as one and the main event was under way.

"You wanta let me in on the secret?" Ozzie said as the field elbowed into turn one.

"The fuel line was split, right after the filter on the left side," I said. "It was dripping gas on the header pipes. It might have started a fire."

"Listen, pal," Ozzie said, poking a finger in my chest. "I'm the tuner here. You're deadwood, along for the ride. If there's any wrenching to be done, I'll do it. We got too much at stake for some skylarkin' desk jockey to go playing race mechanic. Understand?"

"Fine, okay, I get the message," I said. "Here." I shoved the tools at him and stalked off down the fence.

Rusty started on the second row due to having come to the main from the semi instead of his heat. When the green light went on he was already halfway to the front row. It was a blatant jump—the starter should have red-flagged it and sent him to the penalty line.

But he didn't, and Rusty turned a second-row start into a fifth-place spot at the end of the first lap. Ahead of him were Ricky Poe, Al Hendricks, Ted Munson, and Perry Haycock, in that order. Once again Poe's horsepower advantage pulled him to the front. The riders behind him were tied up in a four-bike draft, though, and he couldn't shake them loose.

By the twelfth lap it looked as though Poe might finally see a checkered flag from the saddle instead of the sidelines. The dogfight in his wake was furious, with the order changing five, sometimes six times a lap. But none of them could close the gap on Poe. As soon as one rider pulled ahead of the snarling pack, he lost the draft and had to fall in at the back of the line.

Each rider knew that if he fell behind the others and dropped into the yawning chasm between the front-runners and the rest of the field almost half a lap behind, he was lost. But pass and pass again as they might, by the eighteenth lap they seemed resigned to battling it out for second through fifth, all but conceding the win to Poe.

On lap nineteen a groan rose up from the grandstands. Poe's lead had begun to shrink a lap or two earlier. He might have been backing off, protecting his lead and preserving his engine. But when a thin trail of smoke appeared behind him, growing thicker and darker with every lap, the crowd knew Poe's jinx had struck again.

The lead pack began to close the gap. Poe was riding on sheer guts, running into the corners deep and hard to keep his lead. His bike was smoking like a city bus, and his pursuers were flicking oil-smeared tear-offs in their wake like confetti after a parade. Hendricks and Haycock, running second and third, waved angrily at the starter to black-flag Poe as they came across the finish line. The starter and the referee huddled, but no black flag came out.

Five laps to go. Rusty, running fourth, had been far back from the worst of Poe's oil, and had one tear-off left. Hendricks and Haycock, both long since out, were obviously in trouble, especially along the back straight. The shadows on the wall were lengthening with the setting sun, which hovered over turn three like a blazing orange torch. Riding straight into that searing glare at 130 miles per hour with little or no visibility and then trying to judge when to pitch it into the corner wasn't exactly conducive to a long and prosperous career.

On lap twenty-one Rusty made a move so daring that my own life flashed before my eyes. He took out third and second in one swoop, squaring off the corner and blasting through the cushion with a spray of loose dirt cascading out behind the bike like a comet's tail, and pulled alongside Poe as they crossed the finish line to begin lap twenty-two. His left hand shot up, raked across his helmet, and his last tear-off fluttered to the ground.

Most guys would have spent a lap or two after that just trying to get their hearts out of their throats. But Rusty wasn't most guys, and he didn't have all that long before his own face shield became smeared with Poe's oil. As it turned out he didn't need much time. Half a lap later Poe stuck his arm up in the air to warn the following riders and pulled off the track, looking down forlornly at his silent engine. Rusty sailed by him into the lead. Hendricks and Haycock shot past next, fixing Rusty in their crosshairs.

Me, I was standing on the top rail of the fence, cheering myself hoarse, thinking, *That's my zip-tie out there winning the Springfield Mile!*

Rusty had a clear track ahead and a couple of half-blind pursuers to the rear. His last two laps were smooth, fast, and smart, and the place went crazy as Rusty flashed across the finish line, thrust a victorious fist in the air, overshot turn one, lost it and and fell on his ass, sliding absolutely unhurt into the haybales along the outside of the turn.

Somebody whacked me on the back so hard I almost coughed up my heart.

"Hot damn, Hemingway!" Ozzie shouted in my ear. "We did it! We won!"

Rusty was pushing his bike to the pit gate. The crowd was on its feet, cheering him. He stopped in front of the main section of the grandstand, let the bike fall, and took off his helmet. With a mighty sidearm heave, he flung it high up into the stands. A mob dove for it like it was a home-run ball at a World Series game.

Ozzie and I picked up the bike. The get-off had done only minor damage, but the front header pipe had been flattened against the cylinder head, pinching it shut. The traditional victory lap was out of the question until Al Hendricks rode up, stepped off his bike, and handed it and the checkered flag to Rusty. Rusty insisted that Hendricks ride along behind him, and together they toured the track waving to the fans, who by now were absolutely out of their minds.

"Hey, Hemingway," Ozzie said. "Sorry about what I said out there."

"Forget it. It's history."

"I wasn't pissed at you. I was pissed at my own damn self for not noticing that fuel hose. You mighta won this race for us, you know."

"Rusty did the hard part. That's one of the best races I've ever seen. My pulse is still in triple digits."

"Mine too. Come on, let's go let Rusty spray us with champagne."

As soon as all the bikes were off the track they opened the outside pit gate and the fans came pouring into the infield. Rusty was atop the podium tripping over his tongue and trying to mention every one of his sponsors during the post-race interview. Someone handed up three enormous bottles of champagne. The knowledgeable fans edged away as Rusty, Hendricks, and Haycock shook the bottles, popped the corks, and drenched everyone within twenty-five yards of the podium with champagne spray. When the bubbles ran out, they began pouring it on each other's heads, and when that got old, they poured it into their mouths and sprayed the crowd again.

Our pit was a mob of fans, press, and fellow racers, thumping Rusty on the back, shaking Ozzie's hand, and getting autographs on everything from programs to souvenir hats to well-filled halter tops—Rusty gave priority to the latter. True to Ozzie's prediction, Rusty was once again the horny, scatterbrained kid with a thirty-second attention span and a radar eye for young, awestruck females. I stood off to one side, admiring that fantastic zip-tie job on the left fuel line.

A hand on my shoulder caused me to turn. Angela Bauer said "Congratulations," and before I could thank her planted a warm, wet, and extremely competent kiss on me.

We broke from the clinch and I noticed things had gotten pretty quiet in the Rusty McCann pit, primarily because everyone was grinning at me blushing while Angela dabbed a smear of lipstick off my cheek with the pulled-up tail of her polo shirt. A smattering of awed hoots and whistles followed her as she left.

I began dating Sara three years ago. We moved in together just over one year ago. And since then I had not kissed another woman. Had not wanted to kiss any other woman but Sara. Until now.

The smell of barbecue smoke drifted by. For every van that left the pits another stayed behind and hauled out a gas grill or hibachi. As the afternoon went on, the pits turned into a noisy picnic area, with food and frisbee games and loud retellings of the day's daring deeds, magnified by open ice chests of beer into soaring feats of heroism that made Viking mythology sound like Dick and Jane.

We were invited to half a dozen pit parties and settled for accepting a platter of burgers and eating in the back of the van. Ozzie kept getting up to go over and shake his head at the crushed header pipe. The bike was like his child, and the poor dear had a boo-boo. He wanted to kiss it and make it better.

"Sorry about dumping there after the flag, Ozzie," Rusty said. "It just felt so bitchin' to win, you know? I kinda forgot to keep both hands on the bars."

"Aw, it's okay. But we're gonna have to scare up a welding rig an' a tube bender somewhere so's I can saw off this bent-up chunk and fix it."

"Don't let him touch your bike, youngster," a voice boomed suddenly. "This ten-thumbed excuse for a country blacksmith couldn't find his own ass with both hands and a hunting dog."

"Well, if it ain't Buster Beauchamp," Ozzie said, shaking the fat hand of a man who practically blocked the setting sun. "Jesus Christ, B.B., haven't seen you in donkey's years. Don't know how I missed you, either. Damn if you ain't big enough to be on both side o' your family at once."

Buster Beauchamp wasn't just big, he was monumental. He must have weighed three hundred pounds, before breakfast. His face was sunk down into rolls of fat and he probably hadn't seen his own feet except in a mirror since he was a teenager. There was enough material in his shirt and pants to put a dome over half the racetrack.

Buster astonished Ozzie by turning down a hamburger, claiming he was on a diet. Ozzie said he bet it was the "see food" diet and laughed at his own joke until he almost choked. Buster made a few cracks at his own expense and Ozzie topped him every time until the both of them were wheezing and grabbing things for support, Ozzie hanging onto a canopy pole and Buster leaning against the van, which rocked as he gasped for breath.

"This here's Buster Beauchamp," Ozzie said to Rusty and me, "the motorcycle mogul of Springfield. He owns a Harley shop, two Honda shops, a . . . what the hell else have you bought since the last time I saw you, you ol' pirate?"

"Suzuki and Ducati," Buster said, "and I'm working on Kawasaki. Well? Are you coming over tonight or do I have to pull in a few favors with the local cops and have you thrown in the jug for the perverts and vagrants you obviously are?"

"Much obliged, Buster. We accept your gracious invite."

"All right, then. See you at the house."

We loaded up the van and left the track at the tail end of the spectator traffic. Buster's place was about ten miles north of Springfield in a town called Sherman. It was gentleman farmer country, dotted with homes that ranged from tidy little two-story cottages on a couple of acres all the way up to forty-acre spreads with dairy cows. Buster's place had a red fence around it and an upturned horseshoe nailed to the gate. A wide dirt driveway led to a sprawling ranch-style house with a porch bordered by a split-rail fence. Behind it was a metal building the size of a small blimp hangar. In the dusk I could just make out what looked like a dirt oval track behind the building.

Buster waddled out and met us on the porch. He and Ozzie went way back—so far back, Ozzie said, that Buster could fit into ordinary clothes. They stood in the kitchen holding a couple of beers, ignoring me and Rusty and hacking on one another like old friends. Suddenly Buster slapped his forehead and said, "Dammit, I almost forgot. The pup busted the race bike, didn't he? Well, take it out to the shop, youngster, and we'll see about putting it back together."

Rusty and I unloaded the bike and met Ozzie and Buster outside the metal building. Inside it looked like a small factory. Banks of neon lights blinked to life above thousands of dollars worth of spotless machine tools—a fourteen-inch-swing lathe, a Bridgeport mill, a sand-blasting cabinet, a tube bender, arc and gas welding equipment, the works and then some.

"Everything but a dyno," Rusty marveled.

"That's out there," Buster said, "a half-mile track with a three-eighths-mile short track inside it. That and a stopwatch are the only dyno that really tells you anything."

Ozzie hoisted the bike up onto a lift and he and Rusty began prying the bent exhaust pipe off. Actually, Ozzie did most of the work. Rusty stood close by, ready to hand him tools. It was like watching a father and son working on the family car.

"You boys are staying the night, aren't you, Oz?" Buster said. "Then that can wait until tomorrow."

"I'd rather know what I'm in for, Buster. If I'm gonna need some new tubes sent in I'd rather make the calls first thing in the morning instead of wasting half a day finding it out."

"Suit yourself. I don't believe we've been introduced," Buster said to me.

"Bob," I said, "Bob, uh, Hemingway."

"Nice to meet you, Bob. Why don't we go on inside and sit?"

I declined Buster's offer of a beer. There was a pot of coffee on, though, and I poured a cup. It was rich, dark, and reminded me poignantly of home. I sat on the couch holding the steaming mug to my nose, inhaling the aroma. Buster settled his bulk into a custom-built double-wide leather recliner chair for which no less than two cows had given their all.

The inside of the house didn't go with the Old MacDonald exterior. The living room was quiet and cool, the carpet thick and dark brown. A floor-to-ceiling bookcase along one wall held an impressive array of titles, ones you wouldn't think a bumpkin like Buster would have ever cracked the covers on. I could have spent a week there just browsing through them. There were CDs of Mozart, Rodgers and Hammerstein, and Sting stacked next to a stereo console that looked like the dashboard of the Millenium Falcon. Like Ozzie, Buster was rustic when it suited him. When it didn't, he swung all the way to the other side of the scale.

"This is a great house, Buster," I said. "And that's quite a shop you have. What do you do with it?"

"Thank you. You can see I like my comforts," he said, patting his ample belly. "As for the shop, a man likes to have a hobby. Do you know much about dirt track, Bob?"

Since I wasn't supposed to be who I really was, I couldn't decide whether I should know as much as I do or a whole lot less. So I just shrugged my shoulders.

"Dirt track used to be the most prestigious motorcycle racing series in the country," Buster said. "There were short tracks in every cornfield, and half-mile and mile tracks at every county fairground from coast to coast. You could drive along these old country roads out here and see clouds of dust off in the distance, made by kids on dirt bikes riding around and around in circles all day long pretending to be Buggs Mann or Carroll Resweber. Guys like Bart Markel and Jimmy Chann and Everett Brashear were their heroes. Did you ever see Al Gunter race, or Sammy Tanner, the 'Flying Flea'? Of course not, you're not old enough. They weren't anything like the blow-dried, millionaire, manufactured 'sports legends' of today. They drove ratty old pickups to the races, sat down in the dirt and did their own mechanicking, and were lucky if first-place money would buy them gas to the next race."

Buster took a pull off his beer and wiped his lips with the back of his hand. "These days nobody races for the love of it. They see guys like Roberts and Lawson and Spencer, all fine dirt track racers at one time, go off to Europe to road race and sign million-dollar sponsorship deals with cigarette and soft-drink companies and drive around in forty-foot motorhomes acting like snooty opera stars, and they think they'd like to get rich too. So they go road racing, forgetting where the top American road racers learned their craft, on dirt tracks like—"

Suddenly Buster laughed and shook his head. "Sorry, Bob," he said, "I'm climbing on my high horse again. As you might have figured, I love dirt track. I did some racing myself, back when dinosaurs roamed the earth. Got pretty good at taking soil samples with my face. Then I had a hunch I might get richer selling motorcycles than I ever would racing them. It isn't like I want to give something back to dirt track, because to be honest just about all dirt track ever gave me was a broken nose and a shoulder that clicks like a flamenco dancer's maracas. But I love it just the same, and any racer who loves dirt track like I do is welcome to stay here between races, fix up his bike if it needs it, and eat a good meal. All he has to do in return is listen politely to a boring old fart tell tall tales about the old days. So in answer to your question, what I build out there is a future for anyone who wants it."

Buster went to the kitchen for another beer. I sat in the living room remembering the stories my father used to tell me about the very racers Buster had been talking about. Dad had been one of those kids kicking up dust on the homemade dirt track. He made it to the professional ranks, but lacked both the desire to stick with it and the talent to be good at it. His failure to set the racing world on fire rankled him even today. Whether that failure turned him into a drunk or was the result of him being one was something I'd often wondered about.

Buster returned with a new brew and sat down.

"So, Jason," he said out of the blue, "tell me, how is little Sherry Case these days? Still a hell-raiser like her old man?"

"I—yow! Uh, excuse me?"

"Careful, you spilled some coffee on you there. I apologize for startling you like that, but I couldn't go on calling you Bob, now, could I, and pretending you don't know anything about dirt track racing? Don't worry, son, Sherry called and explained everything. Hmmm. Jason Street, isn't it? I knew a Malcolm Street once, a middlin' good hotshoe from San Francisco. Any relation? "

"Morgan Hill, not San Francisco," I said. So much for traveling incognito. "Mal Street is my father."

"I trust he's well? Remember me to him when you get home."

I went into the kitchen, dabbed the coffee off my shirt with a paper towel, and poured myself another cup. Buster waited patiently in the living room sitting Buddha-like in his chair, his beer cradled in his fat hands.

"Sherman Case was not always a good man," he said. "But he was a friend. Now, how can I help you?"

"I'm not sure. How much did Sherry tell you?"

"Just that she doesn't think Sherm killed himself, and that she hired you to find out who did kill him . . . . You're a writer, aren't you?"

"I'm features editor of a motorcycle magazine, or was. I might still be. I haven't talked to anyone at the office lately."

"And you're being blamed for this?" He shook his head. "It's a shame how adept we Americans have become at shifting blame. A man gets drunk and runs over a child in his car, he blames the drink and sues the liquor company. A politician gets caught with his hand in the till, and he blames the press for snooping around in his private affairs. Whatever happened to taking responsibility for your own actions? Even if Sherm Case did blow his brains out, that's his doing, not yours."

"There are a few dozen lawyers and journalists I'd like you to tell that to. Do you believe he committed suicide?"

"Sherm Case? Never. He'd shoot you and me and every other son-of-a-bitch in the world who got in his way first. If you look up the word 'ruthless' in the dictionary, there's a picture of Sherm Case right next to the entry. Do you know how he got to be president of Case Tires?"

"Ozzie said it had something to do with easing Max Bauer out of his father's company."

"Nobody eased anybody in that deal, son. Sherm just flat blew Max out. Do you know your dirt track history? These days the Number One plate is awarded to the rider who scores the most points over a season of races. But from 1946 to 1953, the winner of a single race, the Springfield Mile, was crowned Number One—the rest of the season didn't matter worth a blown fuse toward the plate. You could lose every race on the calendar, but if you won Springfield, you were Number One.

"In 1950 Sherm Case was a young racer who talked a faster race than he rode. He wasn't among the favorites going into the '50 Springfield Mile, and everyone knew it, including Heinrich Bauer, Max's father. Heinrich went to all the races giving away tires, hoping a big win on his brand would give him some publicity and help sales. But everyone who tried a pair wound up giving them back or throwing them away.

"On the morning of the 1950 Springfield Mile, Sherm, broke as usual, was trying to hustle some free gas, or a chain, anything to nurse his worn-out bike through qualifying. He found Heinrich sitting on a pile of tires, moping. When he heard the old man's story, Sherm graciously consented to accept a free set of tires to use in the race.

"Heinrich thanked him over and over in that thick German accent he had, like it was Sherm doing *him* a favor. He was an old-world gentleman, old Heinrich was, a little too innocent and honorable for the likes of Sherm Case. Sherm must have sensed it, too, because the next thing he did was talk the old man into agreeing that if he won the race, Heinrich would hire him as a salesman. Even Heinrich knew the odds of that were slim at best, but he wanted his product in the main event. So he agreed, and they shook hands on it and Sherm walked off with a new tire under each arm.

"Sherm qualified for the main event and got a good start. He was in the lead pack of riders but slipping back some each lap. There was a lot of jostling going on behind him, some of it pretty rough. Suddenly someone went down in a corner, another rider ran over him, and then all hell broke loose. Six bikes went down, three guys got carted off to the hospital with broken bones, one died on the spot. The race was stopped. When it was restarted all the favorites were either in the hospital or out of contention with broken bikes. Sherm won the race going away, and reported to work Monday morning. Late, too, probably."

"Where does Max Bauer fit in?"

"He was working for his father as a salesman when Sherm joined the company. Young Max inherited his father's quaint notions of honor and loyalty, neither of which served him particularly well in sales. Sherm was everything Max wasn't—a racer, the National Champ at that, friendly, outgoing, devious when it profited him, and shameless when caught. People who couldn't warm up to Max at all liked the hell out of Sherm, even when they caught him with his hand in their pocket. Bauer Tire's fortunes rose on Sherm's reputation and his sales savvy. Max found himself working for Sherm rather than with him when Heinrich made Sherm sales manager. The old man loved his son, but he was no fool. Sherm was the moneymaker, and he treated him accordingly."

"How did Max react to all this?"

"How would you have reacted? He was jealous as hell, but too much of a gentleman to show it. The old man was dazzled by Sherm's act and thought Max was just being childish. He scolded him for not being more like Sherm and for not learning from him instead of complaining about the way he was treated. So Max quit."

"And started his own tire company?"

"Max was better at listening than the old man ever knew. He took what he had learned from his father, and from Sherm, and dragged a struggling rubber company on the verge of bankruptcy up by its bootstraps. Lost that nasty streak of integrity along the way, too, and became as big a son of a bitch as Sherm ever was. Maybe bigger. Then Heinrich had a stroke, and Sherm took over as acting vice-president. He gradually moved the old man farther and farther away from the day-to-day business. Heinrich wasn't getting any better. He knew he didn't have much time left, and when Case offered to buy him out, he agreed. The minute Heinrich died, the Bauer Tire and Rubber Company sign came down, Case Tire and Rubber went up. Sherm Case's name was on the door of the president's office before the old man's body was cold."

"Sherry said Max Bauer has been trying to buy out Case for some time," I said. "Now that Case is dead, it looks like he might pull it off."

Buster frowned. "I see where you're going with this," he said. "But as little use as I have for Max, I don't see him as the kind of man who would kill over a business deal. He's mean but he's not vicious mean."

"Not just a business deal," I said. "You said it yourself. Heinrich shoved his own son aside for a stranger who wound up owning the company which, I gather, Max should have inherited."

"Is that what Sherry thinks? That Max has been carrying a grudge all these years and only now decided to act on it?"

"It's all she has—all I have to go on."

Ozzie came in through the kitchen, wiping his hands on a shop rag. "Hey, Buster, you got any other mandrels for your tube bender?"

"Oh hell, they're scattered all over the place out there," Buster said, heaving himself up. "Come on, I'll help you look." He paused in the doorway. "There's a whole bookcase full of old motorcycle magazines in my office," he said to me, "down the hall and first door on the right. You might want to look up that 1950 Springfield Mile. There might even be a picture of Sherm Case in his glory days."

Buster's office was as orderly and tasteful as the living room, with dark paneling on the walls, a glass-topped desk the size of a tennis court, a Macintosh computer and a pile of spreadsheet printouts. There were framed photographs on the wall of Buster and various racing greats. It was a cozy and efficient place to oversee his empire of dealerships, the kind of seamless and insulated working environment I keep promising myself someday but never quite get around to creating.

Behind the desk was a bookcase full of old magazines in binders and boxes, marked by title and year. Many I had never heard of. I took a chance, pulled down a box marked "Motorcycle Sport/1950," and spread the contents on the desk. I found the issue with the Springfield results and settled into Buster's chair.

Positioning the magazine in the pool of light under the green-shaded desk lamp, I opened it at random and suddenly found Sherm Case grinning up at me from the page, clutching a huge, tacky-looking trophy. He was wearing an old porridge-pot helmet with leather earflaps—real high-tech stuff in those days—and his goggles hung loosely around his neck. His face was dirt-streaked where the goggles hadn't covered it, and he had one greasy hand wrapped around the waist of the blond bombshell trophy girl who was looking down uncertainly at her white bermuda shorts, wondering how she would get that stain out.

The grainy photo didn't tell me anything about Sherm Case that I hadn't already been told. I had only met the man briefly once or twice, and figuring he must have been in his sixties when I saw him last, that made him twenty or so when the photo was taken. In my mind I tried to connect the two across the years, but the funny thing was that the grinning kid in the old bike magazine on the vee-twin Indian looked more real to me than the bloody corpse in the van behind Ascot. Or maybe that's just the way I wanted to remember him.

The race story was unremarkable. It leaned toward straight reporting without any editorializing. In those days the motorcycle manufacturers and the race sanctioning body wielded a lot of power over the motorcycle press, and the press behaved itself accordingly. The sport then as now had image problems, and the magazines routinely swept the controversial and negative aspects of racing under the rug. The crash and subsequent pile-up in the main event were downplayed, the death mentioned and disposed of in a single sentence. Interestingly, the article did note that a rider named Charlie Brand, of Springfield, who had been involved in the crash but was unhurt, had tearfully announced his retirement from racing on the spot and left the track before the race was restarted. The story ended with a run-down of the entrants, their hometowns, and their finishing positions.

The coffee was wearing off, and the yawns came in waves. I flipped idly through the rest of the magazines from the 1950 box. A clock on the desk showed it was almost ten. I thought about calling Sara, decided I was too tired to make much sense, and began putting the magazines back in the box. I picked up the Springfield issue last and a slip of paper that had been stuck between the last page and the back cover fell to the floor.

It was a clipping from a local newspaper, with its own version of the race. It dealt at greater length with the crash and the tragic death of one Jesse Ed Beyer, 19, of Akron, Ohio, who was pronounced dead on arrival at the hospital. The reporter had no qualms whatsoever about characterizing motorcycle racing as a sport that attracted the worst elements of society—drunks, gamblers, non-churchgoers. He hinted that the fix was on before the green flag fell, and that one racer suspected of being involved had hastily left the track right after the crash and before an inquiry could be made. That two of the three riders taken to the hospital were among those favored to win was seen as especially damning. But other than a veiled implication that this sort of thing went on all the time at motorcycle races—no doubt along with unmarried people kissing in public and women showing their legs—there was nothing to back up the claim.

Buster came in. "Find what you were looking for?"

"Maybe," I said. I showed him the magazine story and the clipping and waited while he frowned and chewed his lip. "The magazine says this Charlie Brand was from Springfield. What are the odds he's still alive, and still living here?"

"I don't know the odds," Buster said, pulling open a desk drawer, "but I do know how to use a phone book. Let's see . . . Belcher, Boggs, Brady, here we go, Brand—I'll be damned. Brand, Charles."

"It might not be the same man," I said.

Buster handed me the phone. "It only costs a dime to find out."

I dialed the number and waited through six rings.

"Hello?" a woman's voice said. She sounded old, and not at all pleased at being called at this late hour.

"Is Charles Brand there, please?"

"No, he isn't. This is Mrs. Brand. Who's calling? What do you want with Charles?"

"My name is Jason Street. I'm, uh, writing a book about the old days of motorcycle racing, and my research shows that Mr. Brand was quite, uh, prominent in the sport."

"Prominent? How do you mean, prominent? Who told you to call me? Was it that other man?"

"I found your name in the phone book. Would it be possible to speak with Mr. Brand?"

"I'm not sure I believe you. If I wouldn't let *him* talk to Charles, why should I let you?"

"Mrs. Brand, it's important that I talk to Mr. Brand. There's . . . well, there's a lot at stake for me personally. Can we meet somewhere tomorrow and talk it over? You choose the place. Make it a public place if you want, with lots of people around."

I could hear her breathing in short, agitated gulps of air. Finally she said, "All right, if only to get this over with."

She read off a street number on Rutledge Street in Springfield. "If you want to talk to Charles, meet me there. It's my regular day anyway. I usually arrive at ten in the morning. I'll be waiting."

I hung up and Buster got out a city map and showed me where Rutledge Street was. It was on the west side of the downtown area. "Head south on 55, take Business 55 into town," said. "That turns into 9th Street. Make a right on Carpenter and pretty soon you'll cross Rutledge. I'm sure you can find your way from there."

"Thanks, Buster. I—wait, what if Ozzie and Rusty want to hit the road tomorrow?"

"They won't. Ozzie found a crack in the cylinder head where the header ripped out. It'll take at least a day to get another one here. You'll have plenty of time."

Buster showed me to my room and I tossed my duffel bag onto the bed. I had an inch-thick layer of Springfield dirt on me and my hair felt like steel wool. My room had a bathroom with a shower. I looked at my face in the mirror and rubbed my hand across the stubble. I was at that point where you either have to shave it off or let it grow in. In a devil-may-care mood, I decided to give it a chance and see what it looked like.

I laid out clean clothes for the morning and stripped off my dusty ones. I pulled my shirt over my head and something fell out of the pocket. It was a matchbook from the Holiday Inn East.

Inside, in a flowing feminine hand, were the words "Come see what you've won tonight."

It was signed "Angela."

# 6

I blew the Carpenter Street turn the next morning and wound up in downtown Springfield in Buster's pre-gas-crisis Lincoln Continental, a silent grey monster the size of an aircraft carrier. Despite sitting out a green light reading the map spread across the manhole-sized steering wheel, driving the wrong way down a one-way street—only for two blocks—and getting honked at by every driver in the city with a working horn, I managed not to clip any banks, churches, or government buildings or smash into the quaint and historic site of Abraham Lincoln's law office, or his church, or the place he got his first haircut, and finally eased the battlewagon into a parking space in front of a gloomy old pile of bricks on Rutledge Street.

I bounded up the steps past a crooked hedge dappled with brown spots like mange on an old dog's hide and pushed the heavy glass door open. The smell of antiseptic, and something else nowhere near as delightful, wafted out of the lobby.

Inside I had been expecting to find a row of mailboxes or maybe a sign listing the tenants' names and apartment numbers. What I saw was a desk behind which sat a woman wearing a white starched uniform and a nurse's cap. She had on a pair of reading glasses secured by a gold chain looped around her neck. She peered inquiringly over the tops of the frames.

"I'm looking for Mrs. Charlie Brand," I said.

"Over here, Mr. Street."

Mrs. Brand was sitting on a green vinyl-covered bench, her back straight as a string and an inch from the wall, like a Marine recruit. She was thin and as tough as a piece of old rope. A pair of veined, bony hands were clamped protectively over a shiny black handbag in her lap. Her iron-grey hair was gathered behind her head in a bun so tight it must have taken tremendous effort to frown the way she was. She pursed her lips and looked me up and down like a butcher she'd caught with his thumb on the scale.

"You're late," she sniffed.

"I'm sorry, Mrs. Brand. I got lost. I'm not from around here."

She sniffed again, as if not being from around here was right up there with kidnapping and holding up convenience stores.

"Come along then."

I followed her past the desk where she nodded curtly to the nurse and into an elevator at the far end of the lobby. The ammonia smell almost made me gag. Mrs. Brand endured it stoically. The doors opened on the third floor and at last I knew what kind of place this was.

The man—I'm guessing it was a man—was old and stooped, on the verge of tumbling headlong out of the wheelchair being pushed toward us by the orderly. His head was hairless and mottled with purple spots, and his nose was long and thin. A pair of impossibly slender wrists protruded from the sleeves of a voluminous flannel bathrobe. Pale fingers curled around the chair arms like claws. The bulging eyes, clouded with cataracts, stared sightlessly. He looked like an ancient and infirmed bird.

We got out and the orderly pushed the old man in. He let go of the chair in order to push the button for his floor and the chair rolled on and struck the rear wall. The old man rocked forward stiffly like a mannequin, clutching at the arms of the wheelchair. As the doors closed the orderly was standing at the front of the elevator, admiring the tattoos on his forearms. The old man sat facing the rear, his head bobbing in confusion on the wrinkled neck.

Mrs. Brand marched primly down the corridor, looking neither right nor left. I followed, glancing in open doors, gaping in horrid fascination at the imaginative ways in which the human organism deteriorated and left the mind prisoner in a worthless body.

Charlie Brand was fortunate to have all his body parts intact and functioning more or less normally. It was his mind that had broken down.

"He drifts in and out," Mrs. Brand said. She looked tenderly at the old man dozing fitfully. The eyes behind the closed lids flitted from side to side, and the hand laying on top of the blanket closed into a weak fist and opened again. "Some days he knows my name and what year it is, and other days he's harvesting corn on his family's farm, riding along on the combine and talking to his father who's been dead these fifty-odd years. I'm a total stranger to him then. He doesn't even like me—once he told me to go away and leave him alone or he'd tell his mother. I never know how it will be when I come. But I come every visiting day, Monday, Wednesday, and Friday, like clockwork."

Charlie's eyes opened slowly and stared unseeing for a moment. He blinked rapidly, as if trying to make sense of waking up in the same room as yesterday. Then he saw Mrs. Brand and smiled.

"Hello, Etta," he whispered.

"Hello, Charles, dear," she said, laying her hand gently over his. "How are you today?"

"A little tired. Who is this?"

"This is Mr. Street, dear. He's come to talk to you about your motorcycle racing."

"Oh . . . that was a very long time ago. I'm not sure I can remember much about it any more."

"That's all right," I said. "I'll be grateful for anything you can tell me."

"I'll be happy to try."

"You'll excuse me, I'm sure," Mrs. Brand said, leaving no doubt that motorcycle racing wasn't her favorite topic. "I'll be downstairs, Charles."

I pulled up a chair and sat down next to the bed. The room had a small dresser with a telephone on it, a vase of drooping flowers, and a picture of a stream and an old oak tree on the wall. The idea was to make it seem like a cozy little flat where you could invite your friends for a cup of coffee and maybe a game of bridge. But no matter how hard it tried to look otherwise, it was a place where very old and inconvenient people were left to kill time until time returned the favor.

"Mr. Brand," I said, "I'd like to ask you about one particular race. I'd like to ask you about the 1950 Springfield Mile, when Sherm Case won the Number One plate."

He acted like he hadn't heard me. Then his head gave a little jerk like I had slapped him and he said, "I know why you're here." He was looking at the ceiling, unable or unwilling to meet my eyes. "It's because of him, isn't it?"

"Who? Sherm Case?"

"You know, I can still see his face. He had freckles, hundreds of them, and a big broken nose, and hair the color of straw. He was missing a front tooth. All the rest were straight as could be, and when he laughed it looked like a picket fence with a missing post."

The description fit neither the Sherm Case I had known nor the one in the magazine photo. "Who are you talking about, Mr. Brand?"

"I met him at a hillclimb the summer before and we hit it off right away," he said dreamily. "A farm boy, like me. From then on we always pitted together, shared gas and oil . . . He was a fine young man."

"Mr. Brand—Charlie—Sherman Case won the Springfield race. But first there was a crash and the race was restarted. You were one of the riders who fell in that crash, weren't you?"

"Yes, and so was he."

"No, sir, Sherm Case didn't fall. But you did, didn't you?"

"Of course," Charlie said. "I had to."

"You had to? Why?"

"Because of him. I had to."

"Why did you leave the track before the restart? Was it because of the crash?"

The hand that had been clenching and unclenching started again, this time with all the force it could summon. The skin over the knuckles was bone-white.

"Yes," he said, his chin quivering. He was blinking back tears.

"Because you felt sorry for the riders who got hurt?"

"Jesse was a big dumb farm boy, that's all. He didn't know how it was. I should have told him, warned him to stay back. But he wouldn't have listened, or he might have told . . . A man does things sometimes that he knows he'll regret. But he goes right on ahead and does them anyway, because he has to. Etta was sixteen, pretty as a picture, and her daddy would have killed me if he found out she was . . . so when he came to me and told me what he wanted I said yes, but it has to be more. I told him how much. He knew Etta, you see, and why I . . . why we had to get married. And he laughed and said if he won he'd give me twice that."

"Jesse paid you to do something in the race, is that it?"

"Not Jesse. It was him, with his slick talk and big plans and bright ideas. He said I had to get out out front and keep the rest of them from getting by. He said if I could buy him some room, let him build up a little lead, just a small one, he could maybe win it."

"Are you saying another rider paid you to block for him in the main event?"

"That was all, I swear. I never wanted it to turn out the way it did. Sweet Etta, she's such a pretty little thing, and all those freckles. And now you're here. He sent you. I know it. They're all coming, first Archie and now Jesse." His eyes scrunched up and he took a deep breath. It came out in a ragged sigh. He opened his eyes again and looked right at me. "But you're not Jesse. Jesse's dead. He died in the crash. Three others hurt or crippled, but it's Jesse who died. Did I ever tell you about Jesse? He was a big dumb farm boy, Jesse was, with a big broken nose and hundreds of freckles, and hair the color of . . . of . . ."

Charlie's face contorted into a mask of grief. He sobbed silently, then moaned ". . . oh . . . oh . . . oh . . ." as each expelled breath wracked his frail body.

A throat cleared by the door—a nurse with a tray of food.

"I think Mr. Brand has had enough visitors for today," she said.

Etta Brand was sitting on the green bench, the very picture of prim indignation, when the elevator deposited me in the lobby. She stood up as I approached.

"Well?" she said. "Did you find out what you wanted to know?"

"Mrs. Brand, earlier you mentioned something about another man who wanted to talk to your husband. Who was it?"

"I don't know his name. He called, oh, two months ago. He wanted to talk to Charles about the old motorcycle races, just like you. But he wouldn't say why. I didn't like the sound of him at all. I told him Charles was ill and couldn't see anyone. He tried to get me to tell him where Charles was, but I hung up. A week later I got a call from one of the nurses. A man had come to see Charles without an appointment. She told him I had to approve all visitors, but he said he had already spoken to me, and it was all right for him to see Charles. Well, the silly woman let him go upstairs, and the next thing Charles is crying and carrying on and the man is nowhere to be found. The nurse had to give Charles a a sedative."

"Mrs. Brand, there's no easy way to ask this, so I'll just come out with it. Were you pregnant before you and Mr. Brand were married?"

Her eyes flashed fire and she sputtered. I thought she was going to beat me senseless with her big black handbag. Instead she spun and walked out the door, her back ramrod straight, her heels clattering on the linoleum like gunshots.

I caught her at the bottom of the steps.

"Mrs. Brand—"

"He told you that?" she spat. "He told you that? How dare he—!"

"Did your husband take a bribe to block for another rider in the Springfield race so he could marry you?"

"Why you—"

"He did, didn't he? And there was a crash, and a lot of riders fell down, and a man named Jesse Beyer, a friend of your husband's, was killed, isn't that right?"

"Don't you ever speak to me again—"

"Who's Archie? You husband said someone named Archie had been to see him—was that the man who called you two months ago? Archie who? What's his last name?"

"I don't know any Archie. Now leave me alone or I'll call the police."

When I got back to Buster's that afternoon everyone was out in the shop. The Harley was scattered in pieces on the workbench. Ozzie was scowling at various parts and Rusty was sitting on the bare chassis looking bored.

"I guess I shouldn't ask how it's going," I said.

"It ain't," Ozzie said. "Couldn't scare up a new cylinder head today. The old one's cracked real bad, too bad to weld it up."

"I called my Harley shop in town," Buster said. "They said they'd get on the horn to the factory in Milwaukee and order up a new one. But we don't know if it'll get here in time for Louisville this weekend."

"Can't you afford to miss one race?" I said. "It's still early in the season."

"Early or late don't enter into it. Rusty's third in the standings right now and he's got momentum coming off the win yesterday. If we have to sit one out he might not get it back."

"So what do we do now?"

"You three can sit around dragging your long faces in the dirt," Buster said. "I'm going to rustle up some dinner. Who's for steak and broiled shrimp?"

I might have felt guilty about imposing on Buster's hospitality if it hadn't been so obvious that he loved to entertain. He could wear any number of hats at the same time—businessman, scholar, gourmet cook, raconteur, history professor, and encyclopedist of side-splitting jokes—and made me feel more at home in his house than I had in my own of late.

". . . so the Pope takes a day off from the busy schedule of his visit to America to go for a drive in the country in his stretch limo," Buster said, his hands wrapped around the rim of an imaginary steering wheel, a huge plate of shrimp tails in front of him. "Only he gets bored after a while and tells the driver to pull over.

" 'What's the trouble, Your Holiness?' the driver says.

" 'Nothing. I'm bored. I want to drive.'

" 'But Your Holiness,' the driver says, 'you haven't driven a car in years!'

" 'I don't care. Get in the back. I'm driving.'

"So the driver gets in back and the Pope gets behind the wheel and floors it. He's doing eighty down this country road when he drives by a couple of local cops in a black-and-white. They hit the siren, take off after the limo, and pull it over a couple of miles later.

"The cop behind the wheel gets out while his partner stays in the car. When the cop gets to the limo, the window rolls down and there's the Pope, smiling at him in his white suit and big funny hat. The cop takes one look at him, turns white as a sheet, and goes back to his car.

" 'What's the matter?' his partner says. 'Who'd we collar? Some rich guy?'

" 'It's worse than that,' his partner says.

" 'A senator?'

" 'It's worse than that.'

" 'Don't tell me we pulled over the president!'

" 'It's even worse than that.'

" 'Well, how much worse can it be?'

" 'I'll give you a hint,' the cop says. 'His driver's the Pope.' "

Ozzie and I laughed so hard we almost passed out. When we could breathe again, we explained the joke to a perplexed Rusty. He nodded and grinned politely.

Buster had a couple of mini-motocrossers in a shed behind the shop. After dinner we dragged them out and worked up a fine sweat chasing each other around the short track. Neither Ozzie nor I was any match for Rusty, who rode as effortlessly as either of us breathed. Despite all the off-road riding I had done, I could never quite get the knack of hanging the rear wheel out in a dirt track-type slide for more than a second or two. It was too much like deliberately trying to crash and then changing your mind at the last instant. Instead I rode the mini like a street bike, using the front brake and leaning it over in the corners but keeping both wheels pretty much in line. Ozzie and I ended up hot-lapping the little track, passing and repassing each other while Buster cheered and Rusty stood in the infield shouting bad advice to us until the sun went down.

That night, with Rusty planted in front of a video and Ozzie sitting on the porch sipping a glass of whiskey and listening to the crickets, I told Buster what I had learned that day.

"I think someone paid Charlie Brand to block for him," I said, "and I think it was Sherm Case. Only things went sour, and there was a crash. Jesse Beyer was killed, and three other riders hurt, including one named Archie Jones—I got his last name from the magazine story—who could be easily the Archie who visited Charlie a couple of months ago."

"Why did Archie Jones want to find Charlie Brand?" Buster said. "What was he after? Revenge for causing the crash? Maybe Archie Jones was a friend of Jesse Beyer, too."

I shook my head. "Charlie doesn't even know his own name half the time, or what day it is. What good is revenge on someone who can't remember what it's for? No, it had to be for some other reason—information, maybe. About the race. Or the whereabouts of the other injured riders."

"A lot of questions," Buster said.

"Here's the big one," I said. "Why now? All this happened in 1950. Why is Archie Jones just now looking for Charlie Brand? What tipped him to Charlie's part in the crash in the first place?"

"Only one person can tell you that," Buster said. "Charlie. You have to go talk to him again."

"Mrs. Brand won't let me. All Charlie's visits have to go through her."

Buster smiled, his expression one of bland innocence. "Who said you have to ask her?"

The next day was Tuesday—no visitors allowed. I spent it knocking around Buster's place, watching Ozzie work on the bike—since the engine was apart anyway, he had decided to freshen it up—absorbing some of the ins and outs of tuning dirt track bikes. I learned, for instance, that he ran short intake manifolds for long tracks and long manifolds for short tracks. The short ones, about ten inches long on average, gave the bike more high-rpm power for the long straightaways on mile tracks. On half-miles, the long manifolds—ten-and-a-half to ten-and-three-quarters inches—provided better throttle response and mid-range rpm power, which was more important on shorter, slower tracks than on the miles. It was the same with exhaust pipes. He had a different set for half-miles and miles, tuned for either mid-range response or high-rpm horsepower.

"Everybody's running more or less the same engine setup these days," Ozzie explained, "except for camshafts. Cam timing is where the real horsepower comes from, that and cylinder heads. Get your cam timing right and get your heads to flow a whole lotta air, and you can pull a higher gear, run faster turning the same rpm."

Rusty looked up from the parts washer where he was scraping the carbon off a piston crown with a wire brush. "And kiss the trophy girl a lot."

"So what's the big deal about tuning a dirt track bike," I said, "if the engines are all the same?"

"All the horsepower in the world won't do you any good if you can't get it to the ground," he said. "Chassis tuning is real important, getting the ride height where it oughta be and adjusting the weight distribution to suit the track. Take a track like Springfield, f'rinstance. You mighta noticed the turns are real long and wide, just big arcs connected by short straightaways. That means you're leaned over a long time each lap. What you want to do in that case is raise the bike up as high as it'll go."

"So it's all a matter of ride height?"

"That and weight distribution. Well, you got to get it to steer, too, which you can do by raising the fork tubes in the clamps—"

"Or putting longer rear shocks on it," Rusty said.

"—both of which puts more weight on the front wheel, making it steer better. But that also unweights the rear wheel—"

"—then it'll want to spin out when you gas it coming off the corner," Rusty said.

"Right. If that happens, you want to lengthen the wheelbase. The longer the bike is, the less likely it is to want to come around on you when you get on the throttle."

"Or you could put some more weight on the back end by lowering the fork tubes in the clamps," Rusty said, "to get 'er to hook up better so you can come on the gas sooner and harder."

"Uh huh. Then sometimes the—"

"Okay! I give up!" I said, laughing. "I'm sorry I said anything. There's a lot more to tuning a dirt track bike than I thought."

"You just keep your eyes open, Hemingway," Ozzie said. "Watch what I do the next few races and it'll all make sense to you."

The next morning, Wednesday, I borrowed Buster's Lincoln again. This time I made it to the nursing home on Rutledge without incident or any scenic detours. I parked a block away, where I could see the front steps and where I hoped Mrs. Brand wouldn't notice me.

Visiting hours began at ten. By ten-thirty Mrs. Brand hadn't arrived. I waited another hour just to be sure. By then my stomach was in open revolt, but I was afraid if I broke for a bite to eat I would miss her. So I took a chance.

There was no one behind the desk in the lobby. As it happened the elevator had just arrived and the doors were open. Keeping my eyes straight ahead I went in and hit the button for the third floor.

The corridor was empty. Charlie's room was at the far end. I assumed my I-belong-here look and walked my best I-come-here-all-the-time walk and snuck a peek around the doorway before going in.

I wondered for a split-second if I had come to the wrong room. The bed was empty.

"Help you?" a voice behind me said. I came close to setting a standing high jump record.

The orderly was a short, dark Latino with a Ricky Ricardo mustache and slicked-back hair. A gold chain glittered around his neck, and a gold ring on his finger seconded it.

"I was looking for Charlie . . . Mr. Brand," I said.

He pulled his lips back in a grimace and sucked in a hissing breath. A gold tooth winked. Bingo, hat trick.

"I'm sorry, sir, but Charlie he died las' night."

# 7

I slumped against the wall and rubbed my eyes.

"You a fren' of his?" the orderly said.

"Yeah," I said. " Well, just an acquaintance, really. I would like to have been a friend, though. He looked like he could have used one."

"Poor ol' Charlie. He was so lonely, you know? Nobody ever came to see him but his wife, an' once or twice his daughter, an' that one guy a couple month ago. We useta talk, him an' me."

"What about?"

"Stuff. You know. Wha's happenin', how the baseball teams are doin'. Tell you the truth, I think he din't really care about base-ball. He jus' want someone to talk to. He was all the time calling people on the phone, you know? Just to have someone to talk to. His wife she would complain sometime about the bills. But the daughter, I hear she pay for ever'thing anyhow. She married to some rich guy, she says to the nurses let him call anybody he like."

"Who did he call?"

"Amigos, buddies, you know. This one guy he call maybe t'ree month ago, I come in the room while's he's talkin', he start crying. He sayin' he sorry. 'I'm sorry, Archie, I'm sorry. I din' mean it to happen this way. Don' be mad at me, Archie. I'm dy-ing.' Soun' like maybe he done something to this Archie guy, and he want to go with a clear conscience, you know?"

"Archie? He called a guy named Archie? Was this the same guy who came to see him a couple of months ago?"

He shrugged. "I don' know. I din't see him. Was my day off. Charlie's wife she made a big deal about it. I heard it from one of the nurses. Was a big hassle. They had to give Charlie some medicine to calm him down. Listen, you want to go to the funeral, I can fin' out where they doin' it, huh?"

Things were buzzing back at Buster's. The factory still hadn't come through with a replacement head, but Ozzie had scored a brand new matched set of ported and polished heads from an engine builder in Los Angeles. Federal Express had dropped them off that morning and Ozzie was buttoning up the bike as I walked into the shop.

"Just in time for the break-in," Ozzie said. "Me and Rusty talked it over and decided you should get the first miles on the new engine."

"Thanks," I said, "but I've never ridden one of these."

"It's easy," Rusty said. "Just go straight—"

"—and turn left, yeah, I know. Look, I admit I'd like to give it a try. Just don't expect me to go fast, okay?"

Ozzie and Rusty looked at each other, nodded, then looked at me, smiling like a couple of house cats loose in an aviary.

I wasn't anxious to look like a complete doofus in front of Rusty—*sure, Mr. Horowitz, I'd love to play your piano . . . uh, how about "Chopsticks"?*—but the truth is I had been burning to ride a real dirt tracker for years. There were never all that many Harley-Davidson XR750s in the first place. The factory only built complete bikes in two small production runs in 1972 and 1974, and from then on it just built engines because everyone was junking the stock frames and swingarms and suspension anyway and replacing them with aftermarket stuff. All told, there might have been 600 or so of them in the world at the time.

Not only were they scarce, but like any highly efficient piece of machinery, they were constantly in service, like a hand-me-down suit of clothes. As soon as an Expert-class rider wore one out, a Junior would buy it, rebuild it, and put it back on the track. After the Junior milked the last good mile out of it, some street rider would snap it up, stick lights and a horn on it, and ride it to the Rock Store on Sunday mornings.

Buster scared up a helmet in my size from among a shelf of helmets he kept around for people who wanted to try his track. I jammed my foot into Rusty's left boot—his steel shoe was cus-tom-fitted to it—and sat on the Harley.

The first thing I noticed was that the right footpeg was lower and farther forward than the left, which was perched up high and far back where it wouldn't get in the way when you put your foot down in the turns. With both feet on the pegs, it was like walking down stairs. The foot-activated rear brake and gear shifter were both on the right. There was no room on the left when you were leaned over, and your left foot was pretty busy most of the time anyway. It took a deliberate motion to work either pedal, unlike street bike controls which were placed so as to be easily worked without moving your foot off the peg.

The handlebar was low and wide, making me feel like I was falling over the front of the bike. There was barely enough pad-ding in the seat to satisfy a broad definition of the term. It was like sitting on a vinyl-covered bus bench. The carbs stuck out of the right side of the engine so far I had to crook my knee to avoid hit-ting them, and the huge air cleaners crowded my thigh.

"How's it feel?" Rusty said.

"Is it supposed to feel like it was built for a guy whose right leg has a double-jointed knee and is about a foot longer than his left, and has arms as long as a gorilla's, and no feeling at all in his butt?"

"Yeah."

"Then it feels great."

Rusty gave me a push and I bump-started the engine. The whole world got sort of fuzzy around the edges at low rpm, but when I buzzed the throttle and the revs climbed, everything smoothed out. I let the oil warm up for a minute while Ozzie peered at the engine and twiddled a screw on one of the carbs. He looked a little nervous sending his child out to play with a stranger. I motioned Rusty over.

"Look, I've ridden dirt bikes a lot, and I've done a little sliding in loose gravel. How's this going to be different?"

"It won't be much different except it'll be easier. The bike'll *want* to slide—you'll see."

"What if I fall off?"

"If you fall off the first thing you want to do is get back on and ride that way—" He pointed off in the direction of a small farm house on the neighboring spread, maybe a mile away. "—ask to borrow the phone, and call the cops."

"Call the cops? Why?"

"'Cause Ozzie'll be right behind you with a gun."

I put the gearbox into first and fed the clutch out. The engine wasn't peaky and temperamental like a road-race engine. It just chugged away like a street bike. I rode over the rim of the track and onto the bladed surface. Buster got his dirt hauled in from the same place the Springfield track crew got theirs—dredgings from the Sangamon River. It was dark, rich soil, and with regular care Buster's little playground would have been a fine track in its own right.

Remembering part of the idea was to break the new engine in slowly, I motored around for about ten laps, just getting used to the controls and the awkward feel of the bike. It felt nervous and twitchy on the straights, like the chassis was bent or the wheels were out of alignment. I couldn't see how anyone could ride this thing fast much less ever get comfortable on it.

Rusty jogged to the infield and stood at the entrance to turn one. The next time I came by he held up his arm and made a motion with his right hand like twisting a throttle. I got the hint. Coming out of turn two I goosed it. The rear wheel instantly began to spin and swing around to the right. I snapped the power off and the bike jerked back in line, nearly pitching me over the handlebar.

Rusty gave me a cool-it sign next lap. I slowed as I went by.

"Take it easy!" he yelled. "Smooth! Be smooth!"

Okay, smooth it is. I picked up the pace each lap, carrying a little more straightaway speed into each corner. The faster I went the better the bike felt, especially in the corners. It never felt all that stable in a straight line, but once it was leaned over it was on rails.

Finally, entering turn one, I rolled off the gas and banked into the corner. Engine braking broke the tire loose and the rear end slid gracefully, almost majestically around. Friction generated by the sliding tire began to scrub off speed, and to keep my momentum up I fed in a little power, dropping my left foot off the peg as I leaned to the inside of the turn.

And then some magic equilibrium was achieved, and with my steel shoe skimming along the track and the rear wheel shooting a roostertail of loose dirt behind me, I struck that fragile balance of power and traction and yelled "Yeeaaahah!" inside my helmet so loud Rusty heard it from the infield.

I found I could control the attitude and angle of the slide with the barest twitch of the throttle. If the rear end got too far out, I backed off a fraction and it tucked in again. If I wanted to kick it out further, I just dialed in a few more revs and the bike obliged. The wonkiness of the seating position and the controls vanished in the turns. Everything that was awkward became effortless and the apparently haphazard control layout was revealed to be the end result of decades of refinement toward the single task of negotiating a dirt oval as fast as possible.

I did two, maybe three laps of near perfect broadslides, exulting in the sheer rowdy joy of throwing the Harley to the brink of a crash and then balancing it defiantly on the edge of disaster. Then I went wide in a corner and got off the groove I had been laying down and into the loose stuff up high. In an eyeblink the rear end whipped around, the front wheel slipped sideways, and the bike shot toward the outside of the track like a cue ball on the break. I snapped the throttle shut, both tires regained traction instantly, and the bike lurched upright, throwing me in the air. I held on to the handlebar and came down with the top fork clamp in my chest and my face about an inch from the front tire. Over the banked edge of the track I went, covering at least six feet in mid-air. I did a monster push-up and was more or less on the seat when the wheels hit the ground.

Amazed to find I hadn't killed the engine, I rowed the gearbox around until I found first. Cresting the bank I almost ran over Rusty and Ozzie, who were running toward me full tilt. Buster was pumping along behind them.

"Hey, nice save, Hemingway!" Rusty said, holding a high-five up to me.

I slapped it and took off my helmet and said, "Holy shit, that was *incredible!*" or something equally profound and articulate.

"Getting in some flight time, huh?" Ozzie grinned. "You looked good out there—for a little while, anyway. What happened?"

"Damned if I know. One second I was motoring along and the next second the thing is trying to spit me into the weeds."

"You got up into the marbles," Rusty said. "Stick to the groove until you get the hang of riding the cushion. Take five while I take it around a few times."

We traded helmets and boots and Rusty climbed aboard. We stationed ourselves outside turn one as he came down the front straight. Suddenly the bike slewed sideways in a violent motion not at all like my tentative effort, almost presenting a full-on side view. The rear tire actually squealed on the hard-packed dirt and Rusty wrestled the bike around the turn in a series of small adjustments to the handlebars and a barely audible variation in engine speed. His next ten laps were carbon copies, flawless and fast and scary as hell in light of my new perspective.

I had been feeling pretty good about my performance until then. My hat size shrunk about six sizes.

"Fingers and toes, Hemingway," Ozzie said. "That's what it's all about. Finesse."

"How come the engine sounds like it's straining when he pitches it in?" I said.

"He's using the brake to set up the slide so's he don't have to get off the gas. He doesn't use the tire to scrub off all the speed like you were doing. It saves the tire during the race."

My humbling was complete. Rusty called it a day and rode the bike into the shop. It went up on the lift and Buster went inside to rustle up another feast.

"I imagine we'll be heading out tomorrow, Buster," Ozzie said over dinner. "We don't want to wear out our welcome."

"I'll let you know if you do," Buster snorted. "It's a pleasure having you. Louisville's only a day's drive from here. No sense in spending good money at some fleabag motel. Now, who's for dessert besides me?"

Staying at Buster's place began to feel like taking a paid vacation. But more and more, as I sat watching racing videos with the others or wandered around downtown Springfield doing the tour-

ist tramp, my thoughts drifted toward home and Sara. I called one
night at seven o-clock my time, five L.A. time.

"Hello."

"Hi, it's me. How are you?"

There was a silence that roared through the line.

"Not good," she said.

"What's wrong?"

Silence.

"Sara? Tell me."

"I can't."

"Why not?"

"I just can't."

"Dammit, what's going on? Look, I know we talked about
you leaving if it was the best thing for you to do. Is that it? Do you
want out of our relationship?"

"Jason—"

"Is there some other guy?" There, I said what had been boil-
ing up inside me. "Just tell me. I'll understand." Like hell I would.

"There's no one else."

"How could I have been so stupid? That explains the fights,
the distance, no sex—you want out and you're afraid to say it!"

"No!" She was crying. "That's not it. I need you! I depend on
you. You're all that's holding me together right now."

"Then why send me away? Why is it every time I call I feel
like I'm interrupting something?"

"You don't understand," she said. "You don't care about
what's happening to me."

"I don't know what's happening to you! You won't tell me!"

"It's hard to talk about it on the phone . . ."

"If you hadn't insisted I go on this stupid trip I wouldn't have
to talk to you on the phone in the first place. I'm coming home."

"No! I . . . I'm not ready for you yet."

"Dammit, this is what's been driving me crazy. If I show concern you pull away. If I leave you alone you complain I don't care
about you. You can't have it both ways."

"I'm sorry. I don't know what I'm doing half the time these
days. I can't sleep at night, and I can't seem to stay awake during
the day."

"Sara, look—I know we've already talked about this and you vetoed it. But I want you to do something for me. I want you to see a therapist of some kind, someone who can help you sort all this out. I'll pay for—"

"No!"

I knew she wouldn't budge an inch on this, so after we hung up I cheated and called Aunt Sandy, my mother's sister. Sandy was the closest thing I ever had to a mother. Dad professed to hate her, a feeling that rose out of his lifelong ineptitude at raising two boys on his own and Sandy's infuriating tendency to instinctively know better than him how to go about it. She had been my guardian angel for as long as I could remember. Even though months went by sometimes between my calls, she was there for me at a moment's notice.

She listened to my account of Sara's behavior without interruption. I could almost see her eyebrows huddled together, her head nodding slowly, her lips pressed into a tight thin line of determination.

"You leave her to me," she said. "I'll have a talk with her."

"She won't listen," I said. "I've tried."

"The problem is you're not listening, Jason. She feels as if you're controlling her, isn't that right?"

"That's what she says, yes."

"Then you're the last person who should be telling her what to do."

"I keep forgetting that any time I get to feeling like I understand women, all I have to do is call you, Sandy, and you'll set me straight."

"Humph. Don't flatter me. I never understood why your mother married your father."

I called Sherry Case next and filled her in on what I had found so far.

"What's this Brand person got to do with anything?" she demanded. "I hired you to find out who killed my father, not to dig into some old scandal."

"Your father is implicated in that old scandal," I said. "I think he bribed Charlie Brand to block for him so he could win the National Championship. Two months ago one of the riders who was hurt in the crash, a guy named Archie Jones, found Charlie."

"So?"

"So maybe Charlie told Archie Jones that your father set up the crash. Maybe Archie Jones was still mad about it and went looking for your father and blew his brains out."

"But you don't know for a fact that Brand told Jones anything of the sort, do you?"

"No, but it makes sense that—"

"You're wrong. Max Bauer is behind it."

"How can you be so sure?"

"He stands to gain the most. He wants to buy us out. He couldn't when my father was alive. Now it's almost in the palm of his hand."

And that's the way we left it when we hung up. She wouldn't accept anyone but Max Bauer as Sherm's killer. I talked it over with Buster later and he grudgingly backed her up.

"Just because she's fixated on Max doesn't mean she isn't right," he said. "Even paranoids have enemies. Max had as much reason to hate Sherm as Archie Jones, maybe more. And you *don't* know for a fact, do you, that Brand told Jones it was Sherm who bribed him? Or that there even *was* a bribe? If Charlie Brand was as far gone as you say, you can't take anything he said as gospel."

"Okay, maybe I'm wrong. But what the hell have I got on Max Bauer besides him wanting to buy Case Tires, and the fact that his father snubbed him in favor of Sherm?"

"Let me play devil's advocate here and say what more do you need?"

"Weren't you the one who said you couldn't see Max killing someone over a business deal?"

"Yeah, and in '68 I said Dick Nixon would be one of the greatest presidents this country has ever known."

I laid awake that night wrestling with a battalion of personal demons. I couldn't shake the feeling that Sara's weird behavior boiled down to some flaw of mine. We had always tried to be honest with each other, and by and large we'd done a pretty good job of it. Was I a lousy lover? I wouldn't have thought so from the way she reacted in the days—and nights—before we moved in together. She was imaginative, playful, unquenchable, absolutely unashamed of her body or mine. It seemed as though the minute both our names went on the mailbox she shut all that away and became passive, almost approaching sex as a duty to me rather than a mutual joy.

Then there was *Motorcycle Monthly.* Despite Barry's reassurances to the contrary, I knew my job wouldn't be held open forever, which was coincidentally about how long the lawsuit with Case Tires threatened to drag on. Sherry had not yet come into her father's stock and was in no position to force the suit to be dropped. She sympathized, but from a distance. Her energies were directed toward finding her father's killer. Until that was accomplished, she was powerless to help me or the magazine.

Which left me, wide awake and tossing in an unfamiliar bed, with little else to do but play out the hand I'd drawn. I would do it Sherry's way, starting by finding out where Max Bauer was the night Case died. I wasn't sure how I was going to do it until I got up to get a glass of water and saw the matchbook on the dresser where I had tossed it after it fell out of my shirt pocket.

I turned it over in my fingers, telling myself I had subconsciously saved it only because Angela Bauer might tell me what I needed to know about her husband.

After I told myself the same thing for the third time, I called myself a liar and tossed the matchbook on the dresser and climbed back into bed.

# 8

We left Buster's on Friday with thanks and handshakes all around.

"You have a two-week lay-off between Louisville and Albuquerque," Buster said. "The key's under the mat if you need a place to stay."

"Much obliged, Buster," Ozzie said, "but we intend to hit some of the regionals on the midwest fair circuit and do some cherry-picking, right, Rusty?"

"Yeah," Rusty said. "Gonna see if the local yokels have learned anything since last year."

Ozzie and Rusty were packing the van when Buster motioned me aside.

"If there's anything I can do for you boys while you're on the road," he said, "you give a holler. I've been watching young McCann there. He has what it takes to be National Champ. I'd hate to see him be an also-ran just because Ozzie's too stiff-necked to ask for help."

"Thanks, Buster. I'll keep it in mind. And thanks for helping me out, too."

"Speaking of your problem, I meant to tell you before now, but it slipped my mind. If you want to know all about the 1950 Springfield race, there's a gent in Hagerstown you should talk to. His name is Quince. He sells T-shirts in a booth outside the grandstands. You can't miss him, he's a hunchback. He also has a genuine photographic memory. Any question about tracks, bikes, riders, records, statistics, you name it—it's locked up in Quince's head. He'll be happy to drag it all out for you, too, only be careful. He doesn't know when to stop."

We left around noon and headed for Louisville, Kentucky,

and the Saturday night half-mile at Louisville Downs. It was primarily a harness racing track, with glassed-in grandstands up high and open-air seating down near ground level. There was a big lake filling up most of the infield, with an island for the tote board near the starting line where the officials set up the timing equipment.

We pitted in the stables outside the track, in wooden stalls about eight feet across and a horse-and-a-half deep.

"I wonder if we smell this bad to horses," Rusty said.

"Hey, Hemingway," Ozzie said, "here comes a pretty little filly."

Angela Bauer was strolling up the lane waving to people in various stalls, stopping to chat at one or two. She was wearing tan riding pants that looked sprayed on, polished knee-high black boots, and a loose-fitting blouse. Her long black hair was tied behind her head in, appropriately enough, a pony tail.

Well, it's as good a time as any, I thought, but before I had taken two steps Ozzie was at my side, his hand on my shoulder.

"Uh-oh, cool it, Hemingway. Trouble coming up behind."

A couple of stalls behind her, making his own procession through the pits, was a man in a cream-colored suit with a wide-brimmed Panama hat cocked jauntily on his head. He was tall and slender and fit-looking in a way that suggested he worked on it and was proud of it, and held himself with the unmistakable air of the self-proclaimed aristocrat. He nodded regally in response to shouted greetings, deigned to shake an offered hand or two, and spoke quietly, as if to raise one's voice in public would be unforgivably ill-mannered.

Angela stopped outside our stall.

"Hello, Rusty, Ozzie," she said. "Bob."

"Afternoon, Mrs. Bauer," Ozzie said. Rusty, already descending into the ritual of taping his tear-offs, nodded.

"Hi," I said.

"Didn't you get my message?" Angela said, the corner of her mouth lifting slightly.

I nodded. "Sorry I missed you."

"You could make it up to me later."

"Make what up to you, my dear?" Max Bauer said, suddenly

at her side. He slipped a proprietary arm around her waist, and she snuggled into him, her eyes never wavering from mine as she did.

"Bob, this is my husband, Max. Max, this is Bob, uh . . . ?"

"Hemingway," I said, extending my hand.

"Mr. Hemingway," Max said. His hand was cool and limp. "You know my wife, then?"

"We met at Springfield, dear," Angela said. "Didn't Rusty look good that day?"

"Indeed he did," Max said. "He rode a smart and daring race. And you, Mr. Davidson, you deserve credit, too. The machine ran well. Now if only we could come to some agreement about sponsorship . . ."

At the mention of sponsorship Rusty stopped fussing with his tear-offs and perked up an ear. Ozzie looked away uncomfortably.

"We been through this already, Mr. Bauer," Ozzie said. "I don't feel right talking to you about this kind of thing while we're still under contract with Case Tires."

"But how much longer will that contract be valid, Mr. Davidson? You must know the company is on the brink of financial collapse."

Ozzie shot me a glance. "I don't know nothin' of the sort," he said. "But even if it's true, we're still bound to run Case tires for the rest of the season."

"I admire your sense of loyalty. At the same time it would be a shame if Mr. McCann here were to suddenly find himself on the stretch run to the championship with his sponsor in bankruptcy."

"Ozzie," Rusty said, "what's he—"

With a chop of his hand Ozzie motioned to Rusty to be quiet. "I appreciate your offer, Mr. Bauer," he said slowly, "but that's the way it's got to be for now."

Max shrugged. "As you wish. Angela?"

Angela smiled prettily, like a fashionable accessory to Max's patrician lifestyle, and they continued on down the row of stables.

Ozzie grabbed my sleeve and towed me in the opposite direction. Out behind the vans, he shoved me against the chain link fence and crossed his arms.

"What's he talking about, Street? What all's going on at Case anyway?"

"Max is right," I admitted. "The company's in trouble. Sherm left behind a mess of unfinished business and a mountain of debt."

"So there's more to you tagging along with us than just getting your butt outta the fire, isn't there? Are you keeping tabs on us, making sure we ain't ripping the company off?"

"Sherm Case left Sherry an insurance policy for a million dollars. She can't collect on it if he committed suicide. She can if it turns out he was murdered."

"So the little rich girl gets richer. What the hell's that to me?" Suddenly his face went blank. I could almost hear the wheels turning. "Oh no," he said, glaring at me with narrowed eyes. "Tell me it ain't true! Tell me I'm as crazy as a shithouse rat for even thinkin' it. This million bucks is supposed to keep the company from going under, right?"

"It could. Sherry thinks it will."

"But only if you prove Sherm was murdered, right? Jesus H. Christ in a lifeboat! What if he wasn't? What if maybe ol' Sherm blew his own damn brains out after all? Where's that leave me and Rusty? You know, I don't give a damn if you get your job back or not. What I do care about is Rusty winning the plate. I was willing to drag you along because my sponsor twisted my arm, said you were in a jam, I'd be doing her a favor. Guess she forgot to mention my *own* ass is on the line here, *and* Rusty's. When were you gonna tell me, anyway—when the pump jockeys started cuttin' our gas cards in half?"

"Sherry didn't want word getting out—"

"Well, it's sure the hell out now, ain't it? You think Bauer hasn't told everyone running Case tires that the goddam factory's about to be padlocked? I bet half a dozen teams switched over to his Universals today."

"So what if they did? Does that change anything for Rusty? He still has to run Cases. And you're still under contract to Case for the rest of the season, like you told Max. So what's the difference?"

"The damn difference is I feel like a chump, that's what. I

trusted those people, and look how they . . ." He slumped against a van and ran his fingers through his hair. "Aw, hell, I know it ain't your fault. You're just trying to save your job. So am I. But stay outta my way tonight, okay? Give me a chance to think this over."

We walked to the pits in silence. Suddenly Ozzie pulled up short and turned to me.

*"Bob Hemingway?"* he said.

I shrugged. "I had to think fast."

"Bob Hemingway." He laughed. "Holy shit."

"That's Bob don't-call-me-Ernest Hemingway to you, bub."

I stayed in the background for the rest of the night. There wasn't much for Ozzie to do other than keep the bike full of gas. Rusty liked Louisville and usually placed well there. He went to the main from his heat but qualified out of the running for the Shootout, which Ricky Poe won in spectacular style, bagging Shiloh's $10,000 by riding high up on the cushion while the rest of the field struggled down low on the developing groove.

As the sun lowered I got hungry. The snack bar burgers were rumored to still get skittish at the sound of the starting bell, and the line was moving about as fast as the one painted down the middle of the road. That's when I got to wondering if I could bluff my way into the press room at the top of the grandstands, where there was bound to be something better than tube steaks and watered-down soda on the menu. The only thing that gave me pause was the chance of running into someone who knew me in my editorial capacity.

But the only motorcycle publication likely to send a reporter to Louisville was *Cycle Weekly,* the tabloid that employed Stan Martini. It relied heavily on race reports for its editorial content. The *CW* guy, if there was one, was probably down on the track or in the pits, talking to the riders between races and getting those deathless quotes that are the lumps in the oatmeal of their standard race coverage.

This little inner dialogue went on long enough that the sound of my stomach grumbling began to drown it out, so I said the hell with it, flashed my *Motorcycle Monthly* press card to the rent-a-cop at the bottom of the stairs leading to the skyboxes, and to my surprise and delight was nodded on up.

There was indeed a grand spread laid out for the members of the fourth estate, among which I counted myself, even though I was temporarily on leave. Local newspaper and TV sports reporters made up the bulk of the attendees. They balanced plates heaped high with shrimp and pasta and signalled the waiters for another drink while they argued about the latest stick-and-ball bonus baby whose agent had decided the deal he inked when he came up from the minors might have been binding on a .198 hitter, but was beneath the dignity of one who had averaged .286 at the plate during the last month and brought a struggling franchise to second place in its division.

A stack of press releases with race results and rider bios sat untouched on the end of the bar. The bonus baby's loudest defender was using one for a drink coaster. It was comforting to note the general media still saw motorsports as unworthy of notice unless there was a really horrendous crash they could wow Joe and Mrs. Sixpack with on the eleven o'clock news. There could have been nude ballroom dancing down at the start-finish line and these guys wouldn't have cared.

It was almost dark. The lights around the track were on, and the water truck was circulating slowly, trying to control the billowing limestone dust. From my vantage point I could see the groove, a thin black ribbon of rubber laid down by the fast guys. The track was eighty feet from inside to outside, and the groove maybe twelve inches wide. That's where all the serious racing would take place. With such a narrow racing line it tended to turn into a follow-the-leader affair, and the start would be critical.

The food was good, and there was plenty of it. It wasn't a real dinner, but it would do until later, when we would probably catch a late bite at a local place all the teams went to after the race. I was reaching for a second helping of shrimp when a hand held the big daddy shrimp of all time to my lips.

"I saved one for you," Angela Bauer said.

"Thanks," I said. "Where's Max?"

"Why? Are you afraid he'll see us?"

"No," I lied. "Just curious."

"So am I. Why didn't you call me after Springfield?"

I shrugged. Damn, but she smelled good. "You know."

"Ah, yes, the girlfriend back home."

"We had to do some work on the bike."

"Work on the bike," she said, nodding. "I see. Tell me, how much fun was that?"

"Not much, I guess," I said, glancing around the room to see if Max was nearby.

"Not as much fun, I'll bet, as—" She leaned closer to whisper in my ear.

"Let's go down to the track for the main event," I said, taking her plate and putting it on the table beside mine.

She brightened. "I'd like that."

She picked up her jacket and I held it for her. It was made of glove leather, cut bolero-style, and fit her like skin. We were followed out the door by most of the male eyes in the room.

She stopped on the stairs, a step below me, and turned her face up to mine.

"I like this shy, hard-to-get routine of yours," she said. "It's refreshing. I get so tired of aggressive men."

"Thanks. I think."

"Oh, I mean it as a compliment. Just don't take it too far."

"Can I ask you something? Do you do this just to annoy your husband, or do you really enjoy it?"

Her eyes flashed fire at me. I was really glad the horsey outfit hadn't come with a riding crop.

"Is that supposed to be funny?"

"Sorry. In addition to being shy and hard to get, I also have an inconvenient sense of humor."

"Keep it to yourself." She stomped down to the next landing, her boot heels clacking hollowly in the stairwell.

"Why are you making this so hard?" she said when I caught up. "I like you. Don't you like me?"

"I'd like you a lot more if you were a little more discreet."

"Max doesn't care. He does it himself, all the time."

"Some marriage, huh?"

"Are you married to your little girlfriend back home?"

"No."

"Then you can't know what it's like. In the meantime I'll thank you not to criticize my life."

We found a couple of seats along the front straight and sat down. A breeze came up and Angela moved close to me.

"I won't bite you," she said. "Put your arm around me. I'm freezing."

Despite the night air I was sweating. One part of my mind was trying to convince myself I was only doing this to gain Angela's confidence so I could ask her about Max. Another part muttered—in a venomous voice that belonged to Sara—that I was a lying bastard. I was enjoying her attention, feeling her warmth next to me, responding to her in a way I hadn't been allowed to respond to the only woman in my life for longer than I cared to remember. The worst part was that I knew, regardless of how guilty I felt, regardless if Max Bauer walked right up and sat down next to us, that I wanted to leave my arm around her shoulder, and to put the other one around her other shoulder, and kiss her like she had kissed me at Springfield.

"Do you have a sweater or something?" Angela said. "You're shivering like mad."

"I have a jacket in the van."

"Come on, then."

The pits were dark and mostly deserted. The PA was announcing the starters for the main event. Angela and I walked along the row of stables, bumping hips playfully, glancing into the stalls and at each other.

We passed an empty one with a broken light and suddenly she pulled me into it. There was fresh straw on the floor. We sank to our knees in it, arms around each other, lips mashed together.

"You're not shivering any more," she whispered. She untangled her arms and began to shrug off her jacket. I helped. With a knowing look she began unbuttoning her blouse. I let her get to the one before the blouse disappeared under her belt. Then I stood up.

"I'm sorry," I said, *"really* sorry, but I can't do this."

"What?" she gasped.

"I can't. I don't know how to explain it. It's just not my style."

"Your *style?* What the hell does that mean?"

"You're a ferociously attractive woman, and it's been a long time since I've been this close to one of those. But I made a promise. I have to stick by it."

She stood up and angrily brushed the straw out of her hair. "A long time since—? Then what was that song and dance about a girlfriend back home?"

"It's true. We're having problems."

"Oh, you have a problem, all right, Bob." She fumbled with the buttons on her blouse, her hands shaking.

"It's Jason, not Bob," I said. Damned if I know why I told her. As long as I was being honest with myself I might as well be honest with her. "My name is Jason Street."

"Well, whoever you are, you're a damn fool." She snatched up her jacket and marched out of the stall.

"If it's any consolation," I said, "I'll probably kick myself around the block all night thinking about what I missed."

Suddenly she grinned. Her eyes glowed with a defiant pride.

"You bet you will, buster." Tossing her jacket over her shoulder, she disappeared around the corner with a hip-swinging gait, her pony tail swishing from side to side.

I got to the outside rail just in time to see the main event flag off. Brian Meller, a racer from the Louisville area, had it in the bag from the first lap to the last. He was half a lap ahead of Murdock in second and Hendricks in third. Rusty was mired in sixth, unable to pass on the narrow groove, and was still there when the checkered flag flew.

Rusty's sixth earned him nine points and moved him into second in the overall standings, with 76 points to leader Al Hendricks' 93. Perry Haycock had been second in overall points coming to Louisville, but a broken valve sidelined him early in the race. His overall score stayed at 64.

Rusty was unhappy with his performance, but Ozzie was content.

"You came here in third and left in second," he was saying as I walked into the stall. "What the hell else you want, a brass band and the keys to the Louisville Girls' Academy?"

"I blew the start," Rusty moped. "I should have been up front from the git-go."

"And I shoulda been born handsome and married rich instead of having to sit here listening to the guy in second place in the overall standings pissing and moaning about blowing a start that earned him more points than Perry Haycock, who you mighta noticed got zip for his night's work. Cheer up, ya dope. Hey, Hemingway, how'd you like the race?"

"Nice start, Rusty," I said, slapping him on the shoulder. "You looked liked a real jerk out there. What happened? You go colorblind all of a sudden and miss the green light? Forget which pedal shifts the gears? Jeez, you got such a rotten start you looked like you were going backwards! Ozzie, maybe we better put a back-up light on the bike, huh?"

Rusty laughed. "Knock it off, you guys. I dropped the clutch at the green and the wheel just lit up and started sliding. I gotta practice my starts more, that's all."

"Well, you got a couple weeks of regionals coming up to work on 'em," Ozzie said. "Let's load up and get some chow."

The House O' Pizza in downtown Louisville was a run-down tavern so old that the initials carved in the tables had s's that looked like f's. When we got there it was full of racers, crew members, and anyone who knew a racer or a crew member and had managed to hitch a ride downtown.

We ordered a "huge with everything" and swiped enough empty chairs from various tables to seat ourselves with Chris Murray, his mechanic Jack Something, and a couple of wide-eyed females whose names and ages didn't seem to matter as much to either Chris or Jack as their apparent availability.

Chris was buying the beer that night, pouring from a pitcher the size of a washtub. Rusty was off making the rounds of the other tables. The din was deafening. Nothing short of a shout even made it across the table.

"I don't recall seeing you around before," Chris said to me.

"He's a new engineer from Case HQ in Torrance," Ozzie butted in. "He's learning the ins and outs of dirt track from the ground up. Right, Bob?"

I offered my hand. "Bob Hemingway," I said, following Ozzie's lead. "I'm with Case Tires in the, uh, street tire division." I knew enough about street tires to hold up my end of any semitechnical discussion. "I'm here to learn the ropes, like Ozzie says."

"I run Cases at some of the tracks. I'd be happy to give you some feedback."

"Great. We'll get together at . . . what's the next race?"

"Albuquerque, on the 17th. Gonna make the regional rounds this year, Ozzie?"

"You betcha. We can always use a little gas money, and Rusty wants to practice his starts."

"Looked like he could've used some tonight. How about Ricky Poe blowing up again? Is that routine getting old or what?"

"Poe blew up again?" I said.

"Yeah," Ozzie said. "Where were you?"

"Ah, well—"

I must have been on the universe's shit list that night. As I spoke Angela Bauer came through the door on Max's arm. Max was probably one of about six people in the whole place who owned a tie, and was for sure the only one wearing one. He was struggling gamely to maintain his air of detachment in the face of a rising tide of beer-induced familiarity, but still looked about as comfortable as a tent preacher at a punk rock concert.

Angela's eyes locked onto mine like enemy radar. I felt like a single-celled life form under her withering gaze. She looked down her nose at me with cool disdain for a few long seconds, then dismissed me from the face of the earth with a haughty toss of her hair. Someone yelled and she and Max joined some friends at a table across the room.

Ozzie looked at her, then at me, then back at her. "Never mind," he said. "I think I know. She leave any scars?"

"None you could see."

"Give that one a pass, *Bob*. She'll eat you alive. Besides, what's wrong with that one who dropped you off at Rusty's? She looks to be worth about six or seven of Angela's type."

I shook my head. "Ten or twelve, easy."

The real question remained—was I worthy of her?

# 9

In the two weeks between Louisville and Albuquerque we hit three states, seven races, and every greasy spoon between the Great Plains and the Great Lakes. It didn't seem to faze Ozzie at all, but between the podunk race tracks, the lousy food, and the irregular hours, I was dragging my tail in the dirt by the end of the first week.

Worse, it was getting to Rusty. He rode as hard as he always did, and won two races and some cash, but between starts he began to look hollow-eyed and distracted. Once I caught him going out on a particularly moist track without any tear-offs on his helmet, and another time at a night race, our third in three days, I found him asleep in the van five minutes before the start of the main event. Ozzie said the fair circuit was tough, no doubt about it, but Rusty would rebound by the time the next national rolled around.

To combat my own road fatigue, I bought a mountain bicycle and stowed it in the van, next to the Harley and the single-cylinder Rotax TT bike Rusty rode in short track events and the 600cc regionals. Every morning before breakfast I put in at least five miles. Besides getting my blood pumping and my mind off my troubles, I got to see some pretty country first-hand. The mountain bike came in handy in the pits, too. Pretty soon Rusty was borrowing it regularly, pedaling out to the corners to check the track. But I couldn't get him interested in riding it any farther than from one end of the pits to the other.

Ozzie had an annoying blind spot when it came to any kind of physical training. He and I had a row over it one day while Rusty was lined up for practice at the Albuquerque mile race, the regionals behind us at last.

"This ain't weightlifting, Hemingway," he said. "All's he gotta do is ride the bike flat-out for fifteen minutes at a time. A lot of muscle works against you, gets you all tensed up and holding on too tight."

"I'm not talking about muscle mass," I said. "I'm talking about endurance. The fair circuit wore him out. He needs to lay off the parties, sleep more, eat better food."

"Hell, he's young. As long as his head's on straight by race morning he'll do okay. Besides, you were his age once, weren't you?"

"I sure was. And I was as dumb as the day is long. I'm past thirty now, and I know better than to think I can run at this pace for weeks on end, live on hog slop, run my batteries down every night, and not pay for it in the end."

Ozzie was unmoved. "The best way to keep in shape for racing is to race," he insisted. "Riding the bike is all he needs to do."

"Weren't you the one who said he needed to think like a racer all the time, twenty-four hours a day, if he was going to be Number One? Is he thinking like a racer when he pigs out on pizza and beer the night before a race? Or stays up partying until two in the morning? If he keeps that up he'll burn out before the end of the season, much less before he gets anywhere near winning the plate."

"Look, I've been doing this for longer than you've had a damn driver's license. I don't need some know-it-all from L.A. telling me how to do my job. And I don't want you filling his head with this shit, either, understood? Stay outta my hair and remember why you're here."

By which he meant I should hurry up and pin Sherm Case's murder on someone so Sherry could get her million and save the company—and Rusty's sponsorship deal. If so much as a day went by without me uncovering some new detail of the 1950 Springfield race or Max Bauer's whereabouts the night Case died, he made me feel like a freeloader deadheading around the country at his personal expense.

There were plenty of days just like that, too. A lot of people knew the broad details of how Max's father had brushed him aside in favor of Sherm Case, but what little else they knew was the result of either idle speculation or some grudge against him. The man himself proved to be unapproachable most of the time, and on those few occasions when I managed to strike up a conversation, he deflected all my questions expertly and in turn pumped me for information on the state of Case Tires. Word had gotten around that I was a tire engineer, and I had a few anxious moments trying to maintain the deception under his polite but insistent questioning. Although I could dazzle the average motorcyclist with the breadth if not the depth of my knowledge, he had forgotten more than I ever knew about street bike tires, my putative specialty, and I doubted I fooled him for a minute.

Maintaining interest in hunting Sherry Case's snipe proved increasingly difficult, too. Life on the road lulled me with days of travel, which I've always loved, so that I began to see the racing as an inconvenience. Ozzie pretended I wasn't an important part of the race effort, but if I wasn't nearby come the main he'd get testy about it later.

We came away from Albuquerque with win number two for the season. Al Hendricks had an off day, rare for him even considering the poorly groomed track. He struggled to qualify, had to ride a semi to make the main, started on the back row, and had a tire go down late in the race. His tenth-place finish was worth only five points. Rusty's win earned him 20, boosting him to within two points of the overall points lead. Perry Haycock placed fourth, giving him a solid lock on third overall.

We had another two-week lay-off until the half-mile in Lima, Ohio. Just to prove he was right and I was wrong, Ozzie arranged a punishing schedule of hayseed derbies for Rusty, entering him not only in the relatively lucrative 600cc Series but also in no-name short tracks on rutted barnyard ovals in towns so small that "Now Entering" and "Now Leaving" were painted on opposite sides of the same sign. The first-place money wouldn't buy a good meal at a drive-through, and the locals resented a ranked Expert cherry-picking on their turf and making them look like the amateurs they were in front of their wives and girlfriends.

Rusty fell off at Lima in his semi and failed to qualify. Haycock won it, bumping Rusty from second to third in the overall standings. Ozzie brushed it off as the breaks of the game, oblivious to the fact that Rusty was wrung out.

With Rusty out of the main, I spent the night spectating. Ricky Poe got second in the Shiloh Shootout, and when he pulled off the track after the checker he gassed it and roared straight to his pit. I was walking to the van for my jacket when he almost ran me over in the dim light. I was in a foul mood anyway and had half a mind to find him and chew him out for it, so I followed him to his pit.

While I was still some distance off, I saw Eddie Grimes kneeling by the bike, working on the distributor, and Max Bauer sitting on a toolbox, his legs crossed, looking bored. Poe was pacing like an expectant father, looking a lot more upset than a guy who had just won $3000 had any right to be. But it was Eddie who captured my attention.

First, he looked around to see if anyone was watching. Then he quickly disconnected the fuel lines at the petcocks and yanked the gas tank. The spare bike was parked nearby, and in less than a minute Eddie had swapped tanks, reconnected the fuel lines, and thrown a tarp over the spare. Then he kneeled down and took the distributor cap off the bike Ricky had just brought in and began poking inside with a screwdriver.

Suddenly Poe kneeled beside Eddie and they began an animated conversation, with Poe waving his hands and Eddie trying to calm him down. Eddie stood up and shoved Poe around to the other side of the van, hidden from Max's sight. The argument heated up, and I caught some of what was said.

". . . want to win a goddam race for once, Eddie. I don't care what he says, and I don't care about the money any more."

"You better care about it. And keep your voice down. You could cost us both our licenses. We'll do it his way, understand, 'cause if we don't he'll—"

Something made Eddie turn just then. Our eyes met. He dragged Poe into the shadows and continued to lecture him in a hushed voice.

Later, Poe was running up front in the main but dropped back with a misfire. He pulled into the pits rather than stay out there and fight a losing battle. Once again he rocketed through the pits, and again I jogged along after him and made myself inconspicuous by standing at the edge of a cluster of people watching the race.

Poe stepped off the bike and let it fall before Eddie could grab it. Eddie picked the bike up, ignoring Poe, who was practically ripping his leathers off. I was curious to see what Eddie would do now—change the tanks back, maybe?—and was edging closer for a better view when a shadow blocked the light. Max Bauer stepped out of the gloom.

"Good evening, Mr. Street," he said. "It is Jason Street, isn't it? Features editor of *Motorcycle Monthly?*"

What else could I say? "Evening, Mr. Bauer."

"I'm so very disappointed in you, Mr. Street. How ignoble of you to disguise your identity and try to ingratiate yourself to me. Am I correct in assuming that since your career as a journalist seems to be at an end, you are in fact working for Case Tires as some kind of spy?"

"I'm not spying for anyone. I'm helping Ozzie Davidson and Rusty McCann."

"How odd, since McCann and Davidson are sponsored by the company suing your magazine. I can't help but think you're here for quite another reason."

"I'm on leave from the magazine. I got bored kicking around the house."

"Please don't insult my intelligence, Mr. Street. What lawyer would allow a client to take up with the enemy, and what enemy would accept him? No, Mr. Street, I've been watching you, and I've decided there's more to your presence here than meets the eye."

"Have it your way," I said, and turned to go.

"Just a moment, Mr. Street. You will kindly stop pestering my friends with impertinent questions about me. Further, you will stop interfering in my business affairs and cease to bother my rider and his mechanic. People who continue to annoy me often live to regret it." He bowed slightly from the waist and touched the brim of his hat. "And now, good evening," he said with a chilly smile.

From that point on I was thoroughly sick of Max Bauer and his petty concerns and his faithless wife and Ozzie's stubbornness and just about everything and everybody connected with dirt track. Bickering with Ozzie and watching Rusty burn out had soured me for the racing life. Bouts of homesickness washed over me whenever I saw the latest copy of *Motorcycle Monthly* on the stands.

I got pretty hard to live with. Sherry Case demanded to know what I had learned so far, and got upset when what little I had wasn't enough. I snapped back that the whole idea was ludicrous anyway, and she should just face up to the fact that her father killed himself and get on with her life. The lawsuit against the magazine was dragging on, but Barry hadn't replaced me—yet. He wasn't sure how much longer he'd be able to keep the publisher from overruling him.

I spent my free days riding my mountain bike, and the travel days staring out the window at the landscape scrolling past. I no longer hung out with the guys after the races, preferring to hole up in my room and read. I hated where I was, and I couldn't go home. I was in just such a self-pitying mood the Friday night we arrived in Hagerstown, Maryland, for the half-mile the next night.

We checked in at the Holiday Inn and Ozzie and Rusty went out to dinner with some friends. I went to a restaurant near the hotel but found I just couldn't face another pressed, formed, and standardized surf 'n' turf extravaganza. So I sat in the bar drinking an Irish coffee without the Irish, feeling sorry for myself.

"Hello, stranger," a voice said. It was Angela. She was wearing a white dress, gathered at the waist with a wide brown belt. I had never seen her dressed up, in heels and stockings and makeup. It took a heartbeat to recognize her.

"You look like your dog died," she said, slipping into the booth beside me.

"He might have," I said. "It's been two months since I've seen him. What brings you here?"

"I was supposed to meet Max for dinner. He called and said he missed his flight."

"You don't sound like you believe him."

"It doesn't matter if I do or not. Are you hungry?"

"I was. The menu cured me."

"Come with me. I know just the place."

She handed me the keys to her rental car and we drove north of town past where the city stopped and the country began. We passed a few farms and weathered houses and finally came to a crossroad. We took a left and the road narrowed as it ran alongside a row of trees. There was a white rail fence behind the trees, and then a gate.

We drove through and parked beside an old farm house that had been restored and turned into a restaurant. The house was three stories tall with a peaked roof and gables popping out like mushrooms. The ground floor windows were brightly lit. The ones on the second floor glowed softly.

The hostess greeted Angela like an old friend. If she was surprised to see me instead of Max, she didn't show it. We climbed a broad staircase to the second floor and were seated in what probably used to be a bedroom, but had been converted to a small private dining room. We sat across from each other at a small table with candles in silver holders.

"This is great," I said. "It was getting so I saw Holiday Inn menus in my dreams. What's good here?"

"Just about everything, but order something with crab."

I did, and she was right.

"This is the best meal I've had since leaving home. Thanks for suggesting it."

"My pleasure . . . Jason. Tell me, why the phoney name?"

"It's kind of hard to explain . . ."

"All right, tell me about yourself instead."

The atmosphere was altogether conducive to intimacy. Angela was fast becoming less predatory and more of a friend. I had been missing the comfort of someone I could talk to about things wholly unconnected with racing.

"Well, you know my name, I was born in Morgan Hill, California, thirty-one years ago. Grew up there, went to school there, did some racing, wrote a lot of freelance race reports for motorcycle magazines, and eventually got offered a staff position by *Motorcycle Monthly* and moved to L.A."

"Do you like it there?"

"Yes and no, in roughly equal proportions."

"Why not?"

"Too crowded, too fast, too dirty."

"And what's good about it?"

"Good weather, great riding, and it's the only place I could really do my job. It's where all the manufacturers' U.S. headquarters are, so it's where all the magazines are."

"Any family?"

"My mother died when I was born. My dad's still alive. My older brother was killed last year."

"Oh! I'm so sorry. How did it happen?"

I thought for a second about going into all the details, but settled for just, "Motorcycle accident."

"What's your girlfriend's name?"

"Sara Samuels."

"How did you meet her?"

"At a press gig Kawasaki gave on Catalina Island. She was working for a rival motorcycle magazine, the one my brother wrote for, in the art department. We hit it off but we had to keep it a secret. Bartlett Publications, that's the company that owns *Cycle Journal,* had a no-dating policy. Someone found out anyway, and she got fired. Now we live together."

"Why aren't you home with her? Maybe I'm wrong, but you don't seem too happy with the gypsy life of the professional motorcycle racer."

"I wrote an article," I said, "a tire comparison. I slammed one brand pretty hard. The owner of the company took exception to my test, and killed himself."

"Sherm Case," she whispered, her eyes going big and round. "My God. You blame yourself for that?"

"It hardly matters. Everyone else does. My publisher, Case's lawyers, the rest of the motorcycle press—"

"But that's so unfair!"

"I'm on leave while the lawyers battle it out."

"Why come here? Why make it worse by running off and living with a bunch of strangers for months at a time?"

"The Foreign Legion wouldn't take me. Besides, there's a possibility that Sherm Case didn't commit suicide. That he was murdered."

"By who?"

"I can't really say."

"You can't say as in you won't say, or as in you don't know?"

I shook my head.

Her eyes went unfocused for a few seconds, as though she were deep in private thought.

"Max," she whispered. "You think Max killed him."

"I didn't say that."

"You didn't have to say it. You've been asking everyone about him for two months. You'd better be careful—you can't arouse that much curiosity and not have it get back to him."

"He already knows. I assume you told him my real name? He did some checking and found out I work for *Motorcycle Monthly,* too."

"But how did you find out?"

"Find out what?"

"That Max killed Sherm."

"Are you telling me he did?"

"No, not at all. I . . . it's just that it explains a few things . . ."

A little frown crossed her face and she rested her chin on her steepled fingers, lost in thought.

"You must know," she said after a minute, "that Max has had his eye on Case Tires for some time. What you probably don't know is his hatred for Sherm Case is the only reason he wanted it. Sherm came between Max and his father years ago, and Max has never forgiven him for it, not to this day. We were both at Ascot when we heard about Sherm. After the race I said to Max that I guessed he had gotten his revenge after all. He said, 'Not quite yet, my dear, not completely.'"

"Did you take that to mean that Max had killed Sherm?"

"I didn't think about it much then. Max says things like that all the time. He thinks if he's purposely mysterious people will assume he's deep and profound."

"Where was Max that night at Ascot?"

"I don't know exactly. I was . . . with a friend. In the stands."

"Was Max in the pits?"

"Yes, absolutely. He likes to watch over Eddie Grimes and Ricky."

"Trying to figure out why Ricky's bike always breaks in the main?"

"No, I don't think that particularly bothers him. Other people seem far more worried about it than he is. It's as if he just doesn't care."

"You can see the back pit gate from up in the stands. Did you see him go through it at any time?"

"No, but I wasn't really paying too much attention."

"When you heard the shot and the ambulance left the infield, did you see him come out?"

"I told you, I wasn't watching the pit gate. Besides, I had no idea what had happened until after the race when I overheard some people talking about it."

She was quiet on the drive to the motel, gazing out the window with her elbow propped on the arm rest and her chin in her hand. I parked the car and opened her door for her.

"How do you know I won't tell him?" she said. "If he did it, and I told him you knew or even suspected, you could be in danger."

"Are you going to tell him?"

"I could help you, you know."

"How?"

"I could watch, listen. Tell you things."

"Why would you? He's your husband, after all. Doesn't that mean anything?"

"It used to. Max is sixty. I'm forty-two. Do you know what that's like? Besides, I don't have to tell you it's not an ideal marriage."

"You'd turn him in if it was true?"

"I think so. Yes. I would."

"Could you live with yourself?"

She laughed, not a pretty laugh. "Quite well, thank you. Do you have any idea what he's worth? No, of course not. Would you like your very own motorcycle magazine? I could buy it for you if . . ." A light shined in her eyes like candles beside a coffin.

I walked her to her room. She handed me the key and I opened the door for her.

"Come in for a minute," she said, turning the lights on as she walked to the bathroom and closed the door.

I sat in the chair by the window, feeling lousy. If Max Bauer killed Sherm Case, he should pay for it. But the idea of Angela or anyone else benefitting from it made me feel dirty.

It was a few minutes before I noticed the sound of water running in the shower. I got up to let myself out. As my hand closed over the doorknob the water stopped, and I decided to wait and tell her I was leaving.

She came out of the bathroom wearing a terrycloth hotel bathrobe, like the one in my room, rubbing her hair with a towel. Without make-up the years showed in the mirror under the harsh light above the sink. She was humming a little tune to herself, and there was a far-off look on her face.

"I think I'll be going," I said.

She kept rubbing her hair as if she hadn't heard me.

"Angela, thanks for the dinner. It was fun. I—"

She dropped the towel on the floor and turned around and walked slowly toward me. Without breaking stride she untied the robe and let it fall.

She stopped so close to me I could smell her skin, warm and clean. The pupils of her eyes were enormous, her expression eager and abandoned and at the same time pleading.

"Jason," she said, her voice husky and breathless.

"No," I said. "No. We've been around this track already." I grabbed the doorknob and turned it. She jumped past me and straight-armed the door closed.

"Yes," she said through clenched teeth. "Yes, dammit!"

I picked up the robe and threw it at her. She swiped at it in mid-air and batted it to the floor.

"You son of a bitch," she hissed. "I could help you! I *will* help you! But you have to help me first."

"To do what? Cheat on Max? You don't need me for that."

"Hypocrite! Liar! You wanted me that night, didn't you?"

"Yes."

"And you want me now."

"No."

"Why?" It came out almost as a wail. "Why won't you?"

"Because I want to so bad right now I can't think straight."

"Don't think!"

"I have to. About whether Max is really a murderer, or if you would frame him for it just to be rid of him."

"What difference does it make? He's nothing. To hell with him. We have each other."

"It makes a difference to me. He's never done me any harm. I'm sorry. I have to go."

"Bastard!" she screamed, and lunged at me, her fingers curved like claws. I grabbed her wrists and held her at arm's length. She was screaming, her damp hair flailing like a whip. Suddenly something shoved me hard from behind. I stumbled, almost fell. Angela tumbled backward and landed heavily on her butt.

"Angela, you're making a scene," Max Bauer said coolly. He was wearing a tan sport coat and dark slacks, holding a suitcase in one hand and a room key in the other. "Mr. Street, would you excuse us? I'd like to talk to my wife."

# 10

I met Ozzie in the Denny's across the street the next morning. I was bleary-eyed and badly in need of coffee. He was just finishing, mopping up egg yolk with a slice of toast.

"You look like you been shot at and missed, and shit at and hit," he observed. "Rough night?"

"Nah, the usual," I said. "Nice dinner, romantic setting, attempted murder at the end. You know."

"Yeah. Gets old, don't it?"

"Where's Rusty?"

"Didn't come back to the room last night," he said, challenging me to make an issue out of it. "He'll be along."

That conversation was a dead end, so I changed the subject.

"Eddie Grimes," I said. "Does he know what he's doing?"

"How do you mean?"

"His bikes blow up all the time. Does he really know his way around an XR engine?"

"Beats me. For all the bad-mouthing he gets, his bikes go real fast in the Shootouts. Maybe he just needs to build a longer fuse into 'em."

The waitress brought coffee. A sip or two later I felt more awake, if not any better. I caught a glimpse of myself in the chrome napkin dispenser. The face that looked back at me was that of someone who should be out on the curb with a tin cup full of pencils. I needed a haircut and my new beard needed trimming.

"Why do you ask?" Ozzie said.

"Last night, right after the Shootout, Eddie changed gas tanks on Ricky's bikes. Then he messed with the distributor. Why would he do that?"

Ozzie shrugged. "The XR is a finicky bastard. Some guys can keep one running like clockwork for a hundred miles at a time. Other guys, who maybe don't do the initial set-up and timing all that well in the first place, they have to stay on top of things to keep the bike running strong from the heats to the main. My guess is Eddie is a stay-on-top-of-things kinda guy. He'd rather do a whole lotta quick-and-dirty than one slow-and-steady."

"Okay, maybe that explains the distributor. But what about the gas tank? What goes wrong with a gas tank, anyway?"

"Metal fatigue. They're aluminum. It mighta cracked."

Rusty dragged in and slid into the booth beside Ozzie.

"Hey, champ, you get lucky last night?"

"Yeah," Rusty mumbled. "Hey, Hemingway."

"Hey, Rusty. Want to borrow the mountain bike today, maybe put in a few miles before the race?"

"Hell, yeah," he said around a cavernous yawn. "Let's do ten."

The waitress brought him coffee. He added half a container of cream and drained it off in a couple of gulps. He ordered eggs, scrambled, bacon and toast, orange juice and keep the coffee coming.

I pushed the menu away without opening it.

"What's the number one breakfast?" I said.

"Steak and eggs, hash browns, toast or muffin," the waitress recited.

"Medium, scrambled, and toast," I said. She took my order and walked away. I caught Ozzie's eye, motioned toward Rusty. He was nodding over his coffee, hanging onto the cup the way a sailor hangs onto a life jacket.

We checked out of the rooms and got to the track in the early afternoon. Hagerstown Speedway was built about a hundred yards from a river, with the back straight situated along the steep, tree-lined bank. Early in the program the track was slippery but dry. As the evening wore on, the moisture from the river rose up and changed it to a tacky surface that offered a wide groove and lots of racing room.

While Ozzie ran the bike through tech inspection I crossed the track. On the far side of the grandstands were displays from local dealers and vendors selling everything from souvenir hats to discount tires. There were maybe half a dozen booths selling T-shirts, but there was no mistaking the man Buster had suggested I talk to.

Quince was bent over almost double, wearing one of his own products, a garishly silkscreened T-shirt, on his misshapen back. He moved in a jerky, birdlike way, his eyes darting left and right as he bantered with his customers, crabbing from one side of the counter to the other to show off a design or help judge a size. His specialty was shirts with pictures of past National Champions. He would pluck one shirt from the top of a pile, fan it out to display the design, then deftly fold it and slip it under the pile and repeat the process with the top shirt. All the while he kept up a steady stream of trivia that hardly left him time to take a breath between customers.

"Evening, sir, ma'am, what can I do for you?" he piped in a reedy voice like a rusted-out steam whistle. "Gary Nixon? Sure, I got him, National Champ in '67 and '68, riding a Triumph. Nineteen career wins, first one at a fifty-mile road race in Windber, Pennsylvania, on August 4, 1963, and the last at a seventy-five-mile road race at Loudon, New Hampshire, on June 16, 1974. Fourth Loudon win of his career, only one on a Suzuki—I'd say the little lady's a small, wouldn't you, sir?—the first two were on Triumphs and the third on a Kawasaki. Versatile rider, yes, ma'am. One of the greats of all time—no, ma'am, cold water, tumble dry cool—from Cockeysville, right here in Maryland, did you know that, ma'am? Sure is. Here you go, enjoy your shirt . . . . Yes, sir, can I help you? Bart Markel? You bet. Michigan rider, out of Flint, won the Number One plate in '62, '65, and '66. Black Bart they called him, twenty-eight career wins, first one at . . ."

I edged my way toward the counter and waited for my turn.

"Yes, sir," Quince said at last, cocking his head to look up át me.

"What do you know about Sherm Case?"

"Winner, Springfield Mile, 1950, his one and only career win. Quit racing right after that, went to work for Heinrich Bauer, owner of Bauer Tire and Rubber company, based in Indianapolis, on Water Street on the east side of town at—"

"I heard once that race was fixed. That Case paid some guy to block for him. Do you know anything about that?"

"There were rumors, during and after the race. Big crash in the main, three riders went down in turn three on lap eight. A man named Jesse Ed Beyer died on the spot. Akron boy. Fell off avoiding the wreck and slid between two haybales and smacked the wall. Broke his neck. Good amateur, won the hillclimb at—"

"A rider who went down in that crash, a man named Archie Jones. Whatever happened to him?"

"Quit racing. Had to. Broke his left femur in three places. Caught his leg under the bike as it went down. It never healed right. He moved west, out to California. Got into the law business. Now, I don't have a Sherm Case, no real call for him, but how about Joe Leonard—"

"California? You're sure?"

"I'm sure," Quince snapped. He squinted and fixed a probing eye on me. "Do you want a shirt or not?"

"Where in California?"

"Los Angeles."

"I'll take a Mert Lawwill in a large."

I jogged through the pit gate to the infield just as they were closing it for time trials. You got two chances to qualify, with the option to wave off your first by motioning to the starter as you completed your timed lap. If you did, your second time, even if it was slower than your first would have been, was the one that counted.

Rusty waved off his first time, convinced it wasn't good enough to get him into the program. The clocks backed him up. There was a psychological cushion in having a second chance, but by waving off, Rusty put himself on the spot. He rode the mountain bike out to the corners to see where the fast guys were riding. When he came back he looked uneasy. Since the regional swing he had abandoned his pre-race ritual of shutting out the external world less often. More and more he fretted like a peevish child, sticking close to Ozzie whenever he wasn't actually riding the bike, pestering him for advice.

"They're all over, Ozzie," he said. "Some guys are up high, some guys are down low. I don't know where to try it."

"Keep it low," Ozzie said calmly. "Use your brake a lot, don't slide as much, keep your wheels in line. That way you can come off the corners early and get a run on the straight."

Ozzie's plan turned out to be the right one. Rusty not only got into the program, he qualified for the Shiloh Shootout.

Then he missed the transfer out of his heat and barely made it in from the semi. When he came in he was puffing and sweating and downed a half-gallon of Gatorade in six gulps.

Ozzie sent Rusty out for the Shootout but instead of staying on the grid with him until the start, he faded into the pits. I climbed on top of the van and watched Ricky Poe collect another ten grand bonus check. Rusty got a lousy start and never made up for it. He looked ragged and tired, riding like a drunk, overshooting the turns and running wide. In turn four his left foot caught in a hole in the track and flipped backwards. The heel plate of his heavy steel shoe whacked the exhaust pipe and pinched it almost completely closed. The engine soured immediately, and Rusty limped home in last place.

I jumped down as Rusty pulled up. The bent part of the pipe looked like a roadkill rattlesnake. Rusty was frantic.

"Where's Ozzie?" he whined. "We gotta fix this!"

We yanked the pipes off the bike. I grabbed the biggest hammer I could find and began whacking on the smashed section, trying to round it out. Suddenly Ozzie trotted up.

"What the hell's going on?" he said. Before either of us could answer he saw the problem, snatched the hammer out of my hand, dropped to his knees over the pipes, and began pounding and swearing at himself.

"Where the hell have you been?" Rusty said. "Didn't you see what happened? Jeez, we'll never make the main now—"

Ozzie ignored him. "Hand me them vise grips, Hemingway," he said. "And hey—stick around. We gotta talk when I finish up here."

"What about? What's up?"

He motioned me close and spoke into my ear.

"I got the goods on Max Bauer and Eddie Grimes."

I started to speak but he shook his head emphatically.

"It'll wait."

A mechanic from another team appeared with a portable welding rig. He sparked it to life and centered the flame on the bent section as Ozzie beat on it. A crowd of people had gathered to watch, drawn by the drama of working under pressure against the clock.

Among the onlookers were four tough-looking biker types, with sleeveless jeans jackets and engineer's boots and scruffy beards down to the middle of their chests. Despite the prohibition on alcohol in the pits, one of them was holding an empty long-neck beer bottle.

They shouldered their way to the front of the crowd and stood watching. They looked like four of the uprights at Stonehenge. Ozzie needed something from the van, and as he shouldered by he bumped one of them in his haste.

"'Scuse me, pal," he said. "Would you and your buddies mind givin' us some room? Thanks." He turned and flipped open a spares box.

With a muttered curse the biker grabbed Ozzie's arm and spun him around. The long-neck glittered in the light and flashed down on Ozzie's head.

In the movies the beer bottles are made of spun sugar. They make such a feeble *tink* when they break that the sound man usually has to punch it up in post-production to make it sound like real glass breaking.

This one didn't go *tink,* and it didn't break. The sound was a hollow thunk, coming as much from Ozzie's skull as from the empty bottle.

When the first stunt man hits the second stunt man with the sugar beer bottle, the first one looks cross-eyed for a second, maybe sways on his feet a little. Then he shakes it off and leaps at his attacker, and a fifteen-minute fist fight follows.

Ozzie dropped to the ground like a wet sheet falling off a clothesline.

At the same time one of the bikers lunged toward me and Rusty. He brushed Rusty aside like he was a tumbleweed, cocked an arm that ended in a fist the size of a chuck roast, and launched a haymaker at me. The last thing I remembered was four tattooed knuckles barrelling toward my face like a falling boulder.

I pieced the next few minutes together later, out of second-hand testimony. Somebody yelled, the bikers hesitated, and the racers and mechanics in the adjoining pits jumped them, wading into the fray swinging foot-long crescent wrenches and landing vicious kicks with steel shoe-shod boots. The bikers went down under a heap of bodies but nearly fought their way out again. By the time the security guards got there the bikers were bloodied and groggy, the mob was howling for their scalps, and by most accounts the guards pretty much saved their greasy hides.

I woke up in the back of an ambulance, a place nowhere near the top of my list of favorite places to wake up. My head throbbed like a soccer ball after the World Cup finals and my jaw clacked like a pocketful of marbles. When I opened my mouth to spit out blood and dirt, I yelped from the pain. That just made it hurt more, and I yelped again. I could see where this was leading, so I shut up and suffered in silence.

I got a shot for the pain and ice for the swelling. The X-rays showed no permanent damage—I guess I ducked some at the last second. Ozzie was out cold when they brought him in. He had been whisked away on a gurney the minute the doctor examined him.

Rusty, in jeans and sneakers, was waiting for me in the lobby. He had a butterfly bandage on a cut over his eye and an ice pack on the gauze-wrapped knuckles of his right hand.

"Looks like you got your licks in," I observed.

"Yeah," he grinned. "It was like punching a bank vault. How's Ozzie?"

"Nobody's talking just yet. How about you? Are you okay?"

"Fine, this'll be okay in a day or two . . . Ozzie wasn't moving, was he? Jesus, what the hell was that all about? Where did those guys come from, anyway?"

The race had been stopped when all the ambulances were pressed into service to transport the combatants to the hospital. It got under way again as soon as they returned. Al Hendricks won it, with Evan Martinez second and Perry Haycock third. Another pointless night for Rusty, his second in as many races. Hendricks' total swelled to 126. Haycock had 93 to Rusty's 76. Fourth-place Ted Munson, who was suddenly on a hot streak, was only two points behind Rusty.

With still no new word on Ozzie by Sunday morning, we booked our rooms again and went down to the parking lot to see if we could fix the pipe. There wasn't much else to do, and it beat the hell out of sitting by the phone popping aspirin.

Al Hendricks was coming out of his room with his bags. He stowed them in his car—his mechanic and his van had already left for the race shop—and came over to see how we were doing.

"Tough luck, Rusty," he said, shaking his head at the bent pipe. Hendricks was in his mid-thirties, a phenomenon in the youth-dominated world of dirt track. "You were on a roll there for a while."

Rusty shrugged. "I had a few bad breaks, I guess. I'll be back in the hunt."

"Breaks, hell," Hendricks said. His eyes were blue and narrowed against the sun. He looked more like a cowboy than the poser in the Shiloh ads ever would, with wry lines on his weathered face and a quiet voice that belied his on-track ferocity. "I hear you're a star on the party circuit. Can I give you some advice? Either you race or you party. You can't do both and win. I know."

Rusty's ears reddened. Hendricks pulled a pair of sunglasses out of his pocket and put them on.

"See you at DuQuoin?" he said.

"We'll be there. See ya, Al."

Hendricks started toward his car, then paused and turned.

"You're good, Rusty," he said. "I expect somebody will be handing you the Number One plate one of these days. It might even be me. Don't blow it. And give my best to Ozzie. Tell him we're all pulling for him."

By that evening the hospital would only say that Ozzie had a bad skull fracture, his condition was guarded, and he hadn't regained consciousness.

Rusty was grim that night at dinner. I only then realized how much he depended on Ozzie to keep things moving smoothly. Ozzie always made sure that all Rusty had to do was ride, and as a result that was just about all he knew how to do. It took all his concentration to psyche himself up for the race without worrying about schedules, lodging, paying the bills, and tuning the bike. He could do simple mechanical chores like changing tires or gearing, and he understood more or less which chassis changes had what effect, but everything about the engine from the valve covers on down was a deep, dark mystery to him. Ozzie had spent years getting to know the XR's quirks. Rusty had only a few weeks to get back in the hunt and salvage his fading championship hopes.

Buster Beauchamp called that night. Buster didn't like to travel too far from home. To make up for it, he had an informal spy network that spanned the country and kept him up to date on the flat track circuit. He had just heard about the fight.

"The next race is DuQuoin, a few hours south of here," he said. "You and Rusty get back here and I'll help you get ready."

"I'll send Rusty and fly out later. I want to be there when Ozzie wakes up."

"There's nothing you can do, Jason. He's in good hands."

"You don't understand. Ozzie said he, and I quote, has the goods on Max Bauer and Eddie Grimes, end quote."

"Meaning?"

"I'm not sure. That's why I have to stay."

"Don't wait too long. There are only eight races left in the season, and six of them are miles. We'll have to work our butts off if Rusty's going to get back up in the standings."

Cheered by Buster's sudden personal interest in the team's fortunes, I sent Rusty off on Monday morning in the van and rented a car. After several hours of inactivity in the hospital waiting room, I drove out to the restaurant Angela had taken me to and parked across the road. It looked different in daylight, with spots of peeling paint, a warped plank here and a disjointed rain gutter there. I tried not to think about the obvious comparisons between that night and this day.

I talked to Sara that night. It was a breezy, superficial conversation, the kind acquaintances, not lovers, have. She was sorry about Ozzie, and pretended to care whether Rusty could finish up the season without him. She insisted everything was fine at home. At Sandy's gentle but unyielding insistence, and with her patient help, Sara had found a therapist she liked and jumped right in, going twice a week. It was rough—memories of a terrifying struggle in the dark and something holding her motionless and stiff pounded at the door to her waking mind like burglars outside a locked house—but she was sticking with it.

I got a call on Tuesday from the hospital. Ozzie was awake.

I rushed over there and barged past the duty nurse. Ozzie's head was swathed in bandages and his speech was slurred, his face scrunching up with the effort of forming words. He moved like he was immersed in water, slowly and laboriously. He even blinked slowly.

"Hey, Ozzie," I said, "welcome back."

"Hemingway," he said, "what the hell happened? How did I get here?"

"Don't you remember the fight?"

"Fight?"

"You know, the bikers. The one guy thumped you on the head with a bottle. The other three came after Rusty and me. Then the pits on either side emptied and beat the snot out of 'em—"

I stopped. He wasn't with me at all.

"Does any of this ring a bell?" I said.

He shook his head slowly.

"What's the last thing you recall?"

He thought a moment. "Breakfast. Denny's. You and me and Rusty. How long have I been here?"

"Since Saturday night. Today's Tuesday. Ozzie, listen—do you remember the night of the race, and what you said about Max Bauer and Eddie Grimes? You saw something during the Shootout and never got a chance to tell me what it was. Can you remember?"

He looked surprised. "I did?"

"Come on, Ozzie, try. It's important."

"I don't remember. Can't think. My head hurts."

I had a flashback to Charlie Brand's room.

"It's okay, Ozzie. It'll keep. You get better first."

I stayed and talked with him until he got tired. He took longer and longer to answer, finally closed his eyes and began to breathe deeply. On the way out I left Buster's phone number with the nurse. I drove to the hotel, checked out, and turned in the rental at the airport.

Buster picked me up that afternoon and a little while later I threw my bag on the bed in the middle bedroom. It felt more like home than I could ever remember home feeling.

Without Ozzie we all felt rudderless, especially Rusty. He became sulky and restless. Eventually even Buster, whose equanimity seemed measureless, got fed up with him and sent him out to play on the half-mile.

"He misses Ozzie," I said. "Truth is, so do I. He held this team together."

"Well, he doesn't ride the motorcycle. Rusty does that. But we need someone to tune until Ozzie's on his feet again. What do you know about these things?"

"The XR? I could probably get the engine out of the frame without spilling blood. Beyond that, a chimp with a claw hammer could do just as well."

"I think you underestimate yourself. You just don't want the responsibility."

"You're damn right I don't. There's more at stake here than an article in a magazine. It's just a game to me. It's a career to Rusty. He needs a professional backing him."

"You could learn."

"I can't learn in two days what Ozzie picked up over a decade."

"One of the mechanics at my Harley shop teaches vocational training on the side. He can give you the short course and show you enough to get you through DuQuoin. After that, we'll see about finding someone to fill in until Ozzie's better."

The next morning during breakfast we heard a car pull up in front of the house. The doorbell rang and I was introduced to Roger, who had the world's most correct duck's-ass haircut and a pack of Camels rolled up in the sleeve of his white T-shirt. I looked out the window, expecting a '32 deuce coupe with flames and spinner hub caps. I was a little disappointed to see a white Dodge van mottled with patches of bondo like the spots on a dalmatian.

Roger and I spent the day in the garage, going over every detail of the XR's engine. He watched as I took it out of the frame and tore it down to the base gaskets. We walked through the clutch and the primary chain, Roger telling me every step along the way what might go wrong and what to do about it. Then I took off the cam cover and went on a guided tour of the oiling system.

After he had demonstrated how to time the sump pump to keep the crankcases from filling up with oil at high rpm, I held up my greasy hands and said, "Roger, this just isn't going to work. I'll never remember all this stuff. And even if I do I won't be able to fix it in time. Anyway, you make it sound like 'if A goes wrong then you do B', but it can't be that easy. What if two or three things go wrong all at once?"

"There's no what if about it," Roger said. "They will. But maybe not this weekend. Besides, there's only so much you can do during a race. I'm telling you how to deal with the simple stuff. If you blow a crank, or something in the gearbox goes blooey, it's time to load up and go home and let someone who knows what he's doing fix it. Anything short of that, though, and you should be able to handle it."

"Listen, Roger, how about you come to the race with us? I might need the help."

He shook his head. "Sorry. Can't do it. I used to do this every weekend. It got so my wife and kid didn't recognize me when I came home. She finally put her foot down. She said it was her and the kid, or racing, make up your mind. I made my choice, and it was the right one. No, me going to a race again would be like sticking a needle in a junkie's arm."

I started a notebook like the one Ozzie kept, but instead of recording information on the tracks and chassis settings and jetting, I made a troubleshooting chart. There were so many facts and figures jostling around in my head—ignition timing and spark plug readings and jetting the rear cylinder richer than the front—that I was certain when I woke up in the morning I wouldn't even remember how to pour gas.

I called Sherry Case the next morning. The phone rang about a dozen times before she answered.

"Hello?" she said. It came out almost as a squeak. "Who is it?"

"It's me, Jason Street. What's wrong?"

"Nothing's wrong," she said, putting some steel into her voice. "I was expecting someone else."

"I can call back later if—"

"No! Let's get it over with. What do you want?"

"Just to tell you that Ozzie Davidson is in the hospital. He got hit on the head and his memory's on the blink. But I think he might be able to tie Max Bauer to your father's death."

"Fine," she snapped. "Anything else?"

"I thought that would be great news."

"It is. Now if that's all—"

"One more thing. I want you to contact the California Bar Association or whoever keeps track of lawyers and find one named Archie Jones. Can you do that?"

Slipping that in was a calculated risk. Since we had already been over that ground, with her insisting it was a dead end, I had expected a fight. But I didn't get one.

"I suppose. Yes. Anything else?"

"I guess not—"

"Goodbye then."

I held the phone and stared at the receiver. They say blind people make up for their lack of sight with other senses. I had seen her once for a half hour the night we met, and since then all my dealings with her had been over the phone. I had learned to gauge her moods—haughty, arrogant, impatient, condescending—by her voice. They varied according to some secret inner barometer, the nature of which I couldn't guess. But none were so dominant as her self-assuredness, her confidence that nothing and no one could harm her and that the world was ordered to her liking because she wished it so.

But as I placed the receiver in the cradle the thought entered my mind that this was the first time I had ever heard her scared out of her wits.

# 11

Saturday morning we left for DuQuoin. On the three-hour drive Rusty quizzed me from my troubleshooting notes, making rude noises if I got an answer wrong and high-fiving me on the correct ones. He drilled me on Harley triage until I said "uncle" and complained that if he put his ear to mine he could hear the engine roar.

With Ozzie along I hadn't talked to Rusty all that much, preferring Ozzie's laconic conversation to shallow banter with Rusty. We were separated by more than a decade in age, and a century in cultural terms. Each of us thought the other's favorite music, movies, and TV shows were too stupid for words, and if Rusty had ever read a book past the cover blurb he emerged from the experience unscathed.

Nonetheless we found things to talk about. He was the son of a general contractor who made a comfortable living building strip malls, demolishing them, and putting up newer and better strip malls in their place. All he ever wanted to do was race motorcycles—he won his first race when he was eight years old—and his energy had been narrowly focused to that end to the exclusion of almost everything his peers had taken for granted as normal. He missed Monday classes through most of high school while driving home from far-off Sunday races, and had the gonzo social graces of a kid who had lived on the road for the better part of the last four years. There wasn't a dirt track in the country he hadn't ridden, or a state in the lower forty-eight he hadn't driven through. But he had no idea how to write a business letter or knot a tie.

Or how to cook an edible meal. He had the palate of a trash compactor. At Buster's I watched him turn hundreds of dollars worth of good food into smoking nuclear waste in the microwave and wolf it down like buttered popcorn. He could sense a chili dog ten miles away and home in on it like a grease-seeking missile, and would eat just about anything that didn't eat him first.

"I'm putting you on a diet," I said. "No more junk food. If I ate like you I'd be dead by now."

"You do eat like me," he pointed out. "At least when we're on the road. Besides, I don't need to lose any weight."

"All right, we're both going on a diet. Anyway, I'm not worried about your weight. You're an athlete. You can't perform on the kind of stuff you eat. It's like putting kerosene in the gas tank of the Harley."

"Ozzie says it doesn't matter what you put into yourself, it's what you get out of yourself that counts."

"The one depends on the other. I saw you after the last couple of races. Your tongue was hanging out like a whipped dog. You were exhausted."

"Aw, I was just having an off day—"

"You can have off days when the season's over. Until then you're going to train between races. Start by dropping out of the party circuit. You can't race on three hours' sleep. Then you'll ride the mountain bike every morning—"

"No way, man!"

"—and eat good food. It only costs a little more to go to a restaurant instead of a grease palace. We can fill up the ice chest with fruit and vegetables—"

"Aw, *mom!*" Rusty whined. We both cracked up.

"You're serious, aren't you?" he said. "About this healthy kick?"

"Damn straight. Who was it said 'If you want to win the plate you have to think like Number One'? How often do you run into Al Hendricks when you're making the party rounds? Or chowing down at Burrito King?"

"Not real often."

"And who's the National Champ?"

Rusty nodded. "Okay. I see."

We drove on a while, Rusty lost in thought.

"Hey, Jason," he said.

I took my eyes off the road and looked at him. "That's the first time you ever called me anything but Hemingway."

"Yeah, I guess it is. Listen, you really think I can do it?"

"Win the plate? Sure. Don't you?"

It took him a while to answer.

"Ozzie always talks like it's a done deal, you know. I'm gonna be Number One and we'll make lots of money and everything'll be great. Maybe I heard it so often I stopped hearing it. After these last few races, and now Ozzie getting hurt, I started to wonder—don't tell Ozzie, okay? There's a whole lot more fast racers than there are good mechanics, and I'm lucky to have him—but I started to wonder if he was right, if I could do it. The funny thing is when you first started talking about this health stuff I was kind of interested. Ozzie said you were crazy, that I was doing fine the way I was. But I wasn't, and I think I knew it all along."

"Ozzie's a good man. Let him take care of the bike. You take care of you."

That night I had a chance to test his resolve to the breaking point. I was in my room reading when I heard his key go into the lock next door. Out in the hall Rusty had his arm around a tipsy woman in shorts and a halter top. She was at least a head taller than him, with frizzy blond hair and huge air cleaners.

"Oh. Hiya, Jason. Jason, Lisa. Lisa, Jason."

"It's Linda," Lisa corrected him.

"I'm glad I caught you, Rusty," I said. "Did you remember to take your penicillin? You know those, uh, sores make it hard to sit on the bike for very long."

Lisa-Linda got real sober real quick. "I forgot something in my car," she said, and wobbled away down the hall, leaving Rusty standing in the doorway with his mouth working like Howdy Doody's.

"Nighty night, champ," I said, waggling a finger at him. "It's bedtime. Got a big day tomorrow."

"Coulda had a big night tonight," he grumbled, but he was grinning as he said it.

In the morning he made a face at the breakfast I ordered—fruit, whole wheat toast dry, juice and black coffee—then ordered the same thing and ate it all. In the supermarket he picked out most of the lunch food for the ice chest from the produce section and even ragged on me for buying low-fat yogurt instead of non-fat.

I barely remember what the DuQuoin State Fairgrounds looked like. From the minute we rolled the bike out of the van I hovered over it like a mother hen, ready to pounce on it with tools flying if it so much as got dirty. Rusty played off my uptightness. For a change he was the loose and talkative one, jiving with pass-ers-by and zinging me every chance he got.

He qualified well, not good enough for the Shootout, but good enough for a front row start in his heat. He was fired up from the green light and won it going away. He rode into the pit high on adrenaline, full of predictions of finishing in the top three in the main.

"Don't get cocky," I warned him. "Anything could happen between now and then."

"What's going to happen," he said, "is I'm gonna kick some butt today! I feel great! I'm usually pooped by the end of a ten-lapper like that, but I feel like I could go out there and do another ten."

I doubted one good breakfast and a fifteen-minute bicycle ride had made much difference, but I let him go on thinking it had.

"See, not everyone over thirty is brain-dead. Here, drink some water."

"Thanks. Where's the mountain bike? I want to check out the corners."

By the time the main rolled around my anxiety had given way to resignation. I had done everything I could. Ozzie's notebook had provided the usual set-up for DuQuoin, and during the day we fiddled with it a bit to suit the track, raising the fork tubes in the clamps to put a little more weight on the front end and make it steer better, playing with the carb jetting so the plugs looked just right after a full-throttle run. The bike would either hang together or it wouldn't. It was all up to Rusty now.

Out on the grid I felt a curious calm as I swatted him on top of the helmet and gave a shove on the seat. The engine rumbled, caught, and Rusty whacked the throttle open, lofting the front wheel. He stomped the brake and slid the rear end around so he was facing the starting line. I gave a questioning look. He shot me a thumbs-up. I made a kicking motion with my foot and pointed to the seat of my pants. *Kick butt.*

He was starting from the second row. Hendricks had the pole, and had chosen to start from the outside of the front row. Beside him were Perry Haycock, Ted Munson, and Len Seyfried, with Ricky Poe on the inside. There was maybe a quarter of a century worth of cumulative experience in that front row. Whatever happened, it would be a hell of a race.

And hell is what it turned out to be.

The green light lit up and the field roared toward turn one, bikes slithering from side to side, groping for traction, riders hanging off the bikes like monkeys. Hendricks got a terrible start, lighting his tire up while the second row shot past him.

The leaders went three abreast into turn one and stayed that way until the back straight. They fell into line and drafted each other into turn three.

Poe dropped out at the end of the first lap with a bad misfire. Few were surprised, and fewer still cared, so fierce was the fight up front.

Rusty was running seventh or eighth, swapping places with another rider two or three times a lap. They both wanted to catch the lead pack and if the other got lost in the shuffle, why, gee, that's racing. Hendricks was catching up with them, furious at having blown the start.

Five laps later it had shaken out to a five-bike pack up front, Rusty and his shadow a short distance behind, and Hendricks coming up fast. The rest of the field was embroiled in its own battles, no one rider able to break away.

The draft works better the more bikes are in it. The five-bike pack, which included Haycock and Munson, was running so fast down the straights that the riders were backing off and pitching it in before their usual braking points, using the margin to scrub off the extra speed. Munson was making a move on another rider on lap eight when he misjudged his speed, pitched it in too late, and slipped off the groove into the loose stuff up high.

He headed for the haybales at over a hundred, sawing desperately at the bars, the bike bucking wildly. At one point he had technically fallen off the bike but hadn't actually let go of it. He managed to get the better of it at last, pointed it down the track, and gassed it when the rear wheel slid out from under him. He went down and came to a jarring stop right in the middle of the groove.

The whole drama played itself out in the amount of time it took Rusty to close the gap between himself and the crash site. As he pitched it into the turn he saw a Harley on its side right in his path. In executing a heart-stopping move to avoid the fallen Munson, he ran way off the groove and fell even further behind the leaders.

Al Hendricks, who had been busy putting a pass on the rider behind Rusty, hadn't seen Munson's crash. He swooped around the outside, squared the corner off and came low, and found Munson on his knees in the groove, struggling to pick his bike up.

What Munson didn't know was his bike was in gear, and his engine was still running. As he tilted the bike onto its wheels, the spinning rear tire hit the dirt, caught traction, and the bike pinwheeled around directly into Hendricks' path.

Hendricks hit it absolutely broadside at about a hundred miles per hour. The two bikes practically fused together with Hendricks caught between them like a mouse in a trap. The impact knocked Munson about ten feet. He was spreadeagled on the track, unconscious, when the ambulance arrived.

Hendricks was conscious, trapped under the mangled bikes. His face was ashen and he talked calmly to the paramedics, telling them where it hurt and how best to extricate him while doing the least amount of damage. They had to work fast. A pool of dark fluid was growing under him, and it wasn't engine oil. His left thigh bone was sticking out through the leg of his leathers.

Poor Ted Munson was frantic. When he came to and saw what had happened, he started yanking on the bikes to free Hendricks, yelling for help. A corner worker dragged him away and held him. They put him into one of the ambulances, checked him over, and took him to the pits. Nobody blamed him for what happened except him. He climbed into his van and closed the doors.

After the crash the red flag came out. Rusty finished the lap he was on and stopped out on the corner. When I got there he was kneeling beside the stretcher, talking in a low voice to Hendricks. As they lifted him into the ambulance, Hendricks clasped Rusty's hand.

The infield was hushed as details of the crash and Hendricks' injuries flashed from pit to pit. Hendricks was enormously popular, the grand old man of the sport, and thought to be immortal. Rumors began to fly that his leg had been torn off in the crash, that he was already dead. A woman in the next pit sobbed quietly.

Rusty looked shell-shocked, like a man whose house had just been blown away by a tornado while he hid in the basement.

"Are you all right for the restart?" I asked him.

"Huh? Yeah, I'm cool. Jesus, the bone was just sticking out . . ."

I punched him in the shoulder hard enough to get his undivided attention.

"Hey, what—" he began.

"Forget Al for a minute," I said. "Listen to me. I want you to think about something. When Al was still in it you were 50 points out of first. Now you're just 17 out."

"Huh? I don't get you."

"Al's through for the rest of the season. He had a big lead going into today's race, but not big enough that he could sit out the remaining races and win. So he's out of the running for the plate. That means everyone moves up one spot in the overall points chase—consider yourself second instead of third as of today. You follow me so far?"

"Yeah, but—"

"So Perry Haycock's in first, and you're trailing him by 17. And Ted Munson's not going to score any points today—his bike's bent up like a paper clip. So by the end of the day you'll lead Munson by however many points you score plus the two you had on him coming in. Get the picture?" I put my hands on his shoulders. "You can do it, Rusty. You can win the plate."

A slow grin spread over his face. "Goddam," he said. "I can, can't I?"

"Not if you don't make the restart. Here's your helmet. I'll gas the bike up and meet you at the line."

On a restart the scoring reverted to the last full lap before the red flag came out. The riders lined up single-file, nose to tail, in the order they had been on lap seven. Rusty was in sixth, the gap between him and the fifth place rider now a foot instead of half a straightaway.

At the green light everyone scrambled to get out from behind the rider in front. The single file exploded into fragments as bikes sped for the first turn. You could hear the collective intake of breath over the engine noise, held in until the pack safely completed lap eight.

By lap ten the field had once again sorted itself out into clusters of riders sharing the draft. Rusty was at the tail end of the lead trio. I stood by the railing sending him mental images of ice, polar bears, anything to convey the message: stay cool. A solid third was better than a might-have-had first. If he could just hang on to the spot he had, he could pad his lead over Munson and close up on Haycock, who was stuck in the middle of the second pack of riders to the rear.

For all the drama of the first few laps, the rest of the race was a snoozer. The two riders ahead of Rusty gradually pulled away and swapped the lead every other lap or so, feeling each other out, neither one willing to show his hand completely. There are two schools of thought among mile racers, centering around whether it's better to be in first or second on the last lap. One side of the argument says it's always a good thing to be in the lead, because after all that's what racing is about. The flip side is that the rider in second is perfectly positioned to use the draft coming out of the last turn to slingshot past the defenseless leader at the finish line.

The two lead riders apparently held to the latter theory. They danced around it for a few laps, slowing down so much that Rusty began to catch up. It looked for a fleeting moment as if he would, but then they dialed up the pace in an attempt to outrun each other. In the end it was draft-pass at the line and a photo finish.

It took the officials half an hour to review the tapes and when they announced their decision a chorus of boos went up from the stands. It would have no matter which rider they gave the nod to. What mattered to us was that Rusty was an undisputed third. The overall order was Hendricks, 126; Haycock, 103; Rusty, 89; Munson, 74.

"We only picked up three points on Perry," Rusty said.

"That's three you didn't have when you got up this morning," I said. "You also pulled out to 15 over Munson. It's a long way to Sacramento. A lot can happen by then."

Each of the top three finishers said something about Al Hendricks from the podium, wishing him well, telling him to hurry back even though everyone knew it would be a long time before they saw him on a dirt track bike again. The word from the hospital was that the break was worse than previously thought. The bone was splintered, the knee a mass of bloody jelly. No one would say what everyone was thinking, which was that Hendricks was through for good.

Rusty huddled with the other two, and when the interviews were over and the trophies presented and the trophy girls mauled and the crowd sprayed with champagne, the three motioned the fans to something like silence and drank a toast to the health of Al Hendricks.

Buster was sitting on the porch waiting for us that night.

"Damn fine day, boys!" he bellowed. He grabbed Rusty's hand and worked his arm like a pump handle. "You did good, youngster. You rode hard and finished high. Too bad about Al Hendricks, though. I called Sheldon Jeter right after I heard. He says it doesn't look good."

Jeter was Hendricks' engine builder, based in California, near Riverside. Teams that could afford it had their engines built by an engine specialist like Jeter. The mechanic maintained the engine on the road, but for any major work—crankshaft rebuilding, for instance—it went to the engine man. Jeter was a Harley specialist. He built drag race and hillclimb engines for a number of well-known racers. But he built dirt track engines exclusively for Al Hendricks.

"And how do you like being a big-time dirt track mechanic?" Buster asked me. "Ready to give up journalism for the racing circuit?"

I laughed and said not quite yet, but during dinner and for the rest of the night I tried the idea on cautiously, like a new pair of shoes—not that I was in a buying mood, but just to see if they squeaked too loudly when I walked. Between *Motorcycle Monthly* putting me on leave, and the wall going up between me and Sara, I had felt like a ship adrift in mid-ocean when I joined up with the team. The impermanence of the racing life gradually became the only permanent thing in mine, the shared goal of winning the anchor that held me in place. The team was the center I had been missing, the quest for the plate the goal that gave life meaning and proved I was a worthwhile human being and not just a luckless outcast.

Buster might have sensed my thoughts. He brought me back down to earth with a thud.

"I've been talking to some people about filling in for Ozzie," he said. "I don't guess I have to tell you how lucky you were that things went as smoothly as they did today. Rusty's got a real chance of winning it all this year. He needs a mechanic with experience to back him up."

I bristled at this, but he was right. It was ludicrous to think I could see Rusty through the rest of the season without outside help, my fanciful daydreams of glory notwithstanding. If Rusty was half of the team, Ozzie was the other half. The plate could slip out of Rusty's reach at any race between now and the finale at Sacramento, the season turning on the most insignificant part breaking, or the tiniest error in judgement on my part or Rusty's.

"The engine's going to need some work soon, too," Rusty said. "It's getting tired. I could feel it today. Ozzie was planning to tear it down halfway through the season anyway."

"Funny you should mention that," Buster said. "One of the reasons I was talking to Sheldon tonight was to see what he's going to do now, what with Al Hendricks out of the running. There's a lot of guys out there who'd like to have a Jeter motor."

"You're looking at one of 'em," Rusty said. "Even Ozzie would rather run one of Jeter's than one of his own."

"Well, now, youngster, we just might be able to make that happen. Sheldon's been keeping his eye on you—I might have mentioned your name once or twice, too, just in conversation. Anyway, Sheldon was wondering if you'd like to borrow, on a temporarily permanent basis, like for the rest of the season, one of

Al's engines that's just sitting on the bench gathering dust and getting in the way—"

"Are you serious?" Rusty lit up like a kid on Christmas morning. "He'd do that?"

"Now hold on. Maybe borrow wasn't the right word. More like rent, or lease. And before you two go turning your pockets inside out and pleading poverty, Sheldon's willing to hold off on getting paid until the end of the season. Says he'll take his cut out of your bonus for winning the Number One plate."

"What if I don't win?"

Buster shrugged. "I gather he'll write it off as a bad debt. But just between you and me he doesn't think he'll have to."

Rusty looked back and forth between Buster and me, his eyes wide. Then he let out a whoop like an Indian in a B-western.

"All *right!*" he said. "We're gonna kick us some *major* butt!"

# 12

We had a two-week lay-off before the Peoria TT, so Rusty and I left the bikes and the van with Buster and flew back to California.

I was worried about going home at first, but Sara said she was looking forward to it. I was as nervous as a bridegroom as the plane circled LAX endlessly. I thought I was going to have to get my mail forwarded to Holding Pattern, Runway 5 North, when the plane finally dropped through the layer of airborne sludge onto the runway.

Rusty's father was waiting for him at the gate, a tall, sun-burned man in jeans and a work shirt. Marty McCann had a handshake like a bench vise, and seemed uncomfortable in his work clothes and cement-spattered boots among the power-dressed business passengers and hula-shirted tourists. He and Rusty walked off down the concourse to baggage claim, Rusty jab-bering excitedly and his father nodding at his son's breathless news that he had acquired a Jeter motor, whatever that was.

Most of the passengers on my flight had gone and there was still no sign of Sara. Slumped in one of those awful fiberglass chairs shaped like a slippery catcher's mitt, I scratched my bearded chin absently, wondering where she was, when it sud-denly struck me—maybe she hadn't recognized me and had gone home, thinking I missed the flight.

I was headed for a line of telephones on the wall when I saw her jogging down the ramp, her hair streaming out behind her. She had on jeans and one of my button-down shirts and her grey suede boots. Her eyes met mine for a fraction of a second with no sign of recognition. Then she lurched to a stop, windmilling her arms.

"Jason?" she said. She ran her fingertips over my chin and down my cheek. "My God, what's happened to you?"

More than I could possibly tell you, I thought.

"It's the beard, isn't it?" I said. "You hate it."

In answer she leaped into my arms and wrapped her legs around my waist. I held her, drinking in the feel and the smell and the sheer intoxicating Sara-ness of her. I kissed her like a starving man eating his first real meal in months, smothering her face and neck and shoulders until she laughed and pulled back, held my head in her hands, took careful aim, and pressed her lips gently and fully on mine, putting into that one kiss all the energy of my barrage and more.

"Hi," she said, shyly it seemed.

"Hi yourself."

"Boswell's out in the truck. He missed you terribly."

"How about you?"

"Me too."

"Are you glad I'm back?"

"Yes. Very much. Are you glad to be back?"

"Words fail me."

"That's a first."

Boswell was indeed in the truck, slobbering all over the windows. Due to some freakish neural malfunction both of his brain cells were firing simultaneously and he actually remembered who I was. He bayed like a bloodhound and pawed at the window. Sara opened the door and he leaped out and ran circles around my ankles, sniffing and drooling and pretty much exemplifying the Irish setter's well-deserved reputation for brainlessness and good cheer.

I tied him in the back with my duffel bag and we hit the 405 south to Lakewood. Traffic was sluggish, surging along at thirty, bumper to bumper in the smoggy heat. I was used to driving the wide-open interstates and had no patience for commute traffic. Inside of ten minutes my sweat-soaked shirt was sticking to my back and a tension-induced knot of pain blazed between my shoulder blades.

We got off at Bellflower Boulevard and pulled up in the driveway fifteen minutes later. A cool breeze blew through the trees lining the street, pushing leaves along the sidewalk. Down the block some kids were playing in the street, screeching and yelling. Bos leaped to the porch, pranced at the front door, and once inside zeroed in on his food bowl. He sat there wagging his tail and earnestly willing someone to feed him until Sara got the message and poured his afternoon ration. Thus ended the glad reception. I could have been gone for a day or six months, and when I came back Boswell acted like I'd just been in the next room for ten minutes.

I threw my bag on the bed, then remembering I was really home, unpacked it and put everything either in drawers or the laundry basket. The bathroom, with its mismatched fixtures and missing tiles I kept promising Sara I'd replace, looked like a scene from a bad drug experience compared to the antiseptic and uniform Holiday Inn version I had become accustomed to. The face in the mirror looked strangely out of place.

My office, in the front bedroom, was filled with familiar objects—photos, my computer, my favorite helmet, several trophies—and felt as alien as the surface of the moon. The quiet was eerie, the stillness somehow disorienting.

"I don't really feel like I'm home," I said as I joined Sara on the couch. "There should be a TV with no knobs over there, and a rack of brochures listing all the tourist attractions beside it, and a lamp that looks like a pumpkin with a blue shade on that table."

"We can run out for some mints for your pillow," she said, leaning her head on my shoulder. I kissed the top of her head.

"All I want on my pillow is you," I said.

She stiffened almost imperceptibly, her back and arms becoming rigid before she regained her composure and relaxed. She disentangled herself and went out to the kitchen.

"Is something wrong?" I said.

"Would you like some coffee?"

"Sure. How's therapy coming?"

"Fine. Jeannie is wonderful. We're making progress."

"What kind of progress?"

"Well, I'm learning to recognize my feelings and act on them instead of bottling them up."

"Have you been bottling them up?"

"A lot."

"Is that why you tensed up just now?"

She opened her mouth as if to speak, then shut it. She busied herself with the beans, fussed with the filters, and was rinsing the pot when I took it from her and put it on the counter.

"Why did you tense up when I said I wanted you on my pillow?"

She hugged herself and looked at the floor.

"I don't know."

"I think you do. Are you afraid to tell me?"

She nodded.

"Why?"

"You won't love me any more."

"Try me," I said.

"I saw us in bed together and it made me afraid." Her voice was small and faint.

"Why? I'm not going to hurt you. Is that what you think?"

"No, but he . . ." She paused, unsure of what to say next.

"He who?"

The effort of expressing what she felt overwhelmed her. Her mouth moved but no sound came out. Tears welled in her eyes.

"I don't know who," she said. "I don't know why."

The coffee was ready. She poured and we sat at the table while Boswell sniffed my pant legs to see if I'd been around any other dogs in the last couple of months. Sara stared moodily into her mug.

"Is it because—" I began, but Boswell interrupted before I could finish the thought. There was some important business with a tennis ball that needed attending to. Sara shooed us away with a flick of her hand and we went out to the back yard, leaving her alone with her thoughts.

When we came inside she was washing up. She suggested dinner out and we drove to Hamburger Henry's on Second Street in Long Beach. Her affection for Hawaiian burgers and pineapple shakes was undimmed, but she left half of her burger and barely managed to finish her shake. She had lost weight since I last saw her. She wasn't exactly gaunt, but the muscled sleekness of her arms and shoulders was gone. I didn't even have to ask to know she hadn't gone on her morning run in weeks.

I teased her gently about eating the rest of her burger. She made a face and pushed it away. We walked along Second Street under a full moon. She tensed as I laid my hand on her shoulder. I moved it and we walked on.

I was yawning as we pulled into the driveway. She was distracted, disinclined to talk. I took a shower and she was in bed when I got out, with the covers pulled up to her chin.

"Are you cold?" I said. It was a pretty warm night, actually. "Shall I close the window?"

She shook her head.

I slid in beside her and discovered to my surprise she was wearing underwear and a T-shirt. She always slept in her skin.

If I had been listening to Sara at all for the last few months, I wouldn't have started pawing her as soon as the lights went out. But I had been away for a long time and my body was overruling my brain's objections. Her warmth triggered all the familiar responses—in me, at least. We had always celebrated my return from assignments on the road by joyously and exhaustively reacquainting ourselves with each other's bodies. I was shocked and ashamed to suddenly realize she was lying under me as stiff and lifeless as a cardboard cut-out.

"What?" I said. "What is it?"

"Will you do something for me?" she said.

"Name it."

"Shave your beard off."

I went into the bathroom and began hacking away the foliage. I started with scissors, and finished with an electric razor. I came to bed red-faced and puffy but clean-shaven.

She ran her fingers lightly over my cheeks.

"Better?" I said.

"Yes. Will you hold me?"

We snuggled together under the covers until her breathing became soft and regular. The moonlight bathed her face in a soft pale glow. She looked like an exquisitely beautiful figure made of china, precious and fragile. No one with a face like that deserved whatever hell she was going through.

In the morning I rolled out of bed while Sara slept in. I was in the back yard brushing Boswell when she opened the back door and sat on the porch steps in her bathrobe. She yawned mightily and stretched her legs to let the morning sun warm her feet.

"Tell me about the beard," I said.

She gathered the robe around her and shivered. "It wasn't you."

"As a fashion statement, maybe. But it was me."

"I mean it didn't feel like you. It felt like I was in bed with someone else."

"Someone who isn't safe."

She nodded.

"Have you talked about this with . . . who is it, Jeannie?"

"Uh-huh. Not yet. I will today."

While Sara showered I went into my office and called Sherry Case to see how she was coming with finding Archie Jones. The phone rang a dozen times before a mechanical voice answered.

"The message tape is full," it droned.

I called Case Tires next and asked if Sherry was there. The receptionist put me on hold and a man with a deep and rather irritated voice came on the line.

"Who is this? What do you want with Miss Case?"

"My name is Jason Street. I called Sherry at home but her machine is full and no one picked up. I thought she might be there."

"Miss Case isn't in the office at the moment. Can I take your number and have her call you back?"

"Thanks, I'll just try her later—"

"Wait! Street, the writer? You should know the police have taken her address book. They're checking out everyone whose number is in it. If you've hurt her—"

"Hey, cool it a minute, Mr., uh . . ."

"Wallace. Tyler Wallace, acting CEO of Case Tires."

The guy who was in the business of manufacturing grief for me and *Motorcycle Monthly*. I took a deep breath.

"All right, Mr. Wallace, you want to clue me in? I just got back from two months on the road. Where is Sherry?"

"That's the question of the hour, Mr. Street. She disappeared three days ago."

# 13

According to Wallace, a friend of Sherry's had become concerned when she failed to show up for a lunch date and still hadn't answered her phone by the next day. The friend talked to the manager of Sherry's apartment and he let her in.

On the surface nothing looked out of place. The bed had been slept in, there were a few dishes in the sink, some cigarette butts in the ashtray on the dining room table. Sherry's luggage was in the closet, and no clothes were missing. Her car wasn't in the parking garage. It looked for all the world as if she had just stepped out, meaning to be gone for maybe fifteen minutes. Only she hadn't come back.

I hung up, put my chin on my fist, and stared out the window at the tree on the front lawn. Then I cleared my mind of distractions, and, zen-like, meditated on the connectedness of all things.

Things like Max Bauer and those bikers at Hagerstown. The attack could have been a coincidence. On the other hand, Max could have hired them to stomp me after finding me with Angela. Either way, he probably wasn't steeped in regret over it.

Then there was Max and Sherry Case. Her disappearance could have been a coincidence, too. But it threw a monkey wrench in her last-ditch plan to block Max's takeover attempt with the insurance company's million, something else Max wasn't likely to sit up nights fretting about.

And then there was Archie Jones and Charlie Brand. The connection between them was so tenuous that it might have just been my imagination. But I had a nagging hunch Jones was a player in this, if only because it seemed so improbable that he was, and because he went to a lot of trouble to find Charlie

Brand—but why? So I hauled out the Long Beach phone book and turned to the yellow pages.

There were forty-four pages of attorney listings. A dozen Joneses, none of them Jones, Archibald or Jones, Archie or even Jones, A. But any of the firms listed could have employed Archie Jones, Attorney at Law, and not put his name in the phone book listing.

Sara was out of the shower. I scrambled some eggs and brewed up a pot of high-test coffee.

"I'm having lunch with Dede today," she said. "I hope you don't mind." Sara's sister was three years younger, a feisty and rebellious woman with a sense of humor like a rusty straight razor and a chip on her shoulder the size of the General Sherman tree.

"What's the occasion? Her routine de-clawing?"

"She's having a hard time dealing with me going to a therapist."

"Why? It's not her problem."

"She's making it her problem. Jeannie and I are getting into some family stuff, and last week I called Dede to ask if she remembered a few things the same way I did. She blew up and started yelling at me like I was giving away state secrets. I want to know why it bothers her so much."

After Sara left I called *Motorcycle Monthly*. Cathy Randall, our receptionist, didn't recognize my voice at first. She apologized half a dozen times before switching me over to Barry.

"Jason, it's good to hear from you. Where are you?"

"Home. What are you doing in about half an hour?"

"Buying my features editor lunch. The Hope and Anchor?"

"I'll meet you there."

The Hope and Anchor was a British pub-style eatery in a strip mall near the office. Barry's ancestors had come from the British Isles. It was a fantasy of his to move back there some day, maybe buy a sod farm and raise sod or herd stoats or do whatever it was that British gentleman farmers did. About the closest he had gotten to realizing his dream was the rusting BSA Hornet basket case in his garage and a nifty tweed cap his wife got him for Christmas. My own ancestors came from Kansas. I had been through it several times lately, and to date felt no inner yearning for wheatfields. Give me topography with wrinkles.

Barry shook my hand heartily.

"It's great to see you," he said. "But there are still six or seven races left in the season, aren't there? Have you given up?"

"Seven races," I said, "and no, I haven't given up. But I needed a break. So did Rusty. Running six regionals in two weeks makes putting out a monthly magazine look like mailing a postcard."

"I hope you're keeping detailed notes on all this. I expect at least a three-part series on flat track racing from an insider's viewpoint when you come back to work."

"I've already taken enough notes to fill the next three issues. It helps remind me every day that I'm a writer and not a mechanic. How are things at the office?"

"Not much has changed, at least nothing that need concern you. We have a new staffer, Ken Nakamura. He came to us from an extension journalism class at Cal State Long Beach as an unpaid intern. He's a decent writer and a good rider, and when I asked him if he'd thought about staying on he just about kissed my feet. And since Harry Connor quit—"

"Harry's gone? I thought he'd stay until they tore the building down around him. Who was dumb enough to hire him?"

Barry grinned a Cheshire cat grin. *"Cycle Weekly."*

"Serves the bastards right. I hope he fouls up their operation as much as he did ours. I hope even more sincerely that he screws up Stan Martini's life beyond repair."

"Martini moved to *Cycle Journal . . .*"

I felt like someone recently awakened from a coma as Barry filled me in on what had been happening in the magazine business since I'd been gone. People who I knew when they were green as money were now sitting in offices in downtown highrises writing ad copy for camera companies or working as flacks for speedboat manufacturers with obscene expense accounts and perks that would make a Colombian drug lord envious.

"Stop it," I groaned, "before I go into the men's room and slit my wrists."

"Okay, change of subject. How are you doing? Is there anything I can do for you?"

"As a matter of fact there is. Listen, Barry, I need a favor. I'm looking for a man named Archie Jones." I told him who Jones was, and why I needed to find him. "He's supposed to be a lawyer, or in the law business, somewhere in Southern California. There must be a million lawyers in L.A. alone, not to mention the surrounding counties. Can I talk somebody in the magazine's law firm into giving me a hand?"

"Call Peters. Say I said to give you his full cooperation."

"This isn't strictly magazine business, Barry. What if he balks?"

"Tell him what you just told me about how this Jones could unlock the key to Case's death and make the lawsuit go away. That should get his attention."

I couldn't get his attention if I couldn't get in to see him, and by three-thirty that afternoon it looked like I wasn't going to. I'd been sitting in the outer office since two o'clock reading *People* magazine. I had learned who the sexiest man in the world was that week, and that Cher's entire body had been rebuilt more times than my pickup, but Peters was still holed up in his office "in a meeting," or so his secretary icily informed me every time I asked how much longer he'd be.

Suddenly the door to the inner office opened and Peters stepped out, briefcase in hand. I jumped up to block his way and he leaped back inside like a startled rabbit. The door was swinging shut as I planted my palm against it and shoved. I barged through and closed it behind me, cutting off the indignant screech of the secretary.

"Oh, ah, Mr. Street," Peters stammered, "I'm sorry, but I'm on my way to, ah—"

"An important meeting, I know. Well, this is it. Sit down."

"Really, Mr. Street," he said, puffing himself up and groping for the intercom button, "I really must insist—"

"Do you want Case Tires to drop the lawsuit against Motorcycle Monthly?" I said.

His hand stopped, hovering above the button. "Why, yes, of course."

"Then sit down and listen to me."

Peters sat. I punched the button on the phone. "No messages," I said to the secretary. "He's in a meeting." Just to make sure, I took the receiver off the cradle and dropped it in the wastebasket.

Ten minutes later I had him hooked.

". . . so you see, if this guy Jones turns out to have killed Case, it's the answer to all our problems. We prove that it wasn't my article that drove Sherm Case over the edge, and Sherry Case gets the million bucks and saves the company from bankruptcy. Either way, the motivation for suing *Motorcycle Monthly* evaporates."

"I see," he said. "If you can find this man Jones—"

"Not me. You. You're a lawyer, and the best information I have indicates Jones is, too, or was, or worked in the legal field."

"Yes, of course." He stood up and walked to the door. "Please wait here. I'll just be a moment."

When he returned he had a slip of paper in his hand.

"I checked with the state bar association," he said, "and they have no record of your man practicing law in this state. Perhaps as you say he wasn't a lawyer, but worked in an allied field. A paralegal or court clerk, for instance. In any case, I know someone I can call. We use him now and then for routine jobs like process serving and undemanding investigations like skip-traces. Do you have a description, or anything we can go on beside his name?"

Peters copied what little information I had on the slip of paper and folded it into his pocket. "I'll call our man first thing in the morning," he said.

I took out a business card and wrote my home number and address on the back. "Have him call me or stop by if he has any questions," I said.

I thanked Peters for his time and smiled pleasantly at the fuming secretary in the outer office as I left. In the parking lot it occurred to me that I should have gotten the investigator's name and number, but I shrugged it off. If he needed me he'd call. I'd only get in his way otherwise.

I felt pretty good that night at having accomplished something concrete. My mood was offset by Sara's. Lunch with her combative sister and a session with her therapist had left her exhausted and depressed. I cooked up some burgers, adjusting the size of hers to fit her diminished appetite. Boswell got half of it anyway.

After dinner we settled down on the couch to watch the tube. It might as well have been a potted plant for all Sara knew until a spot ad for a TV movie came on. It was one of those "torn from today's headlines" stories about a man who abuses his children until their teacher calls in a caring social worker—ironically enough played by an actress with about a dozen kids from five different marriages herself—who gets the kids and their mother to a shelter and finally confronts the father on the courthouse steps.

I tuned out about halfway through the promo and was reaching for the *TV Guide* when Sara bolted from the room. I caught up with her in the bathroom where she was throwing up into the toilet.

I helped her into the bedroom and slipped her soiled sweater over her head. She stood motionless like a submissive child while I cleaned her off and got her sweatshirt out of the drawer. I moved to hug her but she backed away.

"No. Please," she said, and walked down the hall.

She sat on the back porch steps, hugging her knees. I sat down beside her, and Bos laid down at her feet. The moon came up and disappeared behind some clouds. The lights in the neighboring houses went out one by one. A chill stole in from the ocean. I wrapped a blanket around her shoulders. She pulled it close around her face, the first real movement in an hour.

We sat like that for a while. Finally she took in a breath, let it out in a ragged sigh, and leaned her head on my knee. I smoothed her hair.

"It'll be fine," I said, not really believing it myself. "Whatever it is, it'll be okay."

"How can you be sure?" she whispered.

I would have given all I had for the right answer to that.

# 14

"What did Sherry do, skip out?" Rusty said. He was behind the wheel of a green Mazda Miata, darting through the traffic on the 91 like a cockroach on a kitchen floor. "She owed a lot of money, didn't she?"

"She owes me a bundle, I can tell you that," I said. I had a death grip on the grab rail over the glove box. Half of my attention was occupied with the conversation with Rusty, the other half with hoping like hell he was as good in a car as he was on a bike. "But I don't think she skipped. She left too much behind, stuff you'd take with you if you were going to be gone for any length of time."

"Maybe that's the way she wants it to look," Rusty said, turning to look at me. "If you were skipping would you leave a note on the door that says so?"

A Porsche with blacked-out windows came up behind us fast and blinked its brights. Rusty scooted over to the number two lane. The Porsche shot past and Rusty snapped the Miata back into the hot lane. He stayed on its tail for a mile. Then the Porsche driver downshifted, the car coughed a burst of oil smoke out its tailpipes, and ten seconds later it was just a dark smudge on the horizon.

"Damn, I gotta get one of those someday," Rusty laughed. "So how's all this affect us? The team, I mean."

"I don't know that it affects it at all. Your deal's with Case Tires, not Sherry, right?"

"I guess, yeah."

"You guess? Jesus, Rusty, haven't you read your contract?"

"Ozzie takes care of that stuff."

"You better hope he read all the fine print. With the expense of the suit against *Motorcycle Monthly* and fending off the takeover and cleaning up after Sherm, I'm surprised they haven't tried to weasel out of the deal already—watch that semi!"

Sheldon Jeter's shop was a couple of miles east of Riverside in an industrial park. A block farther down the street the road ended abruptly. Beyond that lay barren scrub land.

Jeter met us in the lobby, a spare, tidy room with a desk and a telephone and three chairs and not much else. He was a small, neat man with close-cropped hair and an unremarkable pair of thick-rimmed glasses perched on his nose. He had exactly one pen and one pencil clipped in a spotless plastic pocket protector inserted in the pocket of a spotless white lab coat. He looked like an actor playing the part of a researcher in an aspirin commercial, or a nuclear scientist—which wasn't far from the truth.

"I put in eleven years at Lawrence Livermore," he said, "making better and smarter bombs. Then one day they upgraded my security clearance. By the end of the week I knew all kinds of things I just didn't want to know. So I handed back the clearance along with my resignation and took off for the desert in a motorhome with a dirt bike on the back, to sort things out. A couple of guys in a plain-wrap four-door followed me most of the way, keeping their distance and watching me through binoculars."

He laughed and shook his head. "I wound up having to winch them out of the sand, poor bastards. I guess they were finally convinced I wasn't passing classified information to the KGB and left me alone." He glanced out the window at the heat shimmers rising from the asphalt parking lot. "Or they got replaced by two other guys who are too good to be spotted." I involuntarily turned and looked for a nondescript four-door in the parking lot across the street. "How's Ozzie?"

"Not so good," Rusty said. "He's got double vision real bad, and he gets dizzy when he stands up. It'll be a while still, the doctor says."

"Can you put together a program until then?"

Rusty looked at me.

"I'm traveling with Rusty for now," I said. "I'm learning about XR engines, and I'm getting pretty sharp on my chassis tuning . . ."

"You take care of the chassis, then. I'll handle the engines. I had two on the bench when Al got hurt. I assume you can handle the jetting and ignition at the track? Good. If anything major goes wrong, air-freight the dud to me and I'll have a replacement in your hands in twenty-four hours."

"Gee, thanks, Sheldon," Rusty said. "That's great, really. But listen . . ." He looked down at his shoes. "I feel real bad that we can't pay you for any of this, at least not right away . . ."

"We'll talk about it later. Besides, here's something nobody knows yet. Al's out for good. His career is over. And even if he could ride again, it's the right time to quit. He asked me what I thought and I told him it was the smartest thing he'd ever done. Then I asked him what I was supposed to do with all these engines I built for him. He said it was a shame to let them go to waste, and someone ought to get some good out of them. He suggested you."

Rusty gaped. "He did?"

"He thinks a lot of you, Rusty. He pegged you to win the plate someday, back when you were a junior. I'm willing to bet an engine or two that he was right."

"And here I was about to suggest you run off and join the circus," I said later from the driver's seat of the Miata. I had talked Rusty into letting me drive, ostensibly to try out the car. The truth of it was Rusty was so jazzed to hear Al Hendricks had singled him out as heir apparent to the Number One plate he couldn't see around his own grin. "I guess I'm not much of a judge of character."

"I can't believe it!" he kept saying. "You were right. I have a real shot at the plate with Al out. And with his engines—!"

"And a little luck and a continued flow of money from Case Tires," I added.

When we got to Lakewood I invited Rusty in, taking the chance that his excitement would be contagious and drag Sara at least partway out of her gloom. It must have worked. I suggested dinner in Long Beach, and Sara agreed.

We all piled in the Miata, with me driving, Sara in the passenger seat, and Rusty scrunched up in the impossibly small space behind the seats. We found a parking spot a block from Milt's Killer Ribs on Second Street. Sara's appetite made a brief appearance and we strolled the shops until dark. Rusty was bouncing from curb to curb like a puppy on a leash.

When we pulled up in front of the house Rusty hopped behind the wheel, waved, and drove off.

"So what do you think of him?" I asked as I put the key in the front door lock.

"He wears me out just listening to him. How can you stand to be around him for days on end?"

"Try weeks. You get used to him. Most of what he says is just random noise. He saves his real concentration for racing. Right before a race he—" I swung the door open and stopped dead, barring Sara's way with an outstretched arm.

The house was dark, just as we'd left it, but something wasn't right. A smell, a feeling, a sound—I couldn't put my finger on it. Then I heard it, a whimpering sound from the hallway. I flicked on the lights and edged toward it.

Boswell was locked in the hall closet. He cringed from the light and licked his chops reflexively. One eye was swollen closed. His jaw was bleeding, cut near the gum. Drops of blood pooled on the closet floor.

I kneeled and said his name and held my hand out for him to smell. He flinched, then sniffed, and crawled out with his tail tucked up under him. He buried his muzzle between my knees and thumped his tail on the floor.

"What happened?" Sara said, coming down the hall. "Bos? Puppy? Are you all right?" She knelt beside me and stroked his head. He whimpered and rolled over on his back.

My office was a disaster. The desk drawers had been pulled out and emptied onto the floor. The contents of the closet had been piled in the middle of the room. Books and magazines were scattered everywhere. My passport and insurance policies and important papers had been riffled through, but nothing seemed to be missing. My computer was on the desk, untouched.

The bedroom looked pretty much the same. The drawers had been tossed, the closets searched. The stereo, VCR, and TV were untouched. I went back to my office and began sifting through the heap of stuff.

"Jason, what happened?" Sara said from the doorway.

"Somebody broke in, obviously. That, or the maids from the Beirut Hilton dropped by to tidy up."

"Why would they hurt Boswell?"

"He probably came running to say hello. You know how he barks when we come home? If you were a burglar, how would you know he's just a big goofy dog?"

"What did they take?"

"Nothing, apparently. That's what bothers me. What's the point of—shit!"

I yanked my briefcase out from under a pile of jackets and put it on the desk. The lock had been forced and the hasps were twisted and ruined. My tape recorder was still there, and the various maps and pens and whatnot—

"Dammit! My notebooks!"

"What notebooks?"

"All the notes I took during the races—I was going to write up a story on the season after it was over. There were three full notebooks, crammed with details. I'll never remember half of it now."

Sara helped me clean up the office, then we started in on the bedroom. I gave Boswell an aspirin in a piece of cheese and went to the corner store for some canned dog food. His jaw would hurt too much to chew his dry food for a day or two. The walk also gave me time to cool off and think.

If I accepted the notion that Max Bauer was responsible for the Hagerstown brawl and Sherry's disappearance, it was no stretch to give him credit for this, too. All three incidents fit the same pattern—sudden, anonymous, calculated to terrify with their apparent senselessness, methods I had no trouble associating with Max. And the only things missing were three spiral-bound notebooks in which I had jotted down notes for my story—and charted my progress in searching for Sherm Case's killer.

Sara was as jumpy as a cat. It wasn't bad enough that she was having choking nightmares about faceless, threatening strangers—real ones had broken into the house, beaten up the dog, and turned everything upside down. I almost called Rusty and told him I wasn't going to Peoria. Then Dan, the deputy sheriff who lived next door, stopped by to borrow a cup of oil—30-weight, to put in his Triumph's forks—and heard about the break-in. He fetched an emergency air horn he kept in his boat and said if we heard anything during the night, just give the horn a blast and he'd come running with his .357. The next morning I went to the hardware store and bought some window locks and beefed up the deadbolts on the doors anyway.

The day finally came when I had to pack. The plan was to meet Rusty at LAX and fly out to Springfield, pick up the van, and drive to Peoria. Sara drove me to the airport and waited with me for boarding to begin.

"I'll miss you," I said. "Call me if you need to, all right?"

"I will." She smiled. "If I can find you."

"You have Buster's number. He'll always know where to find us. And if you hear anything outside the house, blow that horn and call 911, understand? Don't take any chances."

The PA announced our flight. Rusty went on ahead. I held Sara like it was our last day on earth together.

"I don't want you to go," she whispered.

"I wish I didn't have to," I said. "But I have to finish this. I feel like I owe it to Rusty, and Sherry, and Ozzie—"

"And yourself?"

"I owe it to me, too, to see this through to the end. To prove I'm worth something after all. Even if I never get my job back, I'll be able to say I helped Rusty McCann get the Number One plate."

We kissed as the final call for boarding came. Right on its tail was a tinny announcement summoning Jason Street to the white courtesy telephone.

The flight attendants were glancing at their watches as the final few passengers disappeared up the tunnel. Sara signaled them to wait and I sprinted across the concourse to the row of phones on the wall.

"Jason, I'm glad I caught you," a familiar voice said. "It's Barry. Listen carefully. Case Tires dropped the lawsuit against *Motorcycle Monthly.*"

"What?" I said, dazed. "Why?"

"They filed for Chapter 11 bankruptcy yesterday afternoon. They can't afford to pursue the suit any longer. Don't you understand? It's over. You can come back to work any time. Right now, if you want to."

# 15

"Jason, hurry!" Sara called out. "The plane's leaving!"

"Bankrupt? Barry, are you sure?"

"Absolutely. They closed the doors this morning and sent the entire work force home. Their lawyers called ours this morning and said the suit's been dropped."

I felt as if I were floating in mid-air, as if a crushing weight I'd been carrying for months had suddenly evaporated. Just as suddenly my elation vanished.

"Barry, if Case is bankrupt, that means Rusty's sponsorship is history, too. What'll he do? Our flight's leaving right now!"

"I'm sorry, Jason. I know you've put a lot of your energy into this. But we need you here."

Sara was waving frantically to me. The flight attendant was swinging the door to the boarding tunnel door closed.

"Jason?" Barry said. "Are you there? When can you come back?"

"Listen, Barry," I said. "I have to go to Peoria with Rusty. I'll call you from there."

I hung up the phone and ran to the boarding gate, giving Sara a kiss in passing and squeezing through the door at the last second. I made it to my seat as the engines began powering up. Rusty was already settled in with his Walkman earphones on.

"Thought you weren't gonna make it," he said. "What was the problem?"

I told him. He blinked several times, trying to absorb it, took his headphones off, and stared at the back of the seat in front of him.

"Son of a bitch," he said. "I shoulda known it was too good to be true. Third in the standings with the points leader out of the picture, Sheldon Jeter backing me with engines, and my damn sponsor goes belly-up." He looked about twenty years older. Then he forced a smile and punched my shoulder gently, "But at least you got your job back, huh? Cool. Congratulations. Hey, you guys need any help at your magazine? Someone to sweep up the shop, maybe?"

"Nah, you'd just fall off the broom. Look, don't hang up your steel shoe yet, okay? Something will come up."

But I wasn't so sure it would. Worse, I wasn't too sure I cared anymore if it did or not, and that made me feel like a rat. At least I had a job to go to after Peoria. It was too late in the season for Rusty to get a ride with anyone else, and with me back at work and Ozzie still seeing stars, it looked like he might well finish the season sweeping the floors in Buster's Harley shop after all.

Buster took in the news calmly.

"I'm sorry, Rusty," he said. "I wish there was something more I could do to help out. "

"You've already done plenty, Buster," Rusty said. "Anyway, that's racing, right?"

Rusty had a rough time at Peoria before he even got to the track. We arrived at the motel on Saturday afternoon and the first people we ran into were Chris Murray and his mechanic. Word had already gotten around about Case Tires, and every expression of sympathy or concern only made Rusty feel worse. Chris invited us to dinner. He had a quirky sense of humor that I enjoyed, and we often found things to talk about that weren't connected with racing. I was starting to feel like part of the family of flat track racing at last, and since this would almost certainly be my last race I wanted to savor it while I could. I selfishly goaded Rusty into coming along, hoping he'd get into the swing. The bottle of steak sauce on the table had more to say that night.

On Sunday morning I jollied him as best I could. He trudged past me out to the van with the gait of a condemned man walking the last mile. I grabbed his arm and spun him around.

"I don't know what your problem is," I said, "but you better snap out of it and get your head in gear. You've got a race in a few hours."

"My problem is I got no sponsor," he snapped, shrugging off my hand. "So what difference does it make if I race or not?"

"The difference is how it looks. Okay, so life sucks right now. Maybe you'll have to sit out a race or two, or the rest of the season. But you'll want to come back someday, and when you do, the only thing people will remember is how you left the last time. If you have to go out, do it with some class, not like some whiny kid who got a bloody nose in a schoolyard game and doesn't want to play any more."

"That's real easy for you to say. But don't forget, *I'm* the guy without—"

"Shut up and listen to me. The hell with you. Think of someone besides yourself. Think of Al Hendricks and Sheldon Jeter who're both sticking their necks out for you. Think of Buster who's already bent over backwards, and feels like shit because he can't bend a little more. And Ozzie, who's sitting in a hospital wishing he was here instead of watching little tweety birds fly around the room. Are you going to let them down, or go out there and show everybody what you're made of?"

I thought he was going to take a poke at me. Instead he threw a roundhouse punch into the side of the van.

"Okay," he said, massaging his knuckles. "Let's go racing."

Peoria was the last race of its kind on the circuit. The track was situated at the bottom of a natural amphitheater surrounded by low hills. Spectators brought blankets and lawn chairs or sat on the hillsides under big shade trees, at least the ones who got there early. The rest sweltered on the grassy slopes.

A high overcast hung over the track like a grey cloak. A muggy heat built up quickly and by the time the program started sweat was pouring off me like water in a shower. Most of the riders opted for lightweight motocross gear at Peoria, substituting nylon motocross pants and vented jerseys for the heavy one-piece leather suits they ran on the fast miles and half-miles, and ventilated motocross helmets with goggles to let in as much cool air as possible. The only piece of flat track gear they didn't jettison was the steel shoe.

The track differed from the flat oval mile and half-mile tracks by incorporating a right turn and a jump. It had been years since anyone rode one of the big twin-cylinder Harleys at Peoria. The TT track was now the sole province of the single-cylinder, 600cc four-stroke, usually the same Rotax or Honda that doubled as a short track bike, but with a front brake, which was legal only on TT circuits.

Rusty's bike was a Rotax with a single rear shock on the left side in place of the more conventional twin-shock set-up. The jump worked regular shocks pretty hard, heating up the shock oil until the rebound damping faded and the bike became nothing but a fast, noisy pogo stick. The extremely fade-resistant single shock was taken from a motocross bike, which ordinarily had to deal with jumps that were Everest-like in comparison to Peoria's. It had a large oil reservoir, a hefty spring, and about a zillion possible combinations of rebound and compression damping, spring rate, ride height, and for all I knew blood pressure. I just set it up according to Ozzie's notebook and sent Rusty out.

I was sitting under the canopy during a break, swilling Gatorade and trying to catch my breath in the stifling heat. I mopped the sweat off my face with the tail of my shirt, and when I looked up there was Angela Bauer.

She was wearing white shorts and a halter top. Moisture beaded up on her face and in the cleft between her breasts. Her hair was tied back and she had a green shaded visor on her head. Make-up would have been futile with the temperature and humidity. Without it she looked her age.

"You look better without the beard," she said.

"So I've been told."

"How've you been?"

"Look, Angela, I—"

"Please. I'm not trying to start anything. I heard about Case Tires. I'm sorry. How's Rusty taking it?"

I shrugged. "Something will come up."

"Something just did."

She held out an envelope. I opened it. Inside was a check for $10,000.

"What's this for?" I said.

"The rest of the season."

"Why?"

"Max hired those thugs to beat you up at Hagerstown."

"Because of . . . what went on in your room . . . ?"

She nodded.

I folded the check and put it in my shirt pocket.

"Thanks. I'll give this to Rusty before I leave."

"Where are you going?"

"I'm going back to work. Case Tires dropped the lawsuit against the magazine."

"That's wonderful!" She looked genuinely pleased. "I'll miss you, though."

Rusty came by for another bottle of Gatorade.

"Hey, Hemingway—" he said, then noticed Angela. "Oh. 'Scuse me, Mrs. Bauer. Hey, Jason, listen. I've been talking to Benny Cowens, you know, Art Freitas's sponsor? Well, Art's had a tough year, and he wants to go back to college pretty soon. Benny was thinking he might help me out some for the rest of this season, and maybe we could put something together for next year. What do you think?"

I handed him the check.

"Holy shit! I mean, what's this for, Mrs. Bauer?"

"My way of helping out. And when you need tires, call me at the number on the check. My service will relay the message and I'll have them sent to you. On the house."

"Better tuck that away," I said to Rusty, nodding toward the check in his hand.

Rusty felt the silence between Angela and me. He thanked her, mumbled something about putting the check in the van, and trotted off.

"Ozzie's still in the hospital," I said.

"I know. I'm terribly sorry."

"Yeah." I nodded my head toward the retreating Rusty. "Ten grand worth. Feel better now?"

"I deserve that. But you could be a little nicer."

"Isn't that how this got started in the first place?"

"Max and I are separated," she said. "He's changed. He's secretive and mean and I can't talk to him any more. I think you were right. I think he killed Sherm Case."

"Why?"

"He can't stand to hear his name. He isn't sleeping at night. It's as if he's . . . haunted."

The next practice was called. Rusty reappeared and suited up while I wheeled the bike to the grid.

Rusty wasn't much of a TT rider by his own admission, but he had taken my advice about going out in style to heart. He rode hard and fast, qualifying fourth and earning a spot in what might be his last Shiloh Shootout for a while.

When we lined up for the Shootout he said, "We already made ten grand today. Let's see if we can make it twenty, huh?"

I patted him on the back and gave him a push. The Rotax fired and he took his place on the starting line.

He got a good start at the flag but slipped off the groove coming out of turn one and fell to third. The track was roughly kidney shaped, with a long front straight and a back stretch that featured a jump and a right turn. The jump was situated such that when you went over and were still in mid-air, the track bent away to the left and sloped away under you, forcing you to turn the bike on the way down and hit the track leaned over. Then almost instantly you had to flick it hard to the right, then to the left again to set up for turn four.

There were really only two good places to pass, coming out of turn four, and again going into turn one. Getting the drive out of four was critical to making the turn one move. Passing on the back section was only for the very brave or the very foolish. The racing line on the downside of the jump was about as wide as a first-class stamp, and you had to land on it from six feet in the air while going about sixty miles an hour. Miss it and they'd be picking you and your bike out of the hot dog stand.

Rusty was feeling either very brave or very foolish—possibly both. On the fourth lap he got a good drive out of turn one and pulled alongside the rider in front. They both got to the jump at the same time, but the other guy had the outside line. To hit the groove on landing he would have to cross Rusty's path in mid-air. Rusty would either have to back off and let him by, or hold the gas on long enough to make the pass on the way up, which virtually guaranteed a landing in the weeds.

He stayed on the gas.

The other guy saw him, snapped the throttle shut, and nearly went over the bars on the other side of the jump trying to stay out from under Rusty, who sailed past with his axles level with the other guy's shoulder. Unlike lightweight, long-legged motocross bikes, dirt trackers aren't made for jumps. They're too heavy and don't have enough suspension travel. When Rusty landed his bike clanked like a dumpster full of fishing weights, bounced back almost high enough to throw him out of the saddle, then suddenly squatted down on its haunches and locked the rear wheel tight. Rusty steered it for the catch fence and got it stopped just in time.

I ran out to the corner but he waved me off. He revved the engine, dumped the clutch, and got the rear wheel spinning. Leaning as far forward as he could on the gas tank to get weight off the rear, he rode to the pit, leaving a trail of blue smoke and a hot plastic smell in his wake.

The rear shock's thick shaft had snapped off clean just below the top mounting collar. With the rear suspension collapsed, the tire was rubbing a hole in the fiberglass seat. We only had ten minutes before the main event.

"Get this piece of shit off of here," I said, pointing to the broken shock. Rusty grabbed a socket wrench and attacked the mounting bolts. I jumped on the mountain bike and pedaled out to the back pit where the van was parked. It took me an eternity to take the rear shocks off the Harley, stuff them down the collar of my shirt, and ride back to the pit.

Rusty had the bike on the stand, with the rear end held off the tire with a piece of two-by-four.

"Here," I said, throwing him a shock. We were lucky—when Ozzie converted the frame to a single-shock he had left the stock twin-shock mounts intact. "I'll do this one, you do that one."

"But these are set up for the Harley," Rusty said.

"First things first. Get 'em on the bike, then we'll worry about makin' 'em work. Move!"

A few minutes later we rolled the bike off the stand. Rusty bounced on the seat and shook his head.

"It don't feel right," he muttered.

"You want 'em softer or harder?" I said.

"I don't know, it's kind of like they're—"

"Softer or harder, dammit? There's no time for fine tuning!"

He hesitated a split second. "Softer."

I changed the damping adjustment, eyeballed the ride height, and made a wild guess at the spring preload. We made the grid with a minute to spare.

Rusty still had his doubts.

"I don't know, Jason," he said. "I think—"

"Don't think—ride! Give 'em something to remember you by!"

The flag dropped. Rusty got a lousy start, falling to eighth by the end of the second lap. He wasn't hooking up coming out of four, so he couldn't set up to pass anyone going into one. On lap three he got around one guy who slid off the groove up into the loose stuff, and elbowed another out of the way on lap five.

The bike handled like a bucking bronco with a snootful of speed. It was all Rusty could do to hang on and stay in the saddle. Every time he came down off the jump the rear wheel slewed sideways and the front wheel snapped lock to lock like a terrier with a rat in its jaws. The fans cheered each spectacular landing, and nearly tore the place down when on the last lap Rusty took one hand off the bar in mid-air over the jump and waved to them.

After the checkered flag he brought the bike in and almost fell off it. I propped him up in a lawn chair with a gallon of Gatorade and a shop rag full of ice on his head. The announcer was interviewing the winners out on the front straight but in the pits a steady stream of racers and mechanics came by to congratulate Rusty on the gutsiest ride anyone had seen at Peoria in years.

He finished sixth. What made it all that much sweeter was that the guy he had elbowed out of the way on lap five was Perry Haycock, who came in seventh. I tallied the points totals.

"I only picked up one stinkin' point on him?" Rusty puffed, wiping his hand across his dripping forehead.

"Look at it this way," I said. "He only picked up one point on you."

"Yeah, you're right," he said, rolling his eyes. "It sounds better that way."

We packed up and drove to Buster's house that night. The

front door was locked. We knocked, waited, and finally Buster appeared and let us in.

"I'm on the phone in the office," he said. "Come on back when you're ready."

We threw our bags in our rooms and poured a couple of tall iced teas from the pitcher in the fridge. Buster waved us into his office and we flopped into a couple of chairs.

Buster put his hand over the mouthpiece and said, "How'd you do?"

"Sixth," Rusty said, grinning. "Picked up a point on Perry Haycock."

"Good boy. I—hello, yeah? You're sure? That's not just the first quarter, that's second quarter, too, right? Uh huh. All right. Spool it to my computer. Give me a minute to set the damn thing up. Bye."

He hung up and his fat fingers danced over the keyboard like the hippo ballerinas in *Fantasia*. The phone rang once and the computer emitted a shrill beep—the beginning of a modem transmission.

"I've been doing a little speadsheeting today," Buster said, one eye glued to the screen, "and it looks like . . . aha, there's the rascal. Yep, no doubt about it, boys, I'm financially solvent."

"Glad to hear it, Buster," Rusty said.

"You're damn right you are. I'm also looking for an up-and-coming flat track rider to sponsor. Know any?"

"Do I! Buster, are you kidding me?"

"Watch your mouth, youngster. I don't kid about flat track. Now listen, I'm not rich but I'm not exactly poor, either. Lately my accountant's been telling me I could use a little write-off to help convince the IR-goddam-S that I'm not really doing as good as I am, if you get my drift. Now I can help out with travel expenses, give you a good deal on parts for the XR through my Harley shop, that sort of thing. It won't be anywhere near a full sponsorship, but it's something."

"Something, hell," Rusty said. "Buster, it's great. Thanks a million. Hey, look what else I got today." He waved the check.

Buster whistled. "Got yourself a secret admirer?"

"No secret," I said. "Angela Bauer."

Buster's cocked one eyebrow skyward. "Max know about this?"

I shrugged.

"Cash it first thing in the morning, just in case."

I was beginning to feel like I was leaving the party just as the fun was starting, torn between going back to work and sticking it out with Rusty and grabbing for the gold ring. Suddenly I knew how I could do both.

"Can I use the phone, Buster?" I said. "I promised my editor I'd check in after the race."

"Come on, Rusty," Buster said. "You get the barbecue lit and I'll pick out three good steaks."

I settled into Buster's chair and called Barry's house. As the phone was ringing, the idea was taking shape in my mind. When Barry answered it was all I could do to not laugh out loud at how stupid I had been not to think of it before now.

"Barry, you want a story on the flat track season from an insider's point of view, right? Well, you can't get any more inside than this . . ."

Buster and Rusty were in the kitchen. Rusty was telling Buster the benefits of a low-fat, high-protein diet. Buster was looking at Rusty like he'd just stepped out of a flying saucer.

"What have you been filling this boy's head with, Jason?" he demanded. "He's been telling me about some disgusting glop called yogurt."

"Rusty," I said, "have you ever done any writing?"

He blinked as if it were a totally alien notion, which it might well have been. "Like, what, essays, reports, that sort of thing?"

"Yes. No. It doesn't matter. You tell it to me, I'll turn it into English—"

"Turn what into English?"

"The story of how you won the Number One plate."

"I haven't won it yet."

"Well, if you don't, you're going to disappoint the hell out of *Motorcycle Monthly,* your newest sponsor, not to mention me, your combination race mechanic and biographer for the rest of the season."

Rusty's jaw flopped open. He dropped a frozen steak on the floor.

"Nice work, son," Buster said to me, smiling. "How'd you swing it?"

"I can't believe it took me this long to think of it. Barry wanted me to write up a story about being a flat track mechanic. I told him I could do better than that. I told him I could get him the exclusive rights to the Grand National Champion's story, in his own words. All he had to do was assign me to go to all the remaining races as your mechanic. That, and kick in some sponsorship money. Buster, do you care if Rusty rides under *Motorcycle Monthly's* colors as well as yours?"

"I don't give a damn if he rides under the colors of the King of Siam, as long as he rides!"

"Well, how about it, Rusty? You'll be on your own between races."

"I'll get my brother Kevin to help with the driving—he'd love it. And you'll meet me at the track?"

"Yep. And after Ozzie comes back, I'll still come just to see how my newest freelance contributor's doing. Deal?"

Rusty grabbed my hand and shook it so hard my shoulder hurt when he let go. Just for the hell of it he shook Buster's, too.

"Jesus, everything's happened so fast," he said. "It seems like just yesterday my life had turned to shit, and now it couldn't be better. Jason, Buster, is there any way I can ever repay you guys?"

Buster and I said simultaneously, "Win."

Rusty laughed and shrugged.

"Okay," he said. "I'll win."

# 16

I flew home on Monday and reported to work Tuesday morning. The office hadn't changed much since I'd seen it last. The carpeting was still the same faded green stuff you saw on miniature golf courses, and the portable dividers that formed cubicles made the place look more than ever like a huge rat maze. I expected to find a slab of moldy cheese around a corner any day.

I met the new associate editor, Ken Nakamura. He was replacing the departed Harry Connor, whose sloth had been legendary at Motorcycle Monthly. Ken seemed as determined to live down Harry's reputation as if he were partly responsible for it.

We had a new shop foreman, too, a round-faced Latino named Jos Miraflores. He was a graduate of the motorcycle mechanics program at L.A. Trade Tech. For about the first week he was was so low-key he was almost no-key. No one had been sure if he was painfully shy or just nervous around strangers. So they began kidding him mercilessly every day, and he opened up with a wit sharper than a scalpel. He could cut you off at the knees with a barb and still leave you rolling on the floor with laughter.

I stepped into this new dynamic and found myself in the uncomfortable role of outsider. The staff had lost one member and gained two new ones since I left. The newcomers had already been slotted into the places in the hierarchy, and the regulars had become accustomed to my absence. My return represented a challenge to the established order.

By Wednesday I was restless and impatient with the glacial pace of magazine production. I longed for action, a high point to punctuate the hours of quiet reflection in front of a computer screen and the tedium of product familiarity meetings with advertisers. I spent a lot of time out in the shop, standing in the doorway smelling the salt air blowing in off the nearby Pacific and wondering how Rusty was doing and when Ozzie was getting out of the hospital and where Sherry Case had gone.

I directed a lot of this frustration at Max Bauer, who I slowly but surely came to believe was entirely capable of having murdered Sherm Case, engineering Sherry's disappearance, and arranging the break-in at my house and the theft of my notebooks. I wanted to close the book on him for good, and I found myself looking forward to flying out to Indiana for the Indianapolis Mile with a sense of anticipation that wasn't only for the racing.

It hardly seemed like I'd been home at all when Sara dropped me off at LAX on a Saturday morning and I settled in for another lunch made of some nonspecific edible matter cleverly shaped to resemble food. Rusty and his brother Kevin were waiting for me when I got off the plane. Kevin was two years younger and a head taller than Rusty, with reddish-blond hair and freckles and the friskiness of a basket of puppies. He was eager to help and the interplay between him and his brother took some of the conversational heat off me. It was like having Huck Finn along for the ride down the Mississippi.

Sunday morning dawned clear and hot. With Kevin's help, setting up the pit took only minutes, and while most everyone else was still sipping coffee and unrolling tarps and topping off gas tanks I was pushing the Harley to the tech line.

I was rolling it along, talking over my shoulder to someone walking alongside, when I grazed a man who was standing talking to someone else.

"Excuse me," I said, not slowing down. I had grown accustomed to fans in the pits, rubbernecking and getting in the way of those of us who were there to do a job, and didn't give the man a second thought. Then something made me turn—a tingling in the back of my neck—and there was Max Bauer slapping futilely at the tire dirt on his fawn-colored slacks, glaring at me with the purest malice in his eyes.

"You clumsy bastard," he hissed, and stalked off.

Tech was usually a formality where the inspectors attached a numbered plastic tag to your frame and wrote the number down, knelt on the ground to make sure your drain plugs were safety-wired, and sent you on your way. But the guy in front of me was getting a world-class look-see. When he finally got his sticker and went away I asked the tech guys why.

"Had a little trouble with him once," one of the inspectors confided. "A little displacement discrepancy."

His partner guffawed. "Little like hell."

"So we run the microscope over him every now and then, just so he doesn't get to thinking we forgot about it."

"He hasn't placed in the top three since then, so we haven't had a chance to tear him down post-race. I hope he finishes good today. I'd love to see what's under those cylinder heads."

After the bike was teched and passed I asked Rusty what the inspector had meant. "He said something about finishing in the top three," I said. "Why should that matter?"

"Well," Rusty said, "if you want to protest somebody, first it'd cost you fifty bucks. Then you have to have raced in the same race, too. Say I thought a guy in the main was cheating. I could protest him, but only if I had made the main myself. But the top three finishers' bikes can be torn down after the race at the tech inspector's discretion, whether anybody files a protest or not."

"How often does that happen?"

"Not real often. Just knowing it can happen any time keeps most guys honest."

"What about the Shootout? Do the same rules apply?"

"None of the rules apply in the Shootout because it's not really part of the racing program. It's, you know, a promotional thing the cigarette guys do. It pays money, but no series points—hey, Jason, what's up?"

"I think I know what Ozzie wanted to tell me at Hagerstown about Max and Eddie."

"No shit? What?"

"Not yet. It'll have to wait until after the Shootout."

Rusty qualified in the upper third of the field, then got a second in his semi and transferred to the main. Since we would have nothing to do until then, I got the bike ready and went scouting for a place to watch Ricky Poe's pit from after the Shootout.

The Shootout lined up and flagged off. Poe took the lead and was immediately challenged by Murdock, who pressed him relentlessly until Poe flinched under the pressure and slipped off the groove. It was a good thing for Rusty that the Shootout didn't pay points—Murdock won, and Haycock was second. Poe finished a distant third, far down from his usual spot in the top-heavy Shootout payout.

Poe rode to his pit slowly, probably anticipating the barrage of abuse Eddie Grimes was brewing for him. Max loafed nearby, close enough so he could see and hear the action, far enough away to distance himself from the unpleasantness.

I stood behind a nearby truck, waiting for the tech inspector who had agreed to meet me there. He arrived just as Eddie was undoing the fuel lines from the bike.

"What am I supposed to be looking at?" he said.

"Watch what Eddie does," I said. "See if you can tell me why he's doing it."

Eddie swapped tanks just as I'd seen him do at the Lima half-mile, when he and Ricky had gotten into an argument, then popped the distributor cap and made an adjustment.

"Okay, I give up," the inspector said, glancing at his watch.

"Ricky Poe has been in most of the Shootouts this season, right?"

"I guess. We don't really keep track. That's Shiloh's deal."

"He's won four, placed second in two, third in one and fourth in one. You know what that adds up to? I'll tell you—$47,750."

The inspector nodded, still not understanding.

"What does the Grand National Champ win at the end of the season?" I said.

"The bonus for winning the plate is $100,000."

"Ricky Poe's almost halfway there, and he hasn't finished a main event all year."

He whistled softly. "No kidding. Kind of takes the sting out of his crappy luck, though, don't it?"

"Luck has nothing to do with it. You saw Eddie change tanks, right? I'll bet you $47,750 that the tank he took off is full of illegal fuel—nitromethane, avgas, something that adds a ton of horsepower. That's so Poe can post a fast qualifying time and get into the Shootout. After he runs away with the Shootout and wins the big bucks, off goes the tank full of pop, and on goes the one full of pump gas. Eddie monkeys with the bike a little and sends Ricky out for the main not only down on horsepower but with the wrong carb jets or the ignition timing nudged just far enough so the engine will cook a piston ring or seize. He blows up, every- body says gee, tough luck, Ricky, Eddie Grimes gets a reputation as a lousy tuner—and they laugh all the way to the bank, because the *winner* of the damn main only gets around $4500. There's no way to lodge a protest in the Shootout, and he'll never get caught cheating in the main because who's going to protest a guy who never finishes?"

"Son of a bitch," the inspector said. "Somebody will this time. Wait here." He jogged off toward the starting line. When he came back he had two other officials with him.

"Tell them what you told me," he said.

I stayed out of sight while the three of them approached Poe's pit and asked Eddie if they could have a word with him. Like nuns, officials in threes was a bad omen. The news was circulating through the pits that something was up. Max sensed trouble and melted into the crowd that was quickly gathering to watch the white shirts interrogate an increasingly agitated Eddie.

When one of them made a move toward the spare bike, Eddie pushed him back, shouting angrily that he had no right to inspect a bike that wasn't even qualified. The inspector countered that the bike had been run through tech, and he just wanted to make sure a thorough job had been done for Ricky's sake.

Eddie wasn't buying it. He rolled the bike off the stand and started to load it up. One of the officials put his hand on Eddie's arm. Eddie lashed out and suddenly the man dropped to his knees holding the side of his head. At that point the other two in- spectors each grabbed one of Eddie's arms and threw him against the van, letting the bike fall. The one who had been hit jumped to his feet, tore the tank off the bike, tucked it under his arm, and stalked away, leaving a trail of fuel leaking from the severed lines. Someone ran after him and turned the petcocks off.

Ricky Poe had gone to the john right after coming in from the Shootout and getting his ass chewed. When he came back Eddie was gone, his spare bike was on the ground minus a gas tank, and about a hundred people were standing around trying hard to look like they weren't listening to what the official was saying as he put a fatherly arm around Ricky's shoulder and led him away behind the van.

I turned to go. Suddenly, for the second time that day, I was face to face with Max Bauer.

"You were behind this," he sputtered. "I warned you . . ."

"That was for Ozzie," I said, "and maybe for Sherm Case, too. Screw you, Max, and screw your scummy thugs. I hope they throw your sorry ass out of racing."

I left him standing there with his mouth open.

The Jeter engine ran like a rocket all day. Rusty had so much more horsepower than he was used to that he got in way over his head a couple of times and nearly lunched at the Haybale Hilton. Even so he got a second in the main. Munson won it, and Haycock came in fourth. The overall points race stood like this: Hendricks, 126 points; Haycock, 122; Rusty, 114; Munson, 107. Hendricks had already ceased to be a factor in the race for the Number One plate since his total would easily be surpassed by the four front runners in the remaining races, barring crashes or breakdowns.

By the end of the day the buzz around the pits was that Ricky Poe and Eddie Grimes had had their licenses pulled for life. The Shiloh people were spitting nails and looking for Max Bauer, but no one seemed to know where he was.

# 17

For the next three races I flew to and from the track and spent the time between in my own house instead of seedy roach motels or bunking at Buster's. While things still weren't back to the way they had been—would they ever be? I wondered often—Sara was going to therapy regularly, and we were working hard on redefining the term "normal" as it referred to our life together.

She was a walking lit fuse, subject to wild mood swings. Beneath it all was a barely suppressed dread. I caught her brooding often, frowning into the distance as if struggling to summon some long-forgotten memory, then pulling back abruptly, frightened it would actually come.

"I feel like pressure is building up inside me," she said. "I'm going to explode if I can't find a way to let it out. But I'm terrified of what it might be. It goes with the dreams, Jason."

Rusty finished well at Springfield and Syracuse. He was finally accustomed to real front-row horsepower, and began to believe the Number One plate was within reach. Haycock rode like a man possessed. What possessed him was the sight of Rusty chained to his tailpipe race after race. In the meantime Munson had absolutely caught fire, and was only a handful of points behind the two front runners—a crash or DNF at a critical race by either one could have put him in front. By the time the September Ascot rolled around, the railbirds were scratching their heads, unwilling to stick their necks out and pick a winner by the season finale at Sacramento, just a week away.

I got a night off when Sheldon Jeter himself tuned for Rusty at Ascot. He wanted to see first-hand how Rusty rode under the gun. Sara came along and we sat in the grandstands, shivering in the clammy night air and eating race track food that Boswell would have growled at and circled warily. Compared to being down in the pits on my knees skinning my knuckles and spitting dirt, it was like a month in Hawaii.

Rusty left Ascot that night in second place overall, only five points behind Haycock. With Sacramento a week away, Rusty and Sheldon locked themselves and the Harley in Sheldon's shop and replaced or rebuilt everything but the gas cap. Rusty came out of the clean room one day long enough to phone me with the news that Ozzie was coming home at last, and that he wanted to tune at the race Saturday night.

"He deserves to be there, you know?" Rusty said to me. " I mean, I really appreciate all you've done for me this year, but . . ."

"You don't have to explain. I'll be glad to step aside and let someone else take the responsibility. To tell you the truth, I was nervous as hell about carrying the load myself. With Ozzie and Sheldon behind you, the plate's practically in the bag."

"Yeah, well, let's not jinx it. But just in case, I want you there, too. Not in the stands, but in the pits, okay? Just in case."

"Just in case, right. You got it."

We had the December issue editorial meeting the Monday morning after Ascot. One of my assignments was a road test of an aftermarket company's treatment of a 600 Ninja. We borrowed a stock bike from Kawasaki and took it over to Caliban Engineering. They gutted the engine, filled it with go-fast goodies, tarted up the bodywork with neon stripes and add-on spoilers, bolted on front disc brakes big enough to stop the earth from rotating, and topped it off with an exhaust system that sounded from the saddle like a psychotic chainsaw killer was sitting on the seat behind you.

Like all too many aftermarket makeovers, the Caliban treatment turned an otherwise competent motorcycle into a shrill, demanding, temperamental device which, when ridden in the city with due regard for the vehicle code, was about as exciting as steering a shopping cart down the cereal aisle. I decided I needed some elbow room to see what the surly little mutt could really do. Friday morning I got up early and headed south first on the 405 then the 5, and took the Ortega Highway out of San Juan

Capistrano to Lake Elsinore. I stopped for a breather there, jotted down some notes, took a few snaps of the bike with my pocket camera, and continued south on the 15, picked up Highway 76 at Palo Mesa, skirted Palomar Mountain, and sped past Lake Henshaw toward the town of Julian.

The roads were clean, with little traffic in either direction. I opened up the Ninja's throttles and it leaped forward with a snarl like a sleeping tiger suddenly wakened from a steak dream. At speed the bike's around-town surliness evaporated, and in its place appeared an exhilarating proficiency at straightening out curves and foreshortening long straightaways as if viewing them through a telephoto lens. It was almost worth the compromises that came along with the package to have the bike respond to my input at the speed of thought. It made me feel like a far more skillful and daring rider than I actually was. In what seemed like no time at all, I reached the outskirts of Julian and reluctantly dialed back the nine-tenths pace I had been maintaining for the last hour.

The houses and cabins along the road winding through the mountains became more numerous, gradually increasing in number until that peculiar critical mass was reached at which a town spontaneously erupted out of the collective human presence. Julian attracted swarms of tourists on the weekends, which was odd because there wasn't really much of anything there to attract them, at least not in the usual Southern California sense. No theme parks, no shopping malls, no movie lots, just a small town with a few shops along the main drag selling expensive things to dust and one or two good cafes. I had long since given up trying to fathom the allure the place held for *homo turista* on the weekends. Nevertheless it remained a favorite end point for weekday road testing by virtue of its location at the end of a superlative series of well-paved, highly entertaining, and lightly patrolled back roads.

I parked in front of a small cafe and left my helmet and jacket draped over the bike where I could watch them from inside. I had the place all to myself. The food was great, the prices reasonable, and I was digging an extra generous tip out of my wallet when a small man in faded jeans and a dirty, tan-colored hunting jacket shuffled in. He had a bad limp and dragged his left foot when he walked.

He went up to the counter and spoke to the waitress, who went into the kitchen and brought out two paper plates covered with aluminum foil and a couple of large styrofoam cups in a cardboard holder. The man handed over some bills, exchanged a few words with her, and shuffled out.

As he passed my table he glanced my way. He paused while a frown passed over his face. Then he walked out the door, climbed into a rust-pocked blue Jeep, and drove off.

I took my bill to the counter.

"How was everything?" she asked.

"Just fine," I said. "You know, that man who just left—I know him from somewhere. Is he a local?"

"You mean old man Jones?"

"No, his name isn't Jones, it's something else . . . Hoffer, Haller—" The limp stuck in my mind, and the squinty-eyed stare, and the cocky tone of his voice . . . "Haffner, that's it, Gus Haffner. He works as a security guard at Ascot."

"I think you're mistaken, sir," the waitress said. "That man's name is Jones."

"Jones? Are you sure?"

"Yessir, Archie Jones."

I stood there stunned as I flashed back to Quince telling me that Archie Jones had gone out west and got into the law business—but not the legal profession, as I had assumed, but law *enforcement.* As in security guards and rent-a-cops . . . .

Out in the street the blue Jeep was nowhere in sight. I ran back inside to the counter.

"Where did he go?" I said. "Does he live around here?"

"Timmy," she yelled into the kitchen, "where does Archie Jones live?"

Timmy, a big round man in a chef's hat, ambled out of the kitchen wiping his hands on a towel.

"Lemme think," he said, pushing his hat back and scratching his forehead. "North of town, as I recall. Collins Creek Road, maybe? Yeah, that's it. Collins Creek. Last place before it butts up against the mountain."

I got directions to Collins Creek Road and was halfway out the door when Timmy added, "If you're thinking about calling on Archie unannounced you'll want to be careful. He ain't fond of visitors. Been known to take a potshot at lost hikers. And he's been buying take-out food for two for the last couple months or thereabouts, so he prob'ly has a friend of his up there, too."

Collins Creek Road started out paved and abruptly changed to rutted gravel. The going on the Ninja was slow. I had to slip the clutch constantly to keep the cammy engine from stalling. The thing that worried me most was the growl of the muffler shattering the shady quiet. I might as well have called out *Here I come!* on a bullhorn every ten yards.

A few small cabins and leaning shacks were visible through the trees for the first three or four miles. Farther on the trees grew right down to the edge of the road. The valley through which the creek ran sluggishly, narrowed and steepened and darkened. At some point the road stopped being a road and turned into a driveway. I rode around a sharp corner and there, suddenly, was a tumble-down shack with a blue Jeep parked out front. I jabbed the kill switch to silence the engine, hauled in the clutch lever, and back-pedaled until I was out of sight around the bend.

A hundred yards earlier I had passed a turnout. The brush had almost overgrown it, but there was room for the Ninja. I backed it in and dragged some brush over the eyeball-searing neon paint job.

I left my helmet with the bike and walked up the road toward the house. I ducked into the brush before I turned the corner and made my way to a place where I could see the cabin.

It sat on a small clearing like a cul-de-sac. On one side the hillside rose steeply, covered with gnarled manzanitas and scrub brush. On the other side, the creek burbled at the bottom of a fifteen-foot drop-off. The cabin was small, no more than two or three rooms. An old refrigerator leaned against one wall, surrounded by tin cans, bottles, and trash. Nearby was the charred remains of a burn pile.

The brush was thickest where it stopped at the edge of the clearing. A few feet in, it was mostly bare branches, with enough room to wriggle between them. I was able to almost circle the cabin this way, from the front all the way around to the rear. The only part of the cabin I couldn't see from cover was the side facing the creek.

The afternoon sun was approaching the top of the steep ridge on the creek side. I was trying to calculate how long before it dipped behind it when the front door rasped and Haffner came out with a small metal tool box. He propped open the hood of the Jeep and began working on it. While he was inside I had been reasonably certain he wouldn't hear me thrashing around in the bushes like a wild pig. Now that he was standing not twenty yards away I didn't dare chance it. I sat tight and watched.

Haffner was one of those mechanics whose most frequently used tool was blistering profanity. After about an hour he slammed the hood shut and threw the tools into the box. Then he climbed behind the wheel and hit the starter. The Jeep clattered and wheezed and sputtered to life. He gunned the throttle, cocking an ear to the the engine. With a grinding racket he put it in gear, backed up, turned around, and headed off down the road to test his handiwork.

I had no idea how long he'd be gone, or if the person he'd bought the food for was inside. I crept over to a grimy window and peered in.

The front room was a litter of newspapers, fast-food trash, and unwashed glasses. The furniture was thrift-shop contemporary, a tattered couch with a blanket thrown over it and a couple of thin pillows at one end, a chair with duct tape holding one of the arms together. The small kitchen was a mess, the sink piled high with dishes, empty glasses stacked high. A grocery bag on the floor overflowed with paper plates and pieces of aluminum foil. Haffner had been living off Timmy's cooking for quite some time.

There was a door in the far wall—a bedroom, I guessed. It was open halfway. I looked around, found a fist-sized rock, lobbed it underhanded onto the porch, and ducked around the corner. It hit with a thud.

"Hello?" said a voice from inside. A woman's voice, it sounded like, and a scared woman at that.

The front door wasn't locked. I pushed it slowly open, mindful that whoever was inside might have a shotgun aimed about chest-high at the flimsy wood.

Nothing happened. I stepped inside and edged along the wall until I was standing beside the bedroom door with my back to the wall.

"Hello yourself," I said, trying to sound like the friendliest thing on the face of the earth. "I, uh, I'm looking for Archie. Is he here, or did I just miss him?"

"Jason?" the voice squeaked. "Is that you? Jason Street?"

I knew the voice, but couldn't come up with the name or the face that went with it. I pushed the bedroom door open and stepped into the tiny room.

On the sagging bed, dressed in filthy clothes, her hair matted and dirty, her face tear-streaked and hollow-cheeked, with her wrist handcuffed to a long steel cable attached to an eye-bolt in the floor, was Sherry Case.

# 18

At the foot of the bed was a heap of old blankets and a green sleeping bag with flocks of flying ducks printed on the liner. There was a pitcher of water and a dirty glass on an end table, a box of tissues, and a grotesque lamp in the shape of an elephant with the shade sprouting from the howdah atop its back. It emitted a sickly yellow light that was all but absorbed by the dark wood-grained wall paneling.

Sherry threw her arms around me and began sobbing. Hysterical women were becoming commonplace in my life. I pried her loose and gave the steel cable a yank. No good, the eye bolt was mounted solidly through the floor. The end that looped through the handcuffs had been peened closed with a steel clamp.

"Sherry, listen to me," I said, shaking her. "Is there a key to these handcuffs anywhere?"

She was blubbering incoherently. I did something I'd only seen in the movies. I wasn't sure it was anything but a screenwriter's cliché, but it was worth a try. I slapped her hard across the face.

It's not the kind of thing I've practiced a lot, and I might have put a little too much into it. Her head spun halfway around on her neck, then snapped back. She looked confused for a second, then shook off the blow, put a hand to her stinging cheek, glared at me, and with her free hand planted a shot on the side of my head that made my teeth rattle.

"We could have used you at Hagerstown," I said, rubbing my jaw.

She gave me a crooked smile. "Just let me get my hands on that rotten little son of a bitch who locked me up in here," she said. The tremor in her voice belied the confident words, but she was more or less under control and rational for the moment. "I think there are keys to the cuffs out in the front room somewhere. I can hear him get them when he lets me off the chain to use the bathroom."

I rifled the drawers and found an oddly-shaped key. It slipped into the hole in the cuffs and they clicked open.

"I have a motorcycle parked down the road. It's not far into town. We need to get out of here before Haffner gets back. Can you walk?"

She swung her legs over the side of the bed and leaped up. "Of course I can—" The rest of her words were cut off by the loud thump as she hit the floor in a heap.

"I might need some help," she said. "I haven't been getting out all that much lately . . ."

"How long have you been here?" I said as we went into the living room with my arm around her waist.

"Since August the . . . oh, damn, I don't remember. The end of the month. What's today?"

"October the fifth. Friday."

Tears welled up in her eyes and she sagged in my grasp. "Two months?" she said. "I've been here in this filthy stinking hole for more than two—" She covered her face with her hands.

"Come on, Sherry, stay with me, you're almost out of here. Just down the road and to the bike, and then—"

And then the Jeep came bouncing around the corner and up the driveway. Haffner couldn't have missed the open front door. He skidded to a stop about forty yards from the cabin, scrambled out of the driver's seat holding something shiny in one hand, and ducked down behind the Jeep.

"Shit," I muttered. "Sherry, we . . ."

The spark of defiance had gone out. I looked at her face and saw only a blank and empty look. To be so close to freedom and then have Haffner come back had been too much. I sat her in the corner furthest from the door.

There were two windows flanking the front door. The couch was under one of them. As I edged up to the other and peered around the sill, the whole pane of glass dissolved with a crash. I dove for the floor as two more shots thudded into the far wall.

I crawled to Sherry and pulled her down flat on the floor. A shot boomed outside and the window over the couch exploded. The carpet was a minefield of razor-sharp slivers.

I huddled behind the couch, putting as much cover between me and the flimsy walls as possible. I thought about how many bonehead moves I had made on motorcycles over the years that by all rights should have gotten me killed long ago, and how ironic it was that I was going to buy the farm at the hands of a psychotic part-time security guard in a rat-infested shack quite literally up the creek. At some point during this cheery inner dialogue I leaned wearily against the couch and wound up facing the stone fireplace.

Over the mantel, mounted on two wooden pegs, was a revolver. The thing was huge, with a barrel at least a foot long and an ominous-looking scope mounted on top.

The last thing I wanted to do under the circumstances was stand up. But I would have to in order to reach the gun. I crawled to the middle of the floor and looked back. All I could see out either window was sky. Working on the principle that if I couldn't see him he couldn't see me, I made it to the hearth and rose slowly onto my knees, then to a squat. Nothing but sky so far. I rose a little higher and discovered the front door was between Haffner and me.

Just because he can't see me doesn't mean he won't shoot through the door anyway, I told myself. All right, then, I replied, make it fast. I stood up, reached for the revolver, snatched it off the wall, and hit the floor again, bracing for the hail of bullets that never came.

My heart was pounding audibly. I had been to an indoor shooting range once or twice with Barry, whose interest in firearms was more academic than practical. He tended to view them as interesting mechanical phenomena rather than deadly weapons. Right then I was straining to remember everything he had ever told me about how guns work and how to shoot them well.

I pressed the cylinder latch and the cylinder flopped open. All six chambers were loaded with hollow-point, copper-nosed bullets. I tipped one out. It looked about as big as a roll of Life-savers. I put it back, shut the cylinder, propped the barrel on the back of the couch, and pointed it out the window at the Jeep.

Haffner was hiding behind it, only his feet and ankles visible underneath. I thumbed the hammer back until it came to a stop with a click. The scope was so powerful I could see the oil smears on the rag sticking out of the gas tank filler neck. I didn't want to shoot Haffner, just scare him off. I centered the crosshairs on the rag, held my breath, and squeezed the trigger.

A fireball the size of a watermelon erupted from the barrel and an explosion like a thunderclap made all the bits of glass on the carpet jump an inch. The next thing I knew I sitting on my butt, holding my hand over a sticky wet spot on my forehead where the recoil had tried to push the eyepiece of the scope through my skull like a hole punch.

Outside the Jeep started up. I crept to the window in time to see Haffner crouched down behind the dashboard, backing up the driveway. There was a ragged gash in the fender and an empty hole where the rag had been. I resisted the urge to blow the smoke out of the end of the barrel.

Sherry was still in her own world. I couldn't take her on the bike in her condition, and I didn't want to leave her while I went for help.

I believe it's true that someone watches out for fools and children, because at that moment the phone rang. I hadn't even considered there might be one in that clapboard nightmare. It was underneath a pile of old newspapers on the kitchen table. I picked it up.

"Hey, Arch, this is Donny. You still want me to help ya with your Jeep or not?"

I slammed the phone down to break the connection, picked it up again, and dialed 911. An operator took down my location and promised to have a police car there in minutes. I described Haffner and the Jeep and said he was armed, and if they ran into him coming the other way they might want to shoot him a few dozen times first and I'd answer their questions later.

Two sheriff's cars showed up twenty minutes later. One took Sherry to the hospital while the two deputies from the other one got my story. I got to repeat the whole thing again later at the station. The gash on my forehead throbbed hellishly. A deputy with paramedic training cleaned it out with antiseptic so that it throbbed *and* stung, then bandaged it. The adrenaline was wearing off and I gulped cup after cup of a corrosive coffee-like substance to avoid dropping off to sleep in mid-sentence.

When they finally let me go it was eight o'clock at night. I was still a two-hour freeway ride from home. I called Sara.

"Can you drive the pickup down here and get me?" I said after I explained why I hadn't come home yet. "I'm absolutely hammered, and I have to get up in the morning and fly to Sacramento."

"I'll be there as soon as I can," she said. "Are the tie-downs still under the seat?"

"Right. The ramp's in the garage. And bring a flashlight. It's as dark as the inside of a goat out there."

Sara arrived just before midnight with a sandwich and a thermos of coffee. Good coffee this time, brewed up while she loaded the ramp and packed some tools just in case. But it was fighting a losing battle. I dozed off in the seat before we got to I-5 and didn't know anything else until we pulled into the driveway in Lakewood at some single-digit hour of the morning.

# 19

Later that morning at breakfast, Sara hinted around that she might like to come with me. When I said yes she was visibly relieved.

"Did you think I'd say no?" I asked.

"I wasn't sure," she said. "I thought it might be, you know, one of those *guy* things."

"Oh, you mean one of those tributes to the Y-chromosome where we all stand around grunting and spitting and scratching ourselves, getting in touch with our wild side, maybe doing a little drumming after the race?"

"You have a wild side?" she said, hoisting a skeptical eyebrow.

"Sure do." I held up my mug. "See? Coffee. Black. No cream, no sugar." I took a sip and belted out a passable Tarzan yell.

Boswell picked up on it and began to howl. We harmonized like a couple of out-of-tune dentists' drills.

"Cheetah good dog," I said. "You like song, Jane?"

Sara put her hands over her ears. "Another note and you're both sleeping in the trees tonight."

I caught a few winks on the plane and woke up as the wheels touched down. Rusty and his brother Kevin were waiting for us at the gate. Sara was wearing tight blue jeans, one of my button-down shirts, and white sneakers. Her auburn hair spilled over her shoulders and down to the middle of her back. Kevin's heart leaped out of his chest and landed at her feet with a nearly audible thud.

A pale but otherwise ambulatory Ozzie was waiting for us in the van. I grabbed his hand and pumped it.

"Whoa, easy, Hemingway," he said clearly but slowly. "I'm

better, but I got a way to go yet." He leaned forward and brushed a fingertip across the bandage on my forehead. "Say, what the hell happened to you?"

"I leaned into a scope too far," I said. "I'll fill you in on the way."

We piled into the van and headed for the Cal Expo fairgrounds. Ozzie almost missed the exit off I-5, so enthralled was he by the tale of my daring rescue of Sherry Case.

"Nice going, Hemingway! I hope you drilled the bastard."

"Actually, I missed him. But I winged his Jeep."

"Careful o' them Jeeps. They charge when they're wounded."

As we waited in line to get into the track, Ozzie put his chin in his hand and said, "The gate guard at Ascot, huh? Can't say I recall the name or the face, but then I'm only there twice a year . . . how's Sherry?"

"Physically she's not that bad off," I said, "a bit undernourished, maybe, and fighting off a cold or the flu. But she was scared out of her wits for two months, and didn't say more than a handful of words from the time I found her until the cops took her away. The doctor says it'll take her a while before she feels safe and comes around."

Sara, in the shotgun seat, was only now hearing the grim details for the first time. She gave a little shudder. I put my arm around her shoulder.

"You okay?" I said.

"Trapped in that place, feeling completely powerless for so long, thinking there was no way out . . ." She made a choking sound and put her hands over her mouth.

"Gangway," I said, leaning across her and opening the door. She stumbled out and leaned against the van, her face as grey as dishwater.

"Must have been the airplane food," she said, smiling weakly.

"We could go to the motel," I said, "rest up a bit, and come back later for the main." We were checked into the Residence Inn near the track, with a single for us and a two-story double for Rusty, Kevin, and Ozzie.

"No, I'll be fine. There, the line's moving."

We set up the pit as the afternoon sun began to sink. The

stands filled up quickly, the fans anticipating the last-ditch run for the plate. Sacramento was a horse track with a lush green lawn in the infield and a small lake along the back straight. The tents and awnings flapped in the cool evening breeze, giving the pits the air of a garden party, with the hum of generators and the booming of Harleys warming up taking the place of genteel laughter and the clink of fine china.

The press was getting a lot of mileage out of the slim gap between Rusty and Perry Haycock. If Haycock won tonight's race and Rusty got second, the plate was Haycock's. If Rusty won and Haycock got second, the result was still the same, because the difference between first and second was only four points, three shy of what Rusty needed to beat Haycock. For Rusty to win the plate, he had to win the race, and Haycock had to place third or lower. Ted Munson theoretically had a shot at the plate, but only if a meteor fell on everyone else while he was in the john.

Rusty was calm and loose, as if all he had riding on the race was a five-dollar side bet. I overheard him explaining it to a reporter this way:

"Sometimes you decide to settle for a safe second instead of a maybe first. Other times you hang back a little bit, thinking you can make it up at the next race. This time, though, I know exactly what I gotta do. I gotta win. There's no second place, no next race. That takes a lot of the pressure off, you know what I mean? All I have to concentrate on is one thing, winning . . . What about Perry? He's out of my control, you know? He's riding his race, I'm riding mine. Whatever happens, happens."

Sheldon Jeter overheard this and nodded his head ever so slightly, which for him passed for an overt display of emotion. Rusty had just passed part of his pre-employment interview.

The heats were announced about half an hour after the sun went down. A row of powerful arc lamps along the front of the roof over the grandstands made the grid look like center stage, the racers like actors blinded by the footlights, and the fans like an audience waiting for the curtain to rise on a gripping drama. Bugs flitted here and there in the glare, and a fine mist hovered over the grassy infield.

Rusty, Perry Haycock, and Ted Munson were called by the

announcer to say a few words to the crowd before the program started. They shuffled over to the podium on the start-finish line, their steel shoes clanking, and gave the obligatory shallow answers to the announcer's brainless questions. When it was all over the three of them headed either to the grid or the pits.

Suddenly Haycock, who was just swinging a leg over his bike, held up a hand to the starter and called out to Rusty and Ted Munson. They met in the middle of the track and huddled together for a minute. Haycock lifted his visor and said something to the other two. There was some laughter, and a slow-motion punch missed a smiling face by a mile, but the words were lost in the murmur of the fans and the noise of the engines. Haycock offered his hand to Rusty, who shook it solemnly, followed by Munson. Then Rusty and Munson shook. Finally all three executed a simultaneous three-point high-five and Haycock trotted over to his bike.

Rusty was in the third heat, front row. He was standing by the front straight to see where the best traction was for the start. Sheldon and Ozzie had gone to the head and Sara was off fetching snacks from the van. I knelt beside the bike, giving it what would probably be the last once-over I'd ever give it, running my hand over it like a favorite horse, when I sensed a presence behind me. I was about to look over my shoulder when something hard and cold poked into my ear.

"Say a word and I'll blow your goddam head off right here," a voice said in a harsh, dry whisper. "Get up and go where I tell you."

Something jabbed me in the ribs as I got to my feet.

"This way." A nudge to the right. "Snap it up."

We marched in lock-step toward the vans parked behind the tote board. The lights were all pointed at the track and everyone's attention was focused on the starter. The pitch of the engines rose to a peak as the starter approached the box.

Another jab guided me between two vans. Our van was on the other side of the tote board, maybe fifty yards away.

"Hold it."

"All right," I said, and began to turn toward the voice, "what the hell—"

A blinding flash went off inside my head and a crack like a line drive to center field echoed in my ears. I dropped to my knees on the wet grass with my head throbbing and a fire burning at the base of my skull.

"Knew I'd find you here, smart boy. Shoulda taken care of you at the cabin, but you got off a lucky shot. Took my meal ticket, too. Now they're looking for me. But they won't find me. They'll find you, though. Right here, with a bullet in you."

I forced myself to open my eyes and turned toward the voice. The speaker was a small, wiry man in a security guard's uniform. He held a revolver in front of him, the barrel level with my forehead.

"Haffner?" I croaked.

His face twisted into a malevolent grin. "Or Archie Jones, take your pick. An' I got a few others you don't know about. Leastwise if you do, you didn't write 'em down in those notebooks of yours."

"My notebooks—you're the one who broke into my house? Why?"

"To find out how much you knew. Judging by them notebooks, you knew plenty enough to hang me. I burned 'em, though, so now nobody knows but me and you. And pretty soon you won't know nothing at all."

"How did you find out where I lived?"

"You wrote it down yourself, on the back of your business card." He laughed. "I'm the guy that little prick Peters hired to track down Archie Jones for you. Ain't that a hoot? Paid me to find myself!"

He jerked the barrel of the gun, motioning me to my feet. I stood up and backed slowly away from him, my hands about shoulder level. He let me put a little ground between us and then followed.

Suddenly a voice behind him rose and he spun to see a couple of guys, crew members most likely, opening the rear door of the van to my right. In the split-second he was distracted, I threw open the front door of the van to my right. It whacked the outstretched wrist holding the gun so hard he almost dropped it. Before he did, he brought his other hand up under it and snapped the gun to eye level, aiming it at my head through the window of the door that separated us.

An explosion shook the narrow space between the vans and a bullet dissolved the window glass into a fine spray of particles like a shower of water droplets. But I was already on the ground, rolling under the van to the other side. I laid there and watched Haffner's feet, praying that he hadn't seen where I disappeared to, hoping he wouldn't drop to his knees and start blasting away under the van.

Instead I heard his feet pounding the soft turf like drumbeats. I crawled out from under the van, saw him running toward turn one, and took off after him at what I thought was a safe distance.

The heat race was already under way. The infield gate along the front straight was closed until the short break between the Shootout and the main event. He was trapped inside the track. I stopped and looked around for a real security guard. The two guys at the van *must* have raised the alarm by now, and it would only be a minute until the cops came running.

The pack entered turn one, pitched it sideways, and thundered past where Haffner now stood with a knot of spectators along the inside rail. As the last bike disappeared and a cloud of dust tumbled along after it, Haffner climbed over the fence and scurried across the track.

I sprinted for the rail, sailed over it, and hit the track running. The outside fence was higher and there was a thick shrub, trimmed flat across the top, on the other side. Haffner cleared the fence with surprising agility and crawled over the shrub like a bug on a hotplate. He dropped over the edge and was up on his feet in a flash.

I hopped the fence easily, but I outweighed Haffner by fifty pounds. The shrub opened up under my weight and swallowed me like a Venus flytrap. I thrashed helplessly for maybe half a minute while Haffner vanished into the shadows alongside the grandstands.

I wriggled free and stumbled after him. I turned the corner cautiously against the possibility of a gun barrel waiting for me. Ahead was the main entrance to the grandstands. Lines of people stood waiting to buy tickets, others were queuing up to go inside.

Haffner had just reached the edge of the pool of light that illuminated the area. He glanced over his shoulder, saw me, and melted into the crowd of fans going into the stands.

"Hey!" a voice called. "Hold it!"

Behind me was one of those real security guards I had needed badly about a minute ago, pumping along with his flashlight swinging in one hand and the other hand holding his hat on. But he was after me, not Haffner. If he caught me I'd lose Haffner for sure. On the other hand, if I caught Haffner, I wanted this guy nearby. I let him get close enough to judge his speed—he had a paunch and was already red-faced and puffing from the effort— and then followed Haffner into the stands.

In the middle of the thronged lower concourse I saw a ripple of heads turning indignantly, marking Haffner's trail as if he were running through a field of tall grass. Shouldering my way along behind him, I checked once more to make sure I hadn't shaken my pursuer. When I looked back I barely caught a glimpse of Haffner running up the stairway to the reserved seating and grabbed the iron rail, chinning myself up to the seventh or eighth step and vaulting onto the stairs.

The security guard was falling behind, and I regretfully chose catching Haffner over having him on my side—which I wasn't too sure he'd be, anyway, after the chase I was leading him on.

Haffner was already at the head of the stairs. By the time I got there he was gone.

I swore silently and stopped to think. Why was he going up? There was nowhere to go from there except . . .

Except back down.

The security guard was a dozen steps below. There was another set of stairs leading down to the concourse about twenty yards away. I ran to them and slithered through the crowd until it looked safe to jump, then climbed over the rail and dropped to the ground. Just before I jumped I saw Haffner heading for the bleachers along the front straight.

I could hear the roar of the engines as the starter hit the green light to flag off the next heat. I climbed up onto the outside fence and looked up and down the track. Somebody yelled and tried to haul me down. As I tumbled off I spotted Haffner running along the fence back toward turn one where he knew he could make his way back to the infield. Another dead-end destination, unless he knew something I didn't, which by now seemed more than likely judging by the familiarity he had shown with the Cal-Expo layout so far.

As I reached the corner of the grandstands a huge blue bulk shot out of the crowd and tackled me around the waist. The security guard threw me to the ground, grabbed a handful of hair, and pushed my face into the asphalt. Then he jerked my hands behind my back and knelt on my wrists while he yanked his walkie-talkie off his belt.

"Got him, got him!" he shouted into it. "This is Fred, I got him, man!"

He hauled me to my feet and threw me face-down in the shrub. I almost fell through it again and twisted around so I could see where Haffner was.

As I did a shout went up from the stands and a woman nearby screamed. Haffner was staggering across the track, winded or just lame. The pack was heading down the straight at over 130, everyone tucked in under the paint with the throttle wide open. As the lead rider rolled off the gas and pitched it sideways, Haffner fell to his knees. The rider sat up and planted his steel shoe at the same instant he saw the bent figure smack in the middle of the groove. Whether by design or from sheer panic, he threw the bike clean off its wheels and over on its side, parting company with it in a cloud of dirt and sparks. Bike and rider shot off toward the haybales in a straight line, missing Haffner by inches.

The guy in second wasn't so lucky. There wasn't anywhere he could go except a narrow spot between Haffner and the fence.

Haffner chose that instant to make it to one knee and reach out for the inside rail to pull himself up. The bike hit him low and, leaned over as it was, scooped him up like a cow-catcher on a locomotive and threw him high in the air. He spun like a pinwheel, arms and legs thrown outward, and landed on the infield grass behind the horrified spectators along the inside rail.

The race was red-flagged and both ambulances called out. The first rider was shaken but unhurt. The one who had hit Haffner had a broken arm. Haffner was unconscious and bleeding from several compound fractures. The paramedics, afraid to move him yet, began trying to stabilize him.

The security guard who had tackled me dragged me to the security room and cuffed me to a chair. I kept yelling for him to call the sheriff in Julian and tell him Gus Haffner was here, Gus Haffner who was wanted for kidnapping, goddammit, you stupid hayseed, which is a capital offense last time I looked, and other such reassurances practically guaranteed to ensure cooperation from even the most truculent civil servant. He just stood in front of me fuming and slapping that big flashlight into the palm of his hand like the piggy-eyed deputy in every bad chain gang movie ever made.

The real police showed up a few minutes later and it turned out that one of them knew the Julian area from when he was a Highway Patrolman a few years ago. He quizzed me about the town and the surrounding terrain until he was convinced I had at least been there. When I told him the sheriff's name and described several of the local deputies, he took a chance that I was on the level and made the call. As soon as he hung up I was sprung from the chair and told to get in touch with the Julian sheriff's office the minute I got home, to the obvious dismay of Buford and his pet flashlight.

I limped back to the infield and our pit. I had landed wrong on my weak knee during one of my death leaps down the flights of stairs. Sara was sitting in a folding camp chair. She jumped up and said, "Where have you been? I didn't—" then stopped when she saw me gimping along, spattered with dirt and scratches. "What happened?"

The others gathered around as I told how Haffner had almost popped me for the second time in as many days.

"You get the drop on him again, Hemingway?" Ozzie drawled.

"Sort of. I dropped under a van and he took off. I was chasing him when he got hit."

"You mean that guy who ran out on the track, that was him?"

"Gus Haffner," I said. "The gate guard at Ascot. He kidnapped Sherry Case. He killed Sherm Case, too. He found out from Charlie Brand that Sherm fixed the 1950 Springfield race.

That crash ended his career. He wanted revenge on Sherm, or money to keep the secret, maybe both. He probably talked Sherm into a meeting at Ascot where he was working that night. Maybe he lost his temper. Maybe Sherm lost his. Either way, the gun went off and Sherm ended up dead."

"But why did he kidnap Sherry?

"With Sherm dead, she stood to inherit his estate. What Haffner didn't know, couldn't know, is what a piss-poor mess Sherm had left things in, and how close to bankruptcy the company was. But he didn't find that out until after he already had Sherry. Then he was stuck with her. He couldn't just let her go. So he kept her prisoner in his cabin waiting to see how things shook out with Case Tires, hoping he'd be able to squeeze some money out of someone after all."

Sara gave me a rib-cracking hug. Only then did I realize how scared she had been for me. I felt a tear slipping down her cheek and kissed it away.

More than at any time in the last twenty-four hours I just wanted to crawl into bed and sleep for a week. But there wasn't time. The ambulances came back and the program was under way again within fifteen minutes. Rusty got a clean second place in his heat. Afterward he huddled with Ozzie and Sheldon in the van.

They were discussing whether he should run the last Shiloh Shootout of the season, which he had gotten into with a fifth-fastest qualifying time. Ozzie was adamantly against it, Rusty all for it, and Sheldon sat on the fence.

"I gotta see what Perry's got," Rusty said. "He qualified sixth fastest, but I got a hunch he was sandbagging."

"You can find out from the sidelines," Ozzie argued. "You don't need to be out there with him. Save yourself and the motor until it really counts."

"The track's changing, too, Ozzie," Rusty said. "It's getting tackier, and the groove's narrowing up. It isn't like it was in my heat race an hour ago. If Perry runs the Shootout and I don't, he'll know exactly how to set up for the main and we'll just be guessing."

"The lad's got a point, Ozzie," Sheldon said. "I vote we run the Shootout."

Ozzie started to protest, then shook his head. "Dammit, you're right, Rusty," he said. "I guess I'm gettin' timid in my old age."

Rusty rolled to the line with the five other Shootout finalists. The fans howled in anticipation of a preview of the main, with the two title contenders and a quartet of hungry up-and-comers slugging it out for the big bucks. The announcer was hyping it like it was the opening trumpet blast of the Second Coming.

Rusty and Haycock took off at the green and left the others for dead. They rode like the hounds of hell were at their heels, throwing it in deeper and harder each corner, as if the plate itself went to the winner instead of just another old bucket of money. Neither seemed to have any clear advantage on the straights. If anything Rusty looked just a bit down on power. On the last turn of the last lap Rusty slipped off the groove trying to draft past and Haycock beat him to the line by half a dozen bike lengths.

For a guy who just made a $7,000 error Rusty was awfully chipper. He hardly hid his grin as he handed the bike to Ozzie. He looked around to see if anybody was watching, then pumped his fist and said through clenched teeth, "I got him!"

"Looked to me like he got you," Ozzie said.

"No way," Rusty insisted. "He's mine, as long as he leaves his bike set up just the way it is."

"What're you telling me?" Ozzie said. "Were you sandbagging out there?"

Rusty grinned like a Cheshire cat. "Maybe some," he said with a shrug, and then, "Aw, hell, Ozzie, I coulda passed him almost any time—I got motor on him like you wouldn't believe! Sheldon, this thing's a jet!"

Rusty had let the Shootout money go, choosing instead to scope out—and psych out—Perry Haycock.

"I pulled up alongside him once or twice and made it look like I was making my move," he confided, "then just kind of forgot to open the throttle all the way. I might have touched the kill button once or twice, too, to make it sound like the engine was going sour."

"You sneaky little bastard," Ozzie said, laughing and ruffling Rusty's hair. "I'm proud of you. An' I take full credit for the underhanded side of your personality."

Sheldon gave the bike to Ozzie to roll out to the grid. Ozzie started to protest that it was Sheldon's engine, but Sheldon held up a hand to silence him.

"I'll be nearby if you need me," he said.

I shook hands with Rusty and wished him luck. Sara hugged him and gave him a kiss on the cheek. He clanked off toward the grid behind Ozzie.

Because of the delay earlier, the officials skipped the pre-race interview in the interest of getting the race underway before daybreak. I stood on the sidelines with a strange empty feeling in my gut and a lump in my throat.

"What's wrong?" Sara said.

"Damned if I know why, but I'll miss this," I said. "The dirt and noise and fatigue and frustration, and the incredible high you get when you're a part of a winning team. This must be what it was like to come home from a war and have to wear a tie again and punch a time clock and wash your own socks."

"It's time to let go," she said gently. "You have your world, they have theirs. This isn't your world."

"You're right. It's not my world because you're not in it. I'll still miss it, though . . ."

The green light went on and the pack slithered toward turn one. Rusty's plan was to stick with Haycock in the early stages and then make his move and open up an unbeatable lead in the final laps. But as the bikes bunched up and jockeyed for position on the groove, another rider who had gotten a better start than Rusty suddenly slowed in front of him. In an eyeblink the bike slewed sideways—the chain had broken or slipped off the sprockets and locked the rear wheel.

Rusty, on the gas and accelerating hard, rammed the other bike. The rider went flying one way, the bike another. Rusty almost fell, too. He fought for control, both feet off the pegs and flying wildly, while the pack merged into a single file and entered the back straight.

My heart fell to my feet. I turned away and leaned on the rail.

All that work, a whole year of his life, shot to hell by someone else's faulty master link clip. A fifty-cent piece worth a hundred thousand dollars. The pack came by to complete the first lap and I didn't even look up.

"Jason, look," Sara said, tugging at my sleeve. She was standing on her toes, peering around the tote board at the back straightaway. "He's catching up."

I craned my neck to see down the front straight. Out of turn four came Perry Haycock followed by the tightly bunched field. As they thundered past, I counted . . . seventh, eighth, ninth, tenth, elev—

"Hey, that's Rusty!" I shouted. "He's in eleventh!"

"I told you!" Sara screamed. "Watch him!"

As she spoke Rusty swung wide around two other riders and squared off the corner, beating them to the groove. He passed another rider in mid-corner, caught the next one midway along the back straight, and finally drafted by to beat him into turn three.

"Seventh!" Sara said the next time they came past the finish line. "He's in seventh, isn't he?"

"I think so. Or eighth—no, you're right, seventh!"

"No! No!" She pounded my arm and jumped up and down. "Sixth! There he goes!"

Rusty was carving through the pack, taking them high, low, in the middle, wherever there was an opening. The fans were going out of their minds as Rusty balanced the will to win against the laws of physics.

Still, it looked like that night would go down in racing history as the most spectacular losing effort of all time. Haycock's lead was huge by the tenth lap, and there were still three riders between Rusty and the yawning abyss he needed to cross to catch up. He had little chance of breaking free and reeling in Haycock without a helping draft. He tried nonetheless, wringing the last ounce of horsepower out of Sheldon's engine.

As he completed his pass of the third-place rider, Rusty seemed to realize at last how far behind Haycock he was. You could almost see the fire go out right then. It might have stayed out, had not Ted Munson, who was advancing through the pack, put a move on Rusty and passed him. That got Rusty's attention, and he passed him right back. They went on that way for half a dozen laps, Rusty no longer concerned with catching Haycock . . .

Or was he?

"Is it wishful thinking," I said to Sara, "or are those two catching Haycock?"

"They do seem a little closer than they were a few laps ago," she said.

"That's it! He's using a two-man draft to catch up! Two bikes together are faster than one alone. Haycock's all by himself. Rusty's got help. He still has a chance!"

Rusty and Munson were definitely reeling in Haycock. The crowd sensed it, and so did Perry. He looked over his shoulder coming out of turn four and saw a two-man posse with his butt in their crosshairs. He went too deep into the next corner and almost had the haybales for a late-night snack.

Twenty laps down, five to go. Rusty and Munson were ten lengths behind Haycock now and closing fast. The gap narrowed to three lengths by lap twenty-two. Rusty was giving Munson the tow of his life, spinning Ted's undergeared engine past redline on the straights. It had to hold long enough for Rusty to make his move. If it blew before that . . .

On lap twenty-three Rusty sailed by Haycock on the front straight and closed the door on him going into turn one. Munson tried to slip by in Rusty's wake. Haycock sensed him coming, and moved down low to block him.

Without Rusty's help Munson didn't have a chance. His bike, less powerful than either Rusty's or Haycock's, was geared lower, and couldn't rev high enough on its own to keep up with the front two. He dropped back a bike length.

Rusty glanced over his shoulder and saw Munson falling behind. Whether from that momentary lapse of concentration or by Rusty's design, Haycock slipped by him, back into the lead. I say maybe it was intentional because the next thing Rusty did was fade to the rear just enough for Munson to get back into his slipstream. With the two of them locked in a single draft, Rusty then closed the gap between Haycock's rear wheel and his front.

They crossed the finish line nose-to-tail, Haycock then Rusty then Munson, to end the twenty-fourth lap. As they entered turn one for the final lap, Rusty looked over his shoulder at Munson and waved as if motioning him to pass.

"What's he doing?" Sara yelled. "Is he out of his mind?"

He was far from it. Munson stuck to Rusty's tail as they came onto the back straight. Again Rusty motioned. Munson—who like us hadn't a clue what Rusty was up to but wasn't about to turn down an offer to pass—moved up alongside.

As they entered turn three Munson's momentum carried him past Rusty *and* Haycock, and into the lead. Before the startled Haycock could recover, Rusty rode Munson's draft around Haycock and into second.

Then, coming out of turn four and heading down the straight on the last lap, Rusty gave Munson a final wave—this time waving goodbye—spurred every last horsepower Sheldon Jeter had built into his engine, and slingshotted past him. He pulled out a four-bike-length lead by the finish line. Haycock was stuck in third, unable to pass Munson and regain second in the final fifty yards before the finish line.

As he flashed under the checkered flag Rusty threw a fist in the air, winning the race and—by hauling another rider out of the pack and stuffing him between himself and Perry Haycock—winning the Number One Plate by a single point.

After his victory lap Rusty leaped onto the podium and threw his fists in the air, hooting like a baboon. Al Hendricks hobbled up on his crutches and handed Rusty the front number plate from his own bike. Rusty held it over his head with both hands, displaying the thick, black number one to the fans, who were massing around the pit gate waiting for a chance to rush across the track and mob the new National Champ.

Somehow Ozzie found me in the chaos and thanked me for my help while he was laid up. I said, quite truthfully, that it had been my pleasure.

We stumbled into our hotel room at three in the morning. The first thing Rusty did was phone his father, then Buster, who it turned out had been sitting up all night, swilling coffee and biting his fingernails waiting for someone to call him with the results. Then a bunch of racers showed up and there followed an impromptu victory celebration that got us thrown out of the Residence Inn right around sunup Sunday morning when some fool rode my mountain bike off the diving board into the swimming pool.

Sara and I flew home that afternoon. My shoes were still wet when we got off the plane at LAX.

# 20

On Thursday Rusty's picture was on the cover of *Cycle Weekly*. In the lead feature he mentioned me by name as having been instrumental in helping him win the plate. I stopped getting a kick out of seeing my name in print a long time ago, but that mention put a foolish grin on my face for the rest of the week.

A month later the dizzy elation of that night was little more than a pleasant echo of celebration and back-slapping and champagne showers. By then Gus Haffner had recovered well enough to talk to the police, who suddenly decided they'd been hasty in ruling Sherm a suicide. He admitted kidnapping Sherry Case, more or less for the reason I had guessed. He also admitted trying to shake down Sherm for money to keep the secret of the Springfield race. He and Charlie Brand had been in touch sporadically over the years, but lost contact when Charlie's mind began to go. Through a quirk of memory Charlie still remembered Haffner's phone number long after Haffner lost Charlie's. One night when Charlie was tormented by ghosts from his past, he had called Haffner and confessed to his part in the fixed race.

But despite what the police thought was an iron-clad motive and a golden opportunity, Haffner steadfastly denied killing Sherm or even arranging to meet him that night at Ascot. In his defense he argued that dozens of people went in and out of the back pit that night through his gate. As long as they had the right pass he let them go, and didn't even look at their faces half the time. Any one of them could have pulled the trigger. He clung doggedly to the theory that Sherm must have cracked under the pressure of his blackmail threats and killed himself rather than suffer the humiliation.

The police knew Haffner was lying. After dozens of interviews with people who knew Sherm Case, they couldn't see him as anyone who would sit up nights worrying about a tarnished reputation. But there was actually very little hard evidence to tie Haffner to the murder, especially since the gun found under the window of Sherm's van had been legally purchased by and registered to Sherm, and bore a set of his fingerprints.

The heat for the murder was suddenly off Haffner a week later when Max Bauer committed suicide. Angela came home from shopping and found his body sprawled on the floor of his study, a growing pool of blood from a bullet hole in his temple staining the wine-red carpet even darker. He left a note confessing to the killing of Sherm Case, although he called it an accident.

He claimed they met to discuss a buyout of Case Tires by Universal, but couldn't come to terms. An argument erupted, and Sherm, seated behind the wheel of his van, pulled a gun from the glove box and waved it threateningly. Max grabbed it and a struggle followed during which the gun went off.

When he saw what had happened, Max panicked. There was too much bad blood between him and Sherm for anyone to believe it had been an accident. He fled the pits and made his way back to the stands.

Sherm's death, accidental though it was, gnawed at him for months afterward. But he couldn't bring himself to own up to it. Finally convinced it was too late to come forward and have anyone believe his story, he took the only honorable way out.

Sara had what in therapy circles is called a breakthrough. We were out in the garage one night, putting away the camping stuff for the winter, when she found a box of old family photos she hadn't unpacked since moving in with me. We spread them out on the living room floor. I needled her gently as she blushed at the grainy snapshots of the skinny little girl with the long brown pigtails and the slightly buck-toothed grin.

"I can't tell if you're smiling or grimacing in this one," I said, holding one out for her to look at. It was a group photo of her, her younger sister Dede, her mother, and some man her mother's age who I didn't know. Sara stood in front of the man, who had his hands on her shoulders. She was facing the camera but her eyes were rolled up as if trying to peer through the back of her head at the man behind her. "This guy looks like me when I had my beard," I said. She glanced up from the pile in front of her and frowned at the snapshot.

"That's my uncle Richard," she said. "Mom's brother . . ."

"You look . . . I don't know, kind of wary."

She looked at it a long time, her face clouding over in a manner now familiar to me as heralding the onset of disturbing memories.

". . . like he's about to bite you or something," I said.

She put the photo down and leaned against the couch with her eyes closed, and crossed her hands over her stomach.

"Are you feeling okay?" I said. We had planned on dinner out and a movie later.

"No, not really. Do you mind if we stay home tonight?"

"No problem," I said, trying to hide my disappointment. "I'll cook."

"I'm not hungry."

We spent a tense and quiet night at home. Quiet because Sara responded to my attempts at conversation with nods if she responded at all, and tense because I had been looking forward to a night out and hoping for a small dose of normalcy to dilute the heavy dread that filled the house like smoke.

Later, just before turning in, we fought. It was the kind of rancorous, bare-knuckle skirmish that no one wins and everyone walks away from bloodied. I gave free rein to my temper and all the resentment I had been bottling up for months.

No one fights dirtier than people who are intimate, who each know the other's weaknesses better than they know their own. But Sara, who can ordinarily hold her own in a verbal slugfest with people twice as swinish as I was that night, wasn't in fighting trim. I had her on the ropes from the opening bell, and I kept at her until she was reeling. She slept on the couch with Boswell, the traitorous mutt, on the floor beside her.

I stayed home the next day to work on a piece. That afternoon as Sara got ready for therapy I put on my sport coat and a tie.

"Where are you going?" she said with an affected air of indifference. "Got a hot date?"

"I'm going with you."

"With me? Where?"

"You said I ought to think about sitting in on a session. Well, I thought about it."

"You can't just show up like this. I should ask Jeannie first . . ."

"Don't ask her. Tell her. Who's paying who, anyway?"

"You don't understand how this works—"

"Then let me learn. Dammit, Sara, I'm willing to try this. Do you want me to come or not? Because if you say no now, I might never offer again."

Jeannie was a small, plump woman in her thirties. She had frizzy red hair and wore a flowered vest over a white shirt, a loosely knotted tie, and baggy corduroy pants with the cuffs rolled up. Her office looked like a college dorm room, with notebooks and photocopied reports piled haphazardly on her desk, and kitschy flea-market dustables vying for space with leaning stacks of books and magazines on the shelves along the wall. Next to the professional diploma behind her desk was another one from the California Academy of Juggling.

"I went to conference over the weekend," Jeannie said without preamble after Sara introduced me, "and I'd like to explore some possibilities with you this time. Are you up for that, Sara?"

"All right," Sara mumbled.

"I hate to admit I was behind the curve on this topic," Jeannie said, "but it's a comparatively new field, and I hadn't looked into it too closely until recently. When I finally did, I thought of you right away."

Sara looked up, suddenly interested.

"First, let me ask you a few questions about your relationship with Jason. I know we've already gone over most of this, but bear with me. Jason, are you okay with this?"

"Shoot."

"How old are you, Sara?"

"Twenty-nine."

"How long have you and Jason been living together?"

"About a year now."

"And when did the dreams start?"

Sara shifted in her chair. "A little less than a year ago."

"After you moved in together. Are you two having sex?"

Sara looked away.

"No," I said. "Not for months."

"Any idea why, Sara?"

She shook her head.

"Does the idea scare you?"

A barely perceptible nod.

"Does any intimacy with Jason scare you?"

"Yes."

"Why? Do you feel like you're giving up control, then?"

"Yes."

"And you need to be in control?"

"Of course. Who doesn't?"

"Why do you need to be in control?"

"Because . . . because bad things happen when you lose control."

"What kind of things?"

Sara didn't answer.

"How are you sleeping, Sara?"

"Badly. I can't seem to relax."

"When you do fall asleep, what?"

"The dreams come."

"Tell me about your family. What was it like at home when you were young?"

"Dad left home when I was three, right after my sister was born. Mom worked nights at a dry-cleaning plant."

"Who looked after you and your sister while your mother was at work?"

"Neighbors, mostly. Sometimes her brother."

"Did he live with you?"

"Off and on. He was a truck driver. He'd be gone for a week or two at a time and then come home for three or four days. He'd stay with us while Mom was at work. Then he'd get a job and Mom would call the neighbors again."

"So your mother's brother, your uncle, he'd stay with you sometimes while your mother was working. What was his name?"

"Richard Coburn. We called him Uncle Richie."

"Did you like him?"

Sara shrugged. "I guess."

"Did he like you?"

Another shrug. "He said he did."

"Sara, did Richie ever do anything that made you uncomfortable?"

Sara frowned. "What do you mean? Like what?"

"Like touching you. Saying things that made you uncomfortable."

Sara was quiet for a minute, worrying a knuckle with her teeth. Then in a small voice she said, "He used to watch me dress for school. To make sure I did it right, he said, so my mommy would be proud of me."

"Was that all he did? Did he do anything else that made you uncomfortable?"

Sara leaned back in her chair, closed her eyes tightly, and put her hands over her stomach. A grimace of pain distorted her face. I thought she was going to throw up. I grabbed a wastebasket and slid it next to her chair.

"That's all right, Sara," Jeannie said. "We don't need to go into this any further now."

After Sara's color returned Jeannie said, "The conference I went to over the weekend was on child sexual abuse. The term abuse in this case can mean anything from verbal and emotional abuse to actual physical abuse. Basically it involves the abuse of power by a person with power over a vulnerable person, such as a parent and a child. And although the abuse takes on a sexual form, it involves more than sex. It's a breach of trust that breaks down the abused person's boundaries and violates that person's sense of self.

"Children naturally trust their parents. They count on them for love, safety, food, shelter. So when a parent does something the child thinks is wrong or finds uncomfortable, the child becomes confused. How could this person who I love, and who loves me, do this awful thing to me? the child thinks. The child begins to think that perhaps it isn't the adult's fault that the behavior feels wrong, but the child's. The child grows up full of doubt and confusion about what is good and what is bad, what should be permitted and what should be prohibited, all because the person the child trusted the most violated the child's boundaries. Sometimes it only takes one incident to mar a child for life."

"Why are you telling me this?" Sara said. "What's any of this have to do with me? I wasn't abused as a child."

"Let me finish. Adults who were abused as children—they're called survivors, by the way—survivors grow up with a distorted sense of self-worth. They can come to believe that the abuse they suffered as a child was their fault, and that because of that they're not worthy of having the same things as other people. They may try to sabotage relationships because they feel unworthy of being happy like 'normal' people. Survivors have problems with trust. Since the person they most trusted as a child betrayed them, then it stands to reason that anyone they trust as adults will also betray them. Intimacy terrifies them. The closer their partners get, the more they pull away, because the person in their childhood that they trusted also abused them. They also feel a need to control every aspect of the relationship, because the last time they weren't in control the person they trusted abused them—"

"The towels," I said.

"Jason?"

"The towels. She flamed out once because I didn't fold the towels just right. Is that what you mean?"

"It could be. Sara, you used to live alone, isn't that right? And when you moved in with Jason you began to feel like you were losing control?"

Sara nodded. "It wasn't my house. I wasn't making any money. I sat around the house all day waiting for him to get home."

"I want to ask you one more question, Sara, then I want you to go home and think about what we've been talking about. All right?"

"Go ahead."

Jeannie steepled her fingers on her chest and rested her chin on her fingertips.

"How does it make you feel," she said in a measured voice, "when I suggest that your Uncle Richie came into your room at night, when you were asleep and your mother was at work, and either did things to you, or made you do things to him, that made you feel—"

Sara jackknifed forward and dropped to her knees on the floor, grabbing the rim of the wastebasket I had put there a minute ago. The muffled noise of her heaving was the only sound in the room for half a minute.

"What's happening to me?" she said between gasps. "Jeannie? What's happening to me?"

Jeannie knelt beside her. "It can take years for the memories to surface. We blot them out, stuff them down deep because they're so painful. But they surface sooner or later. For many survivors it starts with vague memories, bad dreams, flashbacks in the middle of normal conversations. I think that's what's happening."

"I had a good family!" Sara wailed. "Nobody hurt me! Uncle Richie would never have done those things to me! He loved me! He told me so!"

"Just think about what we talked about today," Jeannie said later as Sara and I stood in the door of her office. "Call me later if you need to. Okay? Sara?"

"Okay. I'll be all right. See you in a couple of days."

*"Call* me."

For the rest of the night Sara was in a daze. The next morning, though, she brushed off the whole episode in Jeannie's office as if it were just some bug that was going around.

"I'm telling you she's wrong," she said. "I'd know if something like that happened, wouldn't I?"

"You were young, what, four or five years old? Jeannie said the memories—"

"No. I'd know."

"But the things she said, about losing control, being afraid of intimacy—didn't any of that ring a bell with you?"

But she was adamant, and went nova if I so much as brought the subject up. A few nights later I woke up at three in the morning. She wasn't in bed. At the other end of the hall the living room light was on. She was sitting on the floor with Boswell's head in her lap, looking at family photos. Her expression was one of intense concentration as she stared at the picture of her mother, her sister, her Uncle Richie, and herself.

I threw myself into work. I volunteered for every road test, feature story, and product evaluation that Barry scheduled. It helped keep my mind off home, but it didn't necessarily put it into my work. I blew a copy deadline for the first time since I joined the staff. Barry not only reassigned the story to Ken Nakamura, he pulled a feature for the next issue off my desk and assigned it to himself.

"I don't know what's bothering you lately, Jason," he said one day over lunch at the Hope and Anchor, "but get it straightened out soon. Don't make me sorry I went to the mat with the publisher to keep you on staff."

Back at the office the mail was on my desk. I picked up the latest *Cycle Weekly* and took it into the men's room. I turned to the front section called Hot Laps, which consisted of short news items, some of it genuine news, some culled from press releases and foreign sources.

I scanned the lead sentence of each item. If the topic didn't interest me I skipped to the next one. Along about the bottom of the fifth column I spotted the words "Universal Tires"—Max Bauer's company.

> A spokesman for Universal Tires, founded by the late Maximillian Bauer, announced last week that the company has been acquired by a Japanese industrial concern. The spokesman declined to name the concern's principals pending authorization from the new owners.
>
> Bauer, who committed suicide in his home two months ago, is survived by his wife Angela, who along with her husband was a familiar face on the flat track circuit for many seasons. Upon his death, Max Bauer's interest in Universal is said to have passed on to Mrs. Bauer, who immediately expressed interest in selling the company. The Japanese connection was made soon after, and the deal reportedly closed last Monday. Mrs. Bauer plans to leave the country and take up residence in Europe.

Well, I hoped she'd be happy wherever she ended up. I doubted she'd spend too many nights sitting alone by the phone, what with her taste for younger men and the proceeds of Universal's sale tucked away in a Swiss bank account. In a way I was glad she was leaving. A particularly uncomfortable manifestation of Sara's emotional upheaval was sudden jealous accusations that I was seeing other women on the side whenever I did something suspicious, like run down to the corner market for milk. Her reasoning was that since I wasn't getting sex from her, I must be getting it somewhere, since everybody knows men can't live without sex.

I could, at least for the time being, but I was constantly aware of her eyes boring through my head if I so much as glanced at something a good-looking woman happened to be standing near. I had nightmares about being at a press gig with Sara when Angela, wearing a bathrobe, sidled up and offered me a jumbo shrimp with one hand and brushed the hay out of my hair with the other. I could feel my heart hammering just from the memory of that night in Louisville.

I took a deep breath and read the opening sentence of the next item. It only made my heart pound harder.

> Little known fact: Angela Bauer, 42, is the daughter of Charles Brand, a one-time flat track racer whose career ended at the 1950 Springfield Mile after an incident that killed one rider and crippled three others. Brand himself was unhurt in the crash.

I barely got my pants zipped up before I shoved the stall door open and ran to my desk. I had thrown away Angela's business card, but there was a Universal Tire presskit somewhere in my files from that damned sportbike tire test I had written. With the time difference it was almost closing time at Universal headquarters.

"Come on, come on," I snarled at the phone, pounding my fist on the desk. "Answer the goddam—hello? Universal Tires? My name is Jason Street, I work for *Motorcycle Monthly*. I need to speak with Angela Bauer right away . . . I see, yes, can you give me her home number? She knows who I—okay, I understand.

Look, I need to get a message to her. Can you do that? Great. Please tell her I called, and that I want to, need to talk to her right away. She's leaving when? Tonight? *Shit!* I'm sorry, ma'am, forgive me, look, please tell her it's urgent, will you? Here's my home number . . ."

As I hung up the phone I suddenly wondered just what the hell I thought I was doing. Okay, so Angela was Charlie Brand's daughter. She was the one who paid all the nursing home bills, who told the staff to let Charlie make all the calls he wanted, she'd pay for them . . .

The *Cycle Weekly* item said she was 42. Born in 1950. The year of the Springfield Mile when Sherm Case won the plate. Charlie, Archie Jones, Sherm Case, they were all there that day. What had brought them all together again after 42 years?

Angela. It had to be. She was the one who took revenge on Sherm Case for the Springfield crash, not Haffner. But why? She hadn't even been born yet. Etta Brand was only pregnant then. What had Angela lost that was worth killing Sherm over?

Her father Charlie? How had the crash hurt him? He wasn't injured physically. But he might have been emotionally devastated. Had it continued to affect him long after that day? Had it haunted him for the rest of his life, right up until the end when he heard angels' wings and, desperate for forgiveness, tracked down those he had wronged in order to bare his soul to them? Had he told Angela, too, about how Sherm Case conned him into throwing the race? Had she come to blame Sherm for her father's lifelong grief, and exacted the revenge her dying father couldn't?

My phone rang and I practically leaped out of my chair.

"Jason, this is Angela Bauer. I got your message. What can I do for you?"

Fighting down panic, I said, "I hear you're leaving the country. I just wanted to say goodbye first."

"That's sweet of you. I'd like to see you, too. But I'm leaving tonight."

"Oh? Where to?"

"France, eventually. But I'm going to do a little globe-trotting first. I'm flying to Hawaii for a week, then on to Tokyo. From there, who knows?"

"Hawaii? Any chance you'll be passing through L.A.?"

"In fact I have a one-hour layover at LAX tonight. Why don't you meet me at the airport?"

"It's a date. When does your flight get in?"

She gave me the time and gate and said she was looking forward to seeing me. We hung up.

Next I called the Lakewood Sheriff's office and asked for Dan, my next door neighbor. The dispatcher told me Deputy Silver was out on a call. I left an urgent message with the dispatcher, and just to be sure I left another on his home answering machine.

I had until midnight to put everything together. I left the office early and rode home. Sara was asleep on the couch. I used to worry about her sleeping so much. These days it was a blessing. She had the hollow-eyed look of an accident victim half the time, and the other half the frozen stare of a deer in the headlights. Boswell lay on the floor beside her. He had assumed personal responsibility for her safety lately. I scratched him behind the ear and he licked my finger.

I unplugged the kitchen phone and turned down the ringer on the one in my office. I was pouring a cup of coffee when I heard the muted warbling tone.

"Jason? Dan. What's up? You finally decide to buy my Triumph?"

"Dan, what're you doing tonight, say around eleven?"

"There's this thing called sleep I've been meaning to look into. I'm coming off a double I pulled for a buddy with a sick kid. Why?"

"Does the sheriff's department have any of that high-tech wire-tapping stuff, or is that just the cops and the feds?"

"We have a pretty neat Walkman in the lost and found. If no one claims it by Saturday it's mine."

"Seriously, Dan."

"Hmm. Yeah, I might come up with a bug. But I'd have to know why first."

I told him. He stopped me three or four times for more details. Then he made me tell it again.

"Let me go talk to the boss. I'm not familiar enough with this kind of thing to know if we could pull it off without winding up on the wrong end of an entrapment complaint. I'll get back to you in ten."

It was more like thirty before the phone rang again.

"I got permission to use the gear," Dan said, "but before it goes as far as you want it to, the tape comes back here so the boss can hear it. Mrs. Silver didn't raise any kids dumb enough to wake up judges in the wee hours of the morning for nothing."

Sara was rubbing the sleep from her eyes as I was walking out the front door.

"What time is it?" she said. "Where are you going?"

"It's about ten-thirty. I'm going over to Dan's."

"Now? What for?"

"Uh, he wants some help with his Triumph."

I'm good at a lot of stuff, but lying isn't one of them. Not enough practice.

"Are you meeting someone?"

That hit unnervingly close to the mark, since I was actually going to meet Angela, who Sara knew nothing about. If I started in on an explanation, I'd have to tell her who Angela was, how we met, and then I'd probably start sweating or develop some kind of facial tic that would trigger her suspicion gland and the next minute she'd be screaming the house down around my ears—not that I wouldn't have deserved it, but I'd only get one chance at Angela, and I didn't want to miss it.

"We're, uh, going over to some guy's house who has some parts Dan needs. He wants me along to look at them. The guy, uh, he said—oh, shit, Sara, nothing's going on, really, it's just I have to go now. I'll be home as soon as I can, all right?"

Dan drove us the mile or so to the sheriff's office. In a concrete-walled squad room I stripped off my shirt and Dan taped the microphone to my chest. It was about the size of a gumball, with a thin wire antenna about a foot long.

"The latest spook stuff," he said. "We seized it from some drug dealer. All those guys are super-paranoid—the blow does it to 'em after a while. This guy had his girlfriend's bedroom wired with this thing, trying to see who she was doing on the side. Want a laugh? Turns out it was his wife."

"Yeah, it's a funny old world, all right. What's the range?"

"Thirty yards out in the open. We shouldn't have any problem in the airport."

We drove out to LAX in an unmarked Ford four-door. The tape was pulling at my chest hairs. I scratched absently.

"Quit that," Dan said. "People will think you have fleas. Besides, you can't be doing that while you talk to her. She'll start to wonder."

Traffic on the 405 was light and moving along at a brisk pace. Dan slid the Ford through gaps like a pro. Right around the tank farm in Carson, brake lights flashed ahead and formed a solid line of cars stretching into the distance.

"Shit," Dan grumbled as traffic slowed to a crawl. He groped for the radio and found a police frequency. There was a three-car pile-up a mile or so ahead, all but one lane blocked.

"Hang on," he said. He pulled a flashing red light from under the seat and stuck it on the dashboard. Hauling at the wheel he darted for the number two lane. The guy who was already there honked and flipped him off.

For all the cooperation it got us the flashing red light might as well have been a cartoon animal suction-cupped to the window. Dan jammed three or four other drivers on his way to the shoulder, snarled at the last one and floored it. We took the next off-ramp and sped north on the 110. He made a left where the 91 becomes Artesia—only a block or so from Ascot Park Raceway—and picked up the 405 again just south of Lawndale.

"Take Imperial westbound," I said as we neared the airport.

"Not Century?"

"Imperial's quicker. Fewer stoplights. Then north on Sepulveda. It takes you under the south runways and straight to the terminal."

We had been cutting the time factor to the bone to start with, and it was twenty past midnight as Dan nosed the car into the curb outside the departure area. A skycap came over to help with our luggage.

"We'll just be a minute," Dan said, hanging onto the duffel bag containing the rest of the listening gear.

"You can't park here, sir," the skycap said.

"Look," Dan said, pulling out his badge, "gimme a break here, okay?"

"Sir, I don't make the rules . . ."

A small scene ensued that attracted an airport cop, another skycap, and a cab driver with nothing better to do. In the midst of the argument Dan motioned for me to go on ahead, he'd catch up.

Inside I checked the overhead TV screen. Angela's flight had arrived on time, and was due to take off at 1:05 a.m. She had said she'd meet me in the boarding lounge, so I had to go through the metal detector. I had no idea what I would say if the microphone set it off, but it didn't. The gate was at the far end of the concourse. It was twelve-thirty. Christ, they'd begin boarding any time. I ran.

Angela was sitting by herself reading a magazine. She was dressed for first-class travel in a skirt and jacket with a matching handbag on the chair beside her. Her hair was down and fell around her shoulders. She wore glasses with gem-studded designer frames which she hastily removed and put in her handbag when she saw me.

"How nice to see you," she said, giving me a sisterly peck on the cheek. "How's your lady friend, umm . . . ?"

"Sara."

"Of course. I trust she's well?"

"The grand dame bit suits you, Angela. You'll be good at it."

Her eyes narrowed but the smile stayed. "I don't know what you mean."

"Sure you do. You're shedding your old life like a bad habit. No more race tracks, no more tires, just the Riviera and good champagne from now on."

"And what's wrong with that?"

I glanced over my shoulder for Dan. He was nowhere in sight.

"Jason," Angela said, "maybe we should just say our goodbyes now. I'm afraid this is becoming tedious—"

I couldn't wait any longer. I blurted it out.

"You killed Sherm Case to get it, that's what's wrong."

She blinked. She was good. Better than me.

"I beg your pardon? Max killed Sherm. He confessed to it right before he killed himself."

"Yeah, I read that," I said, "but I'm not sure I believe it. I have a hard time saying 'Max' and 'conscience' in the same breath."

"It's not nice to speak ill of the dead."

"Let's talk about the living, then. You're Charlie Brand's daughter. Sherm Case talked him into blocking for him at the Springfield race in 1950 so Sherm could win the Grand National Championship. A friend of Charlie's got killed in the crash, and Charlie never forgave himself for it. He probably didn't even own up to it to anyone until right before he died. He told you, didn't he? You visited him a couple of times in the nursing home. I know. So did I."

Her eyes went soft, as if seeing the past in vivid detail. I looked over my shoulder. Still no sign of Dan. Angela was lost in thought.

"Come on, Angela, level with me. What harm can it do now? You're practically home free."

She seemed to make up her mind. "All right," she said. "What harm indeed?" She smoothed her skirt and folded her hands on her lap.

"Charlie was a beaten man from that day on," she said. "He never forgave himself for what he did. All his life he felt he was unworthy of anything good. He took menial jobs for low pay because he didn't deserve anything better. You're right, Mother and I never knew why until just before he died. But it hardly mattered, because we paid for Charlie's sin right along with him. We lived in run-down apartments, wore hand-me-down clothes. Our lives were miserable because of Charlie, and because of what Sherm Case had talked him into doing."

"So you killed Sherm because of what he did to your father."

"Charlie Brand was not my father."

"But the *Cycle Weekly* article said—and you just—"

"Charlie Brand was the man who raised me. Sherm Case was my father."

The PA announced the first boarding call for Angela's flight. I barely heard it.

"Etta, my mother, and Charlie Brand grew up together. They were childhood sweethearts. As they grew older Etta began looking at other boys, but Charlie never had eyes for another girl. He followed her like a puppy. She liked the attention, and led him on. But she didn't let him stop her from seeing other boys. She went to the races with him often, which is how she met Sherm Case. He was handsome, brash, confident. He stole her heart, and as soon as he got what he wanted he tossed her aside.

"By then she was pregnant and terrified. In those days it wasn't like it is now. Unmarried mothers were outcasts. Families, relatives, whole towns drove them away in disgrace. Etta went to Charlie and told him what she had done, but not with who. Poor, kind Charlie couldn't find it in him to hate her. He offered to marry her and raise the child as his own. But he knew he'd need money, lots of it, to raise a family. So when Sherm Case offered him a bribe he accepted.

"You've already guessed how it turned out. Charlie spent the rest of his life doing penance in his own way. His only joy was taking his little girl to motorcycle races. Even then he wouldn't go near the track. We sat in the car in the parking lot where we could hear the engines. I can still see his hand on the steering wheel, the ash of the cigarette between his fingers getting longer and longer, and the tears that ran down his face.

"Well, you can imagine what a happy life that was. I left home when I was seventeen. I had been to dozens of motorcycle races without ever having seen one. So one day I bought a ticket and went inside. That's where I met Max Bauer. He was like the father I had always wished for but never had, and soon I grew to love him."

"What happened between you and Max?"

"Maybe there was too much of my real father in me. Maybe it wasn't a father figure I was really after. It doesn't matter any more. We grew apart. He had his life, I had mine."

"And now you have it all. But you haven't answered my question. Did you kill Sherm Case?"

"I told you, Sherm Case was my father. I wouldn't deliberately kill my own father."

"Are you saying it was an accident?"

"You could call it that," she said. "When Charlie told me who my real father was I was furious. All those years of poverty and hardship, and never once did Sherm Case offer to help. I had known the man socially for years, for God's sake, and never once did he give the slightest hint that I was his daughter. So I asked to meet him that night at Ascot. I told him Max had a proposal to buy out Case Tires, and that he wanted me to deliver it so their animosity wouldn't get in the way of his seeing the deal objectively. All I wanted to do was confront him, make him own up to abandoning my mother and me. I just wanted the satisfaction of hearing him say he was sorry.

"He wouldn't even give me that. He was sitting in his van reading a magazine, fuming about the story you wrote. I got into the passenger seat and tried to tell him I knew he was my father, but the words wouldn't come. He wasn't paying any attention to me anyway. I grabbed the magazine away from him and opened the glove box door, meaning to throw it inside so he'd have to listen to me. The little light went on and there was the gun. Maybe he misunderstood what I was doing, thought I was going for the gun. He slapped me. He was getting ready to slap me again when I swatted him with the magazine and as he flinched I grabbed the gun and jumped out. I held the gun in both hands and kept it pointed at him through the windshield as I circled around to the driver's side.

" 'Look at me, you bastard,' I said. 'I'm your daughter! Doesn't that mean anything to you?'

" 'I already have a daughter,' he said. 'Sherry. You know her. Now give me the gun. You're hysterical.'

" 'I'm not either. I just want to hear you say it.'

" 'Say what?'

" 'You're my father! Say it!'

" 'All right, so I'm your father. So what?'

" 'How could you leave us? How could you leave me with *them?*'

" 'You mean Charlie and Etta? She was okay, a lively little girl in her day. Charlie, now you're right about him. A milktoast, as I recall, with no spine and as dumb as the day is long. You know what he used to do?'

"As he said that he slid his left arm out the van window, resting his elbow on the sill and drumming his fingers on the roof.

"He said, 'I hear the old clown used to go to the races and sit out in the parking lot the whole time. Never even went inside! Can you imagine anything as *cowardly*—'

"On that word he lunged for the gun. He grabbed the barrel and pulled it toward him. I pulled back, as hard as I could. And of course it went off . . ."

She was quiet for a few seconds, her face smooth and expressionless. Then she blinked and went on.

"Oddly enough, I was able to think very clearly after that. I was wearing gloves, so I hadn't left any fingerprints. I put the gun in Sherm's hand and pressed his fingers against it, then let it drop to the ground under the window. Then the fear came and I began to shiver. I heard someone running toward me so I ducked between two vans. When he was past I walked out the pit gate and around to the main grandstands and went back to my seat."

"So it was an accident," I said. "You didn't intend to kill Sherm."

"I'm not so sure," she said. "I wonder."

"But something's still not right. If you shot Sherm Case, why did Max kill himself—"

Our eyes met. Hers probed mine, then glanced at her watch as the PA system barked the final boarding announcement.

"My flight," she said, standing. "Well, Jason, it's been pleasant—"

"You killed Max," I said. "You had to in order to cover for yourself in case anyone found out about you and Sherm."

"Nonsense."

"And you were counting on me to back you up. You laid the groundwork for your alibi by telling me that Max began behaving strangely after Sherm's death. Tell me something, Angela, did Max really hire those bikers to beat us up at Hagerstown?"

She looked away.

"Or did you? To make me even more certain that Max had something to hide? That was a nice touch, too, giving Rusty that check to make up for putting Ozzie in the hospital. I guess ten grand is a cheap price to pay to get out from under a murder charge."

"Max was going to divorce me," she said. "Besides, the police couldn't crack that security guard's story. They needed someone to pin Sherm's death on. I gave them Max." She smiled. "You see, I can take care of myself. I would have taken care of you, too, if you'd played along in the beginning."

"I bet you would have," I said.

Angela picked up her bag and gave her ticket to the boarding agent. She disappeared up the ramp to the plane without looking back.

A hand landed on my shoulder and I almost swallowed my tongue.

"Case closed, Sherlock?" Dan grinned.

"Goddammit, you missed her! She's getting away!"

"Relax." He held up the duffel bag. Inside was a black box with a meter and some knobs on it. A cable ran from it to a battery-operated tape recorder in which a cassette was rewinding. "I got most of it."

"Oh, Jesus." I sat down, my breath coming in gulps. "I'm having a damn heart attack."

"Naw, it's the wire. Here." He reached inside my shirt and yanked the microphone, tape and all, off my chest.

"Ow! Hey, that hair's mine! Where the hell were you, anyway?"

"I got held up at the metal detector—damn airport cops think they're the FBI or something. The bug does look like a bomb, though, I'll give 'em that. Anyway, I was sitting over there at that row of courtesy telephones, well within range. Had my back to you. That way you wouldn't give me away if you saw me. Come on, let's fly."

"Where to?"

"Got to audition this tape for the brass, see if we have enough to file murder charges on your lady friend."

I got home at four in the morning. Sara was sitting in the kitchen. A cold cup of tea sat on the table in front of her. Boswell snored at her feet.

"How were those parts?" she said, her chin trembling. "Did you buy them?"

"There weren't any parts," I said. "Here's what really happened . . ."

It took me an hour to tell her the whole story, from my first meeting with Angela to watching her walk away for the last time. I left absolutely nothing out.

When I was through I sat back and wiped my face with my hands. It was getting light outside. Boswell stirred and asked to be let outside.

"You hurt me," Sara said at last.

"I know," I said. "I'm so sorry. It won't happen again."

"How can you be sure?"

We both knew I couldn't.

"I'll do my best," I said at last. "That's all I can do."

"I don't know if that's enough."

A knock came at the front door. I opened it to find Dan standing on the porch.

"We got her," he said. "We got an arrest warrant based on the tape. They'll detain her in Honolulu and send her back on the next plane. We'll need a formal statement from you this afternoon. Meet me at the station at four."

I closed the door. Sara was standing in the middle of the living room, hugging herself. She looked small and alone and as fragile as glass.

"I'm scared," she whispered.

I put my arms around her as gently as I could. She slowly relaxed into my embrace.

"Scared of what?" I said.

"Of what Jeannie said. I'm scared it's true. Oh, Jason, how could something that happened so long ago affect me now? How could it affect me like this? Why? Why?"

The why didn't seem to matter. The how would be evident soon enough for both of us. What I couldn't tell her then, what I wouldn't have believed myself if I hadn't seen the dead look in Angela Bauer's eyes when she told me she had killed her husband for his money and nothing else, was that it could have been worse.

"Stay with me," she said. "Please don't leave me."

"I'm here," I said, I rocking her in my arms as she cried. "I'm here."

# About the Author

Veteran motojournalist Jerry Smith has served on the editorial staff of *Rider, Cycle Guide,* and *Motorcyclist,* and currently freelances for motorcycle consumer and trade magazines from his home in Oregon. *Deadman's Throttle,* the first Jason Street motorcycle murder mystery, and *Motorcycle Maintenance Made Easy,* both by Jerry Smith, are also available from Whitehorse Press.